Billable

Hours

By
Susan Dakers

It's 5:30 a.m. one Friday morning in Brighton. The black SUV creeps along like a hearse on Terminus Road as a blood-orange sun kisses the sky awake with the promise of another wonderful spring day. As the car parks outside a grimy pink launderette, Ethel Hargreaves is sleeping with no notion of the spectacle she will witness later that morning.

An unshaven man dressed in a black suit gets out of the car, fumbles for keys, and opens the reinforced glass door to the launderette. He signals to his passenger, also dressed in a suit, at the front of the car. Slowly, they walk together to the rear of the SUV and lift its tailgate. They pull a large hessian bag from the car and carry it into the launderette, clearly struggling with its weight. The bag fastened with a tied rope is placed carefully on the black-and-white tiled floor. The unshaven man looks back at the bag and sniggers to his companion. They leave after locking the door. Having made their delivery and within the safe confines of the SUV, they congratulate each other with a high five and speed off along the dusty, littered road.

At precisely 7 a.m., Ethel with her hair in curlers held in place by a silk scarf, waddles up to the launderette.

1

Keys jingle in her hand, which resembles a fistful of pink sausages. She opens the door. Fighting against the rolls of fat between her and the floor, she bends down to pick up the mail. Out of breath, she turns around and immediately notices a hessian bag on the floor.

"Well, wot the bleeding 'ell is this then?" She searches for her eyeglasses in her red handbag, too small for her hands. "Jesus Christ!! I 'ope it ain't a dead body!" she mutters to herself, all the time staring at the motionless bag lying on the floor.

Ethel opens the door and looks over the street to the newsagent owned by Mr. Singh. Scratching her forehead, she decides to investigate and lightly taps her fat foot, squished into a moderately heeled shoe, against the bag. She concludes that whatever is in the bag is some form of flesh but is most concerned that the flesh is not moving. Not moving at all.....

Like a plump pigeon, she runs across the road, seeking the assistance of Mr. Singh - who is seeing his last paperboy out on a delivery.

"Oh, thank gawd you are here!"

"Well, of course I am here, Mrs. Hargreaves. Where else would you suppose I would be at this time in the morning? I have a business to run."

"Oh, Mr. Singh, please come quickly - I think something terrible has happened at the launderette!"

"Whatever is it Ethel? Have you run out of soap powder?" He chuckles. Shaking his head from side to side he states, "You know, this really isn't a good time."

"Sorry, but this is serious Mr. Singh. I think I may have a dead body in the launderette – please come quickly! Bring your mobile thingey-me-jig with you – I have a feeling we are going to have to call the police!"

They hurry across the road, Ethel wheezing with every step. They arrive at the launderette to find that the hessian bag is no longer motionless - something appears to be moving vigorously inside.

"Ethel, I thought you said it was a *dead?*"

"Well, it was when I left ....What the hell is it?"

"I have no idea. How did *it* get in to the launderette?"

"I don't bleeding know! Did you see anything this morning from your shop?"

"Nothing at all. Well, Ethel there's only one way to find out what it is." Mr. Singh moves toward the bag attempting to rip it open against the vigorous motion coming from inside.

"Please be careful Mr. Singh – it could be dangerous!"

Ethel runs to the back of the launderette to stand on a bench by the dryers, anticipating the imminent escape of a wild animal. After some desperate motion, the bag is ripped open revealing a pale and naked man, hands tied behind his back, mouth covered with duct tape, and a pink feather boa wrapped around his head. He pleads with his eyes for freedom, while Ethel averts her eyes to save embarrassment.

Mr. Singh unties the boa while reassuring the captive. Finally free from restraint, the naked man runs immediately to the door of the launderette, covers his genitals with his hands, and runs down the street.

A wild animal? How could Ethel have known? This was indeed a wild animal and difficult to tame.

PILKINGTON, ISLEY & SIMEON
Est. 1892

P.I.S. (or known by some as PISS) was a highly respected and proudly traditional law firm. Its Georgian-style building with red brick exterior was home to a handful of youthful articling students eager to impress with academic prowess; secretaries weary from daily demands of perfection; aspiring partners; established partners flagrantly enjoying the fruits of their labour; and crusty second-generation lawyers that come into the office every day primarily to escape their families to read the newspaper in peace.

As lawyers, we were here to service every important stage of life. We handled first house purchases; pre-nuptial agreements for the sensible minority; visits to courts (often with vociferous spouses in tow) for the not-so-sensible majority; emotional adoptions; troublesome litigants; drafting of generous (and not-so-generous) wills; exercising discretion as appointed trustees; but ultimately profiting from every step of a person's life - from birth to death.

4

CHAPTER 1 - MONDAY MAY 8, 2000

I had been told that in the early days of legal practice, lawyers had been paid by the word for conveyances of land. This, of course, explained why lawyers had a habit of expressing themselves with languid verbosity.

Early on in my own career, I had learned the difference between a fixed fee arrangement (a good deal for a lawyer able to work fast and efficiently) and the popular hourly billing. I became acutely aware that much like Captain Hook from Peter Pan; lawyers were mentally tortured by the sound of a ticking clock inside their heads. Ticking to remind them that time is money and tocking to remind them of their target of "billable hours." Of course, the ticking and tocking was also there to remind them that partnership is attainable only to those who consistently meet their targets.

It was a gloomy day in Brighton. Rain gently tapped on window panes, shaking in their frames while umbrellas battled against blustery winds.

At the age of 23, somehow I had decided that a profession in law would provide me with a meaningful existence. The firm I decided on as the vehicle for my substantial amount of ambition was Pilkington, Isley and Simeon (referred to by the competition as "PISS" and all lawyers who worked for "PISS" being known as "Piss Artists.")

I arrived at the office at the usual time of 8:45 a.m. While grabbing mail from my mailbox with one hand, coffee cup in the other, I made my way down the hallway to my office. Some time ago, I had developed the art of opening doors with an elbow rather than a smile, all natural charm having departed at around month three of my employment as an associate lawyer.

One year into the job, I was no longer living the life of a third-class citizen (also known as an articled student). I now had my own office, which was definitely preferable to the dimly lit corner of a room I previously occupied.

As clients were always seen in interview rooms, I was free to make my office as comfortable as possible. After the fluorescent lights had been removed, I brought in a couple of lamps and an old leather couch purchased from a flea market. A couple of Turner prints in contemporary frames hung on the wall and a few photographs of friends were placed on my desk and bookshelves - there to remind me that I *did* actually have a life outside of these four walls.

My desk was an antique desk inherited from the previous occupant with a leather insert tabletop. An old fashioned pillar box red telephone sat on the desktop (another find from a flea market, and the bain of the tech department since it took around four times longer to install *at my insistence*).

I put down my coffee cup, took off my trench coat, hanging it as I did every day, behind my office door. Checking my appearance in the mirror, I pulled my hair in various directions in attempt to bring it to order. Sweeping back my fringe, I tucked my long, brown hair behind my ears and sighed at the pointless exercise.

Sitting at my desk, I switched on the computer:

Please enter password....
*1Philisadick!

INBOX (3)

From: Lord Oscar Hanley
To: Penny Banfield
Date: May 8, 2000
Re: New Client

Penny would you be so kind as to drop by my office this morning, I need to brief you on a new client matter. Thank you.
Oscar

From: Anthony Jarvis
To: Penny Banfield
Date: May 8, 2000
Re: Meeting 2 p.m. today, re: Football Club

Please let me know immediately if you are for some reason unavailable.
AJ

From: Phil Stevens
To: Penny Banfield
Date: May 8, 2000
Re: I need to talk to you

Come see me as soon as you get in.
Phil

Of course you need to talk to me Phil...... I rolled my eyes and picked up the phone.

"Nigel, it's me." I straightened the buff files on my desk while talking.

"Yes Penn, I do have caller ID you know. What can I do for you? Did I not load up the dishwasher properly or something?"

"No, nothing like that ... I was just wondering ... is it wrong that it's only 9 o'clock in the morning, and I already want a gin and tonic?"

"Bad morning?"

"Nothing ... yet, but I have a feeling that Phil is about to dump something on me again."

"Most likely I'd say, unless he just wants to ask you for some Nurofen.*"

"First thing on a Monday morning? Surely not? Did you feed Liam and Noel last night? I did leave a note."

"Of course, I'm very well trained and always do what I'm told, especially when it comes to feeding your bloody goldfish."

"Thanks Nigel. Guess I should make my way down the hallway to see what nightmare I have to clean up for Phil. See you at home tonight?"

"Yep, but not until later. I'm playing cricket, remember?"

"Right. Oh well, see you later … have a nice day." I said, in a phoney American accent.

I picked up my coffee cup and headed to Phil's office at the end of the corridor.

Phil liked to work in the end office because it was next to a fire exit and provided a very convenient method of exiting the office without being noticed. This way, he was able to keep up with his social responsibilities like (a) playing golf, (b) drinking at the pub, or (c) gambling at the casino with the boys. I nodded to his assistant, Julie, who was on the phone diligently scribbling notes, taking instructions from a client.

Unusually, the door to Phil's office was closed. He didn't like to spend inordinate amounts of time in his office (especially if work was involved.) I peered through the glass panel on his door and saw he was on the phone. So I turned back toward my office. He beckoned me in and hung up the phone. Phil was remarkably groomed, although his eyes were not their usual sparkling blue. They had redness to them this morning. His dark hair was tied back in a ponytail. And although he wasn't a bad looking guy, he was vertically challenged and had started to put some weight on around the waist due to his drinking.

"Here she is – Penny Banfield! Jesus, what a blinder last night Penn – you should have been there. Mickey Fat Boy was on the dance floor dancing up a storm with some brunette with false knockers. Don't ask me how, but somehow he managed to convince her that he was an ex-SAS officer," he said, as he started laughing.

"What - Mickey from the casino? Good God, she must have had a lot to drink - he's totally vile!"

"What a night. God, I can't keep this up for much longer," he said, loosening his tie. "I would kill for something to get rid of this bloody mother of all headaches." *So Nigel was right, seems like Phil was in dire need of some Nurofen.*

"Hmmmm, what did you say Phil ... a headache? Oh, you mean HANGOVER! What's wrong, the sauce getting to you in your old age?" He started to look a little green around the gills.

"I used to be able to handle my drink. Well, I can handle my drink. It's just the drinking till three in the morning that's a killer. Not to mention the pain in the neck I get in the morning from Lisa."

Anticipating the Nurofen he would need, I popped out two white pills from the packet and handed them to Phil. He promptly jolted them down with a glass of water.

"Well, I'm sure you deserve every minute of that pain in the neck Phil. I'll never know how Lisa puts up with you."

"Yeah, she's golden, that one. A *keeper* as they say."

"Well then, it's about time you made an honest woman out of her, isn't it Phil?" He looked at me with utter disgust.

"Yeah ... I don't think so Penn. You know me ... I'm happily single."

"Single with all the home comforts you mean." I glanced around his untidy office scattered with various groups of client files. He had around 10 CDs on his desk; complimentary theatre tickets; a lottery ticket; and a print that needed to be hung on his wall next to a few golf trophies displayed on dust-covered shelves. The only thing that appeared to be pristine in his office was the set of golf clubs that had evidently been cleaned by some caddy and stood in the corner of his office.

I wondered just what it was that had established Phil as the "go-to" person for the senior lawyers, yet also had made him overtly nonchalant when it came to the number of hours he spent in the office. It had to be his ability to bring in new clients. A "rainmaker" was the American term. It seemed to me that there were three types of lawyers: the socialites, usually great at bringing in and maintaining relationships with clients; the academics, who basically had excelled at law school in the area of jurisprudence and constitutional law; and the multi-faceted who seemed to be able to keep the clients happy without getting too bogged down in the academia.

"God, what a dog's breakfast this office is Phil. How can you work in this mess?"

"Yeah, I was thinking that it could do with a bit of a tidy up - but then again, I'm not really in my office enough to warrant any special attention, am I?" He chuckled.

"Anyway, what's up? Why the cryptic email? Did you really just want some Nurofen?"

"Oh that ... nothing to worry about, I just wanted to talk to you about this new application we are going to apply for. It's called an Anton Piller Order. I want you to be my right-hand man ... er ... sorry. I mean *person* on the football club file. The whole operation is going to involve a lot of manpower, and I want to know that I can delegate as much as possible to somebody who can handle it."

"Oh Phil, you are too kind. Somebody competent you mean? Or do you mean somebody who doesn't have a life outside of the office and can work multiple hours of overtime without complaining?" I watched him shift his weight uncomfortably in his very comfortable high-backed chair.

"Oh, don't be like that Penn. You know I depend on you whenever I need to get something done."

"Oh, I am painfully aware of that Phil. The problem is that it's *always* me. Can't you use pretty boy Fairhurst? He's always looking for an opportunity to boss everyone around."

"Yeah ... unfortunately Mr. Fairhurst is too busy working on the Annual General Meeting for the partnership, and he is getting a little bit too high on the totem pole these days to be at my beck and call."

"What do you mean too high on the totem pole? Jesus, he's not on the partner list this year is he?"

"Well, let's just say that pretty soon, we might have to have the doors widened to accommodate his beautiful, *big*, blonde head."

"Oh, that just about makes my day doesn't it? Bloody Fairhurst a partner of the firm! I can just imagine his smug, little face. Poor Raj ... he must be so disappointed."

"I think not Ms. Banfield. The word is that Raj *also* got partnership. You need to keep that under your hat, goes without saying. Anyway, enough about them. Let's talk about *me*. Are you going to help or not?"

It seemed that Phil didn't want to talk about partnership. Why? Was he surprised that he had been passed over? Everyone knew you had to work your arse off to get partnership. To many, it appeared that Phil's heart just wasn't in it. He didn't look at all concerned that he had been passed over for being a partner.

"So, do I have a choice on whether I work on this thing?"

"Of course not, but it always sounds better when you acquiesce," he said and grinned.

"You are a nightmare Phil."

"I know – a reoccurring one, right?"

I rolled my eyes. "So, this Anton Piller order, what does it involve?"

"An Anton Piller Order is a civil order granted to a party and used like a search warrant for evidence in a *civil* case."

"Yes, I know *what* it is. I mean, who are we going after?

"According to AJ, we are going to be raiding several different addresses at the same time; mainly homes of the directors of the football club. It's not common knowledge yet though, so make sure you keep schtum over it. Practically everyone is going to have to get involved - even that little, fat bloke up on fifth floor that works for debt collection."

"His name is Andrew Barker, as you well know Phil."

"Is it?" He started to play with his desktop Zen garden.

"Phil, what's going on? You seem even more distracted than usual. I mean, I'm not just talking about the usual ADD, but more hyperactive than usual."

"Oh, I'm OK … .probably just lack of sleep making me edgy. Perhaps I need to get out on the golf course?"

I sighed. "So, this Anton Piller Order - is there any chance that we *won't* get the Order?"

"Well, that depends on you I guess and how well you draft the application."

I had worked for Phil for more than a year now and was quite used to his constant delegation. But that's not to say it didn't irritate me. More often than not, I would work my arse off on a file but he would be credited for my billable hours on a file. A billable hour is the means by which a junior lawyer builds credibility and earns partnership. Every hour of billable time is a service of professional time. Time the client pays for. The more billable hours you have for the year, the more likely you are to make partnership, after serving your time of course. I had recently started to be more assertive with Phil, insisting that my time was billed under my name.

Misinterpreting the frown on my face for worry, Phil said, "Don't worry Penn, it's all billed under your name. I know you can handle this file, and AJ will provide us with all the information we need at the meeting this afternoon."

"I'm counting on it." My mood suddenly improved. "Oh well ...onward and upward, I have to pay Oscar a visit."

"*Lord Hanley* to you," he said as he gave me a royal wave.

"His Nobleness, His Royal Highness, or whatever you want to call him. As you know, I'm not really impressed by all that crap. He may have a title, but I'm told he's practically penniless. He told me the other day that he had rainwater pouring through the roof to their bedroom. Guess it's hard at the top, eh Phil?"

14

"Those stately homes cost a fortune to maintain you know."

"Why doesn't he sell the place then?"

"Penny Banfield – I can't believe you would even suggest that he should sell the family home. His wife would leave him in an instant."

"Poor Oscar. I guess that's why he's so insistent on trying to get partnership; he just needs the extra cash?"

"Personally, between you and me, I think he has more of a chance winning the lottery."

"I know. But I do feel sorry for him, holding on to a dream that will never come true." I stared out the window at the drizzling rain. "Not a good day for golf Phil. Guess we might just have you in the office all day today." I grinned.

"Don't forget, there is always my friend at the Ship and Anchor."

"Oh yes, how remiss of me! I'll call the landlord if I need anything then?"

"That's my girl" he said and chuckled.

"Don't drink too much!" I yelled at the top of my voice as I strutted down the corridor from his office to my next call of the day, Lord Oscar Hanley.

Of course it annoyed me that Phil was so thoroughly comfortable delegating virtually anything to me; however the upside was that I'd managed to gain three years of practical experience in one year. My peers seemed to have spent most of their time begging for scraps of "interesting" work. For this reason alone, my relationship with Phil was what you might call a necessary evil.

Lord Oscar Hanley worked at the opposite end of the corridor to Phil. His office was that of an "old school" lawyer furnished featuring a captain's leather chair with worn armrests, large oak desk with leather tabletop, and brass lamps. In keeping with tradition (probably from Victorian days), Oscar would cover his desk with calico dust sheets every night, taking them off in the morning and folding them neatly in piles on top of his filing cabinet. When I first saw them, I thought he was having his office decorated.

Oscar was a tall, pale faced weakling with huge glasses that swamped his face and hair that flopped over his face uncontrollably. With ill-fitting false teeth, he spoke with a slight hiss and would often run his tongue along his teeth in an effort to perhaps check they were still intact. I found him smoking a cigarette. His ashtray was overflowing from previous cadavers of the day, and his files and papers were ash covered as if a volcano had erupted overhead. He was a total gentleman, Eton educated, the sort of personality you would like to mother. I also happened to feel great sympathy for him. Close to retirement age, he had been passed over for partnership many times. Though not a brilliant lawyer, he had his place within the firm, still managing to bring in new clients.

"Good morning Lord Hanley. How are you?"

"Oh fine, thank you dear," he said smiling. "Do sit down – here let me clear a space for you." He picked up files and placed them carefully on the floor beside his desk.

"Wow, you look really busy. There's no shortage of files in your office is there?" I looked around at the clutter.

"Not at all – lots of work and lots of clients … always good for a lawyer seeking partnership." He looked serious.

"I suppose so, if that's what you really want." I raised my eyebrows.

"Oh my dear, of course it's what I want. It is, after all, every lawyer's *destiny*." He made it sound like the Holy Grail. I was not totally convinced at this stage in my career that it was totally worth the sacrifice.

"Maybe it's not as wonderful as you think Lord Hanley. Imagine all that responsibility, not to mention having to work longer hours."

"Well, I'm no stranger to responsibility. The longer hours would give me … well, let's just say a *welcome* escape." What could he mean by that?

"Oh, from home you mean?" I smiled.

"Now, I'm not saying that I don't love my family, but sometimes it does get a little tiresome with three women in the house and not one gentleman to keep me company," he chuckled. "Now then Penny, what can I do for you?" He looked at me quizzically.

"Oh I'm here because of your email. I think you wanted to speak to me about a new client?"

"Oh yes, of course … of course! My Wobbly-Table-Man Jeremy Peters. Let's see, I have his file somewhere." He started to pick files up, brushing the ash from each file as if swotting flies. "Oh, here it is. Now, let me see ..." he said as he started to look through the file carefully.

"I'm sorry, did you just say, 'wobbly table'?" *Dear God ... surely not?*

"Yes dear, exactly right. You know how it seems every time you sit down at a restaurant table or outside cafe it jigs around because it's not on level ground?"

"Well yes, I suppose so ... occasionally anyway."

"My client, Mr. Peters, has designed a device that can rectify the situation immediately. He wants to patent his product."

"Oh, I see. Do you think that there is a market for a product like that?" I could not believe that he was seriously going to make a patent application for something that could be solved by a couple of paper tissues shoved under a table leg.

"The point is my dear that Mr. Peters *thinks* so and that's all we need to concern ourselves with. I was hoping you could help with the usual filings – it's a little difficult for me to handle this file."

"Really? Why's that?" I couldn't imagine at this stage of his career that any file would be too difficult.

"Technically, it's called a conflict of interest." I could not imagine why he would take on a client that involved a conflict. Lawyers are prevented from acting for a client if that client has any issues or relationship that could possibly conflict with those of another client.

"Well, maybe he should go to another law firm?"

"No, it's not as simple as that my dear. He is my wife's ex-husband, and I said I would handle it for him as a favour."

"I'm sorry Lord Hanley, where is the conflict?" I was confused. There couldn't possibly be a conflict unless we had sued the client in the past or were involved in something current where he was on the opposing side.

"The conflict is that I cannot stand the wretched man, and I was hoping that you could take him off my hands." He pressed his palms together as if to plead his case.

"Oh, I see. In that case, I'd be happy to oblige Lord Hanley. I presume that the billing for this file will be under my name?"

"Well naturally." He seemed so surprised to have been asked the question. I guess that I had become so used to Phil having me work under his name so he could take the credit for my billable time that I had forgotten the usual honourable way of crediting lawyers for their time.

"And he is aware of my charging rate?" Oscar nodded. "OK then." I stood up to take the file from him just as his telephone rang.

"Hold on a moment dear, this shouldn't take too long." He gestured me back down into my seat and picked up the phone before I was able to snatch the file and make a hasty retreat.

"Hello darling. How is your day going so far?" I could hear an animated shrill voice coming from the receiver as Oscar tried to placate his spoiled wife. "Oh no, that's really too bad for you. I am soooo sorry darling. Why don't you go back to bed and get some rest?" He seemed to hit a nerve as there was more shrillness. "Of course, yes ... of course. No, I expect it must be absolutely awful for you. Did you take something for it my darling?" Oscar had a pitiful look on his face resembling a bullied child, and the volume of shrillness had increased to such a point that I was now able to hear every word. "Of course I took something for it! What do you take me for – a complete fool Oscar?!"

"A fool? Of course not! You know I would never think of you that way, darling. You are a wonderful, beautiful, intelligent goddess."

Having met his wife at the Christmas party, I knew for a fact that this was simply *not* true. The woman had the face of a horse, the arse of an ox, and the laugh of a hyena on heat.

"You simply don't care Oscar. I *cannot believe* you left me this morning and went to the office!!"

"Darling, please don't upset yourself. You'll only make the headache worse. You know I had to go to the office ... it's my profession." He started to play with the telephone cord while I looked around the room, trying to create some diversion from the exhibition of marital discord and biting my bottom lip in an effort to suppress an emerging smile.

"Sometimes I think you don't love me at all Oscar."

"Oh *please*, don't say that darling! You know I love you. I love you very, very, very much." He spoke like he was stroking a tiger in a cat's skin.

In many ways, it could have been a conversation between my parents - only my father was not so subservient. I grabbed the file from him and mouthed, "I will call you." Then I fled from his office to the refuge of my own.

Usually at 11 a.m., my roommate and colleague Nigel would come by my office for a cup of coffee and a chat, which was welcome relief from the "billable time" target that hovered over our heads like a clockwork anvil.

Starbucks had just opened in Brighton, and we were gradually familiarizing ourselves with various terms, such as grande, latte, Frappuccino, and mochaccino. My first visit there had been a life changing event – so many choices! Before I had frequented a local cafe and had a choice of either black or white, involving only milk and certainly no cream. I had to admit I was intrigued at first by the wooden stir sticks replacing the familiar plastic spoon, but soon got the hang of buying coffee at an exorbitant price for the trendy experience of walking around sporting a Starbucks coffee cup.

It was Nigel's turn to get the order today. Who am I kidding ... I should start again. Nigel had gone for the coffee today, as he invariably did. He had turned out to be a great roommate and a wonderful confidante.

It was still gloomy outside, so I switched on all three lamps in my office and sat on the floor practising a few yoga poses to relieve the tightness in my neck. Like an exuberant pup, Nigel rushed through the door. His chestnut hair dripped down his freckled nose and his raincoat was splattered with raindrops. "Jesus, it's filthy out there Penn. I must remember once in a while to ask *you* to go and get the coffee."

"Oh, but you are so much better at it than I, Nigel." I pulled myself to my feet.

"They have a new barista over there – *very* nice....lovely smile and the body of a goddess."

"Wow, that's the second time I've heard that word today."

"Really? What context?"

"As in, Lady Hanley."

Nigel almost choked on his coffee. "Lady Hanley? A *goddess*? *Don*'t make me laugh."

"At least her husband seems to think so. They do say that beauty is in the eye of the beholder."

Nigel had a look of total disbelief on his face. "Well, I knew his glasses were old, but I'd say he definitely needs a new prescription."

"Yes, the words 'Red Rum' spring immediately to mind." I started to laugh. "Now, that's real breeding for you. God, I think I am going straight to hell when I die."

"Red Rum? Oh right, you mean the horse! What are you working on?" He scanned my desk, always on the lookout for something interesting to talk about.

"Nothing you'd be interested in." I found myself covering my notes relating to my meeting with Phil and the Anton Pillar Order.

"I'm completely bored upstairs at the moment. I had no idea working for the commercial department was going to be like this." He started playing with his hair, in an effort to help it dry.

"What did you expect? Did you think it would be any different from your articling experience?"

"I think I believed that I'd be doing a little bit more than form filling."

"Oh, just think about the money Nigel. In two years' time, you will be making more than any of us mere *'pee-ons'* that started out with you."

"Maybe." He didn't look convinced.

"How's Jenny? I haven't seen her at the flat much?" I suddenly lost eye contact.

"That would be because Jenny is no longer my girlfriend." He started fiddling with the lid on his coffee cup.

"Really? When did *that* happen?"

"About a week ago."

I really should pay more attention to the people in my life. "You never told me." I searched his face for signs of emotion, but could detect nothing other than evasion.

"It's not that important really. You know we barely had anything in common. Anyway, Jenny fell in love with some other guy at the polo club. So, thankfully I'm off the hook .... footloose and fancy free again!"

I stood up in full theatrical mode. "Is the world able to cope? Mothers lock up your daughters - Mr. Nigel Wilkinson is back on the market! Special one-time offer, roll up, roll up!!"

"I can think of a much better way of marketing myself thank you," he said, as he grabbed his crotch and started strutting around my office like Freddie Mercury, right about the same time as Anthony Jarvis, also known as "AJ," entered the room, coughing loudly enough to bring us both to our senses.

"Ah, Ms. Banfield, I thought I might interrupt your ... er ... whatever it is ... for a moment. There's something I wanted to talk to you about, if it's not too much to ask."

Wow, so sarcastic, still I expect he had every right – I was in fact supposed to be working. A very embarrassed Nigel gathered himself together, grabbed his coffee, and bolted out the door.

"So sorry about that sir." I looked in the general direction of the fleeting image of Nigel.

"I must say that I didn't realize that the two of you were ... *friends.*"

"Oh no nothing like that sir. We are just friends, well roommates actually."

"I see." He slowly surveyed my office in a very disapproving manner. "Well I must say, it's certainly very *cosy* in here."

"Yes, yes it is. I find I can concentrate way more when I'm relaxed."

"Really? Whereas I on the other hand insist on keeping the window open even on the coldest day, just to put me on edge and keep me *from* relaxing."

OUCH.

Aware of the personal dig, the litigator in me just couldn't let it go. "I wasn't aware that relaxing was a *bad* thing, sir?"

And there you have it, the very reason why I likely will never make partnership. When others just grin or smile, I simply have to have the last word. AJ inhaled deeply, speaking to me much like a judge delivering a verdict.

"Because I had not heard from you, I wanted to check that you are in fact in the office and going to be at the meeting this afternoon. Philip has told me that he intends to have you working very closely with him on the Seaton

Football Club case. It's therefore absolutely *imperative* that you are there."

SHIT! I forgot to reply to his bloody email! I found myself worrying about the implications of such insubordination in this world of hierarchy. Had I already earned a black mark beside my name?

"Of course sir. I'm sorry I haven't had time to respond yet to your email."

"No, well I can see you've been *busy,*" he sneered and with a dismissive nod, he left my office for the next victim of his ridicule.

Picking up the phone, I virtually spat out the words. "Nigel, I hope to God that you are *not* home when I get back to the flat because I seriously might throw you off the balcony."

"Hi Penn."

"What on Earth were you thinking?"

"Sorry about that, I just got a bit carried away. You'll have to wait until I get home from cricket if you want to throw me over the balcony."

"Not if this weather continues – you won't be playing in the rain will you?"

"It's possible I might prefer playing in the rain to enduring the wrath of Ms. Penny Banfield."

"Well, thanks to you Nigel, any ideas of longevity I ever had for my career with this firm have just flown out the window. He thinks I am a total imbecile now."

"Wow, that's a bit harsh Penn. If I recall, he might just as well have found you doing the downward dog – especially if he'd decided to walk in a few minutes earlier."

"OK, ok. Fair point. Oh bloody hell Nigel, he's going to be watching me like a hawk now."

"Better to be *noticed* than unnoticed my dear."

"Yes, but noticed for all the *right* reasons, not the wrong reasons. Sometimes I wonder how the hell you managed to pass the bar exams."

"Pure genius darling. You've either got it or you haven't."

"I hate you." I hung up, picked up the wobbly table file, thought better of it, and threw it back onto the desk. *How is a girl supposed to work when she doesn't have any damn chocolate!*

From: Penny Banfield
To: Reception
Date: May 8, 2000
Re: Supplies

Just gone out to Gita's for supplies, be back in 10 minutes.
Penny

Monday, May 8, 2000 (Afternoon)

Lunch for me was often a rushed affair. Today, I decided to miss lunch altogether having satisfied my hunger with a Lion Bar and packet of Revels picked up from my previous sugar run to Gita's. Incredibly thirsty due to the chocolate I had consumed and having completely blown any chance of having a "good day" calorie-wise, I decide to go all out and drink a can of Coke before my meeting at 2 p.m. AJ might need to keep the window open to keep alert, but I had other ways of achieving the same goal. God knows I had to be alert for this meeting, especially after the earlier debacle in my office.

I decided to get a head start on the intellectual property file and to help Mr. Peters solve the ever-taxing problem of getting through life without a wobbly table. I also needed to review the Rules of Court and get up to speed with Anton Piller Orders.

After drafting a Patent Form and Statement of Inventorship as far as I was able to, I drafted a letter to Mr. Peters asking for detailed drawings of his riveting invention. I then focused on a review of the rules surrounding the very draconian civil remedy of an Anton Piller Order and was able to make the following entries for my timesheet:

0.1 Unit – Legal discussion with Phil, re: Anton Piller Order - Montgomery #44654

0.1 Unit – Legal discussion with Oscar, re: Patent application - Peter #65576

1.2 Units – Draft Application for Patent - Peters #65576

0.2 Units – Draft correspondence to client – Peters #65576

0.5 Units – Brief review of Court Rules, re: Anton Piller Order – Montgomery #44654

On a normal day, I was expected to bill six hours per day. Well, 0.5 units = 30 minutes, 0.2 units = 12 minutes, with each unit representing six minutes. Today, in all honesty, the additional records could have been entered, yet sadly could not be regarded as legitimate "billable time."

0.4 units – Meeting with Phil to discuss golf, Tim Fairhurst, Raj Gosavi, the Ship and Anchor and Lord Oscar Hanley

0.1 unit – Unfortunate witness to ridiculous telephone conversation between Oscar and his wife, Red Rum

0.2 units – Yoga practice

0.3 units – Coffee meeting with Nigel; spectator to burlesque show by Nigel exhibiting masculine attributes

0.2 Visit to Gita's Newsagent to pick up sugar supplies

0.1 Eating sugar supplies

As there was no category of non-billable time reserved for *"Time wasting,"* I was unable to enter this time and would therefore have to find ways of making up the lost time, which inevitably meant working late. Ever wondered why lawyers often speak quickly or want to hurry along a conversation to the point where you can't speak quickly enough for them? Well, that is because they are trying to make up lost time and are being mentally tortured by that ticking clock inside their head.

The briefing meeting with AJ would however be a perfect billing opportunity, requiring very little effort other than the ability to listen and take notes. I was excited to learn about the order and how it was going to be implemented. It was such a rare occurrence in law that you would be hard pushed to find a senior litigator who had in fact ever applied for such an order. I was pleased to be given the opportunity to learn about it because in this business, opportunity means experience.

I picked up my perfectly organized handbag, pulled out my lip gloss and some gum, glanced at my reflection in the mirror behind my office door, and brushed back my hair with my hands again. My hair was driving me insane. After writing a sticky note, "Hair Appt," and sticking it to the screen of my computer, I made my way to the boardroom armed with the requisite yellow legal pad and a couple of pens. The bolt of sugar had kicked in, and I felt completely wired for the meeting. They always say the key to litigation is preparation, and I felt prepared.

Situated on the third floor, the boardroom was a spectacle of opulence with dark wood panelled walls, a crystal chandelier, Arabian rugs, and crystal-cut glasses set out on a silver tray beside the bar. The oval-shaped cherry wood table was surrounded by high-backed chairs and could comfortably accommodate 20 people at a time. I grabbed a seat next to Phil, relieved to see that he was at the meeting and on time.

"Here she is," he said as he mocked me as I set my things on the table, arranging them in an OCD fashion.

"Oh Phil, so glad you could make it." I whispered into his ear, "And what is more ... you don't even smell of alcohol. Very impressive."

Fairhurst and Gosavi were standing at the back of the room having a private conversation in muted tones, no doubt discussing their upcoming partnerships.

"Oh I wonder what they could possibly have to talk about?" I asked, unable to contain my jealousy.

"Who cares? They are both wankers as far as I'm concerned." Phil straightened his tie and started playing with his cufflinks.

"Because they've made partner, and you haven't!"
Surprisingly, he did not look at all bothered by the jab.

"No. It's because they are a couple of arse-lickers."
He smiled.

Leading my witness, I threw in another inflammatory
remark. "Wow ... do I detect a little bit of the green devil
rising to the surface?" Rather than irked, he seemed
amused.

"Are you kidding me? Why on Earth would I want to
be a partner? Can you just imagine being a partner with
this bunch of wankers? I like the freedom I have, thank
you very much."

"Good point, and I suspect your golf game would
suffer irreparable damage." I smiled.

Andrew Barker, "The fat boy from the 5th floor,"
appeared with his colleague Gavin Preston. Andrew
resembled a shaven pig wrapped in a suit, and Gavin was
dressed in a grey pinstripe suit, seemingly fashioned by a
Saville Row tailor. He wore it with a deep blue shirt and
muted gold tie.

I'd known Gavin for years. In fact, we had been to
law school together. Working on different floors,
however, we very rarely got to see each other except
perhaps at the firm's Annual General Meeting or Xmas
Party. Gavin was tall, blonde, and completely modest.
When talking to him, I found my hard exterior
completely dissolving and often had to look away,
concerned that I may be drooling too much while
marvelling at the sheer beauty of this Adonis (which
believe me is a rarity in the legal world).

To my knowledge, he was not gay and did not
currently have a girlfriend. Gavin was the object of desire

of practically every assistant and no doubt many of the female lawyers. He was, and always had been, out of my league. But that did not stop me from wishing and hoping, much like when one buys a lottery ticket every week.

"Hi Phil." Gavin smiled, offering his hand to Phil, who sprung up and shook his hand.

"Mr. Preston, sir. Nice to see you. How are things going on the 5th floor?"

"Busy. I'm in court practically four out of five these days."

"Good grief. I think you probably have more court experience than I do!" Phil said jokingly.

I found myself thinking that Phil would have way more court experience if in fact he spent more time in the office.

"Well, let me know if you want any more experience, we could certainly do with a hand up there." Gavin grinned.

"Hi Phil," said Fat Boy.

"Oh, hi Andrew – didn't see you there." Phil was so obviously lying, seeing as Andrew was practically impossible to miss, all 20 stone of him.

"I think you know Penny, don't you Gavin?" asked Phil.

"Of course. Hi Penny, good to see you again." Gavin smiled across the table as I started to blush.

"Hi Gavin, good to see you are on the team - it looks like it is going to be an interesting case."

"I think so. I've heard that many senior litigators don't even know what an Anton Piller Order is, as the circumstances arise so rarely."

"I know. I'm quite excited about it, although it's probably going to mean that we will all be working 24/7 for the next week or so."

"Hopefully you have an understanding boyfriend?" He smiled.

"Oh, I'm not with anyone at the moment." I suddenly felt like a complete loser.

"Really? I must say I find that hard to believe." I blushed so hard that I could feel heat coming off my cheeks. Sensing my embarrassment, and for once, Phil came to my aid.

"Penny, didn't you go to University with Gavin?"

"Yes, and I also spent a couple of months under his tutelage one summer."

Andrew interrupted, "Hey Penny. Are you sure we can't persuade you to join us up on the 5th floor permanently?" *Only if I can sit permanently at Gavin's desk ....*

"No, I think I'm quite happy in my current office, thanks."

"Christ, have you seen her office?" Phil said. "It's like a bloody cocktail lounge, nice cosy furniture, dimmed lights. My God, she even plays opera music in there!"

"Well, I must say that sounds very relaxing," said Gavin.

"I like to think so. My friend Nigel often pops in for coffee in the morning, just to relax in my office. I'm not sure if you know him - Nigel Wilkinson from commercial?"

"No, I'm sorry I don't think we've met." He seemed genuinely interested.

"Sounds like we should all *'pop in'* for a coffee or maybe even tea? I know I certainly could do with some relaxation," Phil said jokingly.

"Give over Phil ... as if your golf games aren't relaxing enough!" I said.

"It does sound like a good idea though," said Gavin.

"What? Golf? Or tea?" I tried to suppress my excitement as I fiddled with the strap of my handbag.

"Oh, I'm not a golfer. I was referring to the tea."

"Well, I do have an opening at three. *'Tea at Three'* would perhaps be fun?" I smiled.

"Pencil me in then. I'm definitely up for that." *My God, he was serious!*

"OK, will do – you know where my office is?"

"I think that if I can track down deadbeats that don't pay their bills, I should be able to find you Ms. Banfield."

0.1 Unit - Flirting with Gavin Preston

A sense of humour was so important in a man. I guess that was the one thing I did actually enjoy about Phil - he could always make me laugh - that is when he was not driving me insane. I hadn't realised that while I had been flirting, AJ had arrived.

AJ did look impressive for his age. He had quite an imposing effect on the room being so tall. Although, I liked his distinguished grey hair, I was very wary of those steele-blue eyes. He wore a plain, grey wool suit with a white shirt and red tie and had walked over to the bar to pour a glass of mineral water. I noticed that he did not invite us all to partake in libations with him. After finishing his refreshment, he sat at one end of the boardroom table and cleared his throat to garner attention from the group of lawyers and paralegals.

"OK everybody, I assume we all know what we are doing here. So I'm not going to waste your time. As most of you are aware, the firm has been acting for Seaton Football Club for some time now. A lawsuit has been brought in the High Court over an agency issue. I won't get into the full details of our case because everybody will receive copies of the pleadings and can read these later.

"In short, we act for Richard Montgomery, an ex-director of the club. He claims that Chairman Jim Bateman took a large fee for accepting their new player Steven Graham with full knowledge that the player was in fact badly injured at the time of the transfer.

"Our client believes that a few of the directors have deliberately withheld information and have documents that are relevant and helpful to our case. There is a real concern that the directors may even resort to destroying evidence if they get desperate enough. For this reason, we shall be making an application shortly to the Court for an Anton Piller Order. The Order, if granted, will provide us with a civil search warrant for a number of addresses relating to the directors in question. Some addresses are office premises, but most of them are residential addresses and homes of the current directors of the club.

"Please take a look around the room. These are your teammates. As a team, we will work together to ensure that the execution of the Order goes as efficiently as possible. Since preparation is the key to litigation, we will be meeting regularly to discuss progress on the Order and how it will take place. As you can imagine, it is *absolutely imperative* that this exercise goes well and without any hitch. We will need to ensure that all addresses are effectively *raided* at the same time to prevent the possibility of one party calling another to give them advanced warning of our visit, thereby providing an opportunity for them to destroy evidence.

"It goes without saying that everything that is discussed in this room is completely confidential, and I absolutely forbid you to talk about this to anyone, excluding those people currently in this room.

"This is an extremely unusual experience in the world of litigation as the Courts consider this remedy as an extreme, draconian remedy. We have therefore been provided with a rare opportunity to expand our expertise and demonstrate to our commercial clients that our firm's litigation department is able to practice litigation at the highest level.

"If anybody has any leave coming up or is not available within the next week or so, I would ask that you let me know immediately. At this stage, I can confirm that the raids will be taking place during the daytime and on a weekday. However, I need to know now if you are for some reason not able to accept the responsibility that is being placed on you."

There was complete silence in the room. I could see why AJ was a legendary litigator. He had a way of talking that commanded attention, and it was hard not to respect such an eloquent speaker.

"Within the next day or so, Philip Stevens - assisted by Penelope Banfield - will be submitting our application to the Court. I anticipate that they will obtain the Order without a hitch, and we will meet again at that time to go over the planned itinerary. Any questions?"

"Sir?" All eyes were on *"Fat Boy."*

"Barker?" AJ stared at Andrew with his steele-blue eyes while Andrew fidgeted with the cuffs to his shirt.

"If we have to work late, will we be able to claim overtime?"

I held my breath, anxious for him, as he had just committed career suicide in the presence of all his colleagues. *Of course* we would be paid overtime, but who in their right mind would have the audacity to show such entitlement publicly? I heard somebody further up the table, trying to suppress a laugh.

"Well of course, Mr. Barker. I had however hoped that the questions might relate to our *client's* needs rather than our own, but be rest assured that the firm will be paying full compensation for any personal time that may be lost."

Andrew slumped down like a huge sack of potatoes, and I felt sorry for his lack of awareness. Obviously, he had no concept of office politics and the fact that his question would be regarded as *"bad form"* by AJ. As I looked away from Andrew, I caught the eye of Gavin who looked equally as embarrassed for his friend. *Poor Andrew.*

"Any other questions?" AJ surveyed his team to see who would be brave enough to come forward now. This time, Phil stepped into the ring of fire.

"Although I am absolutely positive that there will be no issue with obtaining the Order, what alternatives would the firm have *other* than obtaining an Anton Piller

Order? I see that we have already obtained an order for specific discovery, but that proved to be fruitless."

Wow! Phil could certainly sound like a professional when he had to. I guess that was why they tolerated his golf escapades and casual attitude.

A stern looking AJ replied, "There are *no* alternatives. This is our last resort and that's why it's so important that we get it right."

As much as I tried to keep a tight grip on myself and despite my reluctance to draw further attention to myself in view of the episode earlier that morning in my office, I was unable to resist.

"Assuming the Order is granted without any issues sir, how much preparation time do you think we need to spend before executing the Order? Also, I believe it's necessary to have a supervising solicitor present. Have we decided which firm will be assuming this role?" I blushed, waiting for the inevitable sarcastic reply.

"Thank you Ms. Banfield. With respect to your former question, I anticipate we would need at least three days to prepare for the execution of the Order from the time the Order has been granted by the Court. With respect to the latter, the firm of Dinning Baker and Humphreys have agreed to act as supervising solicitors."

What no sarcasm? I waited and waited again, but there was no scorching reply. I threw a quick glance over to Gavin, who was nodding his head with approval.

"Anybody else?" The room was silent. "OK then, team. Meeting adjourned. I will email everyone when the Order has been obtained and will at that time, set our next meeting date." He picked up his notepad and marched out of the room with the stiffness of a flight commander.

I picked up my notes and hurried past Phil and the younger lawyers, who seemed to be extremely pleased at having been picked for the mission, like an elite team under orders from their flight commander.

"See you later Penny. Remember, our 'tea at three'?" Gavin said, as I brushed by.

"Fabulous. I'll see you then." With my back to him and fists clenched with excitement, I mouthed the words, *"Thank you God."* Never before had a cup of tea held so much promise.

At 3 p.m., Gavin arrived to a scene that unbeknownst to him had been totally staged. The kettle had boiled and was piping hot. I sat at my desk, lipstick freshly applied and hair perfectly groomed, and had just spritzed the room with Guerlain before sitting at my desk, seemingly engrossed in my work. I looked up slowly, but managed to look surprised at just the right time saying, "Oh Gavin, is it that time already? Please ... come in."

"My God, this office *is* incredible, and it smells so nice in here. Now, I know why the other lawyers call this the cocktail lounge." He laughed.

"Do they really?" I had in fact heard this comment from Phil more than once a week over the past year.

"Well, as much as I would love to share a cocktail with you, I know that we are both professional people. So, I'm sure we can make do with an Earl Grey instead."

I picked up some china cups from the tea tray and opened the mahogany box with a full tea selection.

"Let me see now, Earl Grey ... chamomile ... or would you like to check out the selection yourself?" I beckoned him over to the tea. He came over to my side and started to run his slender fingers over the various sachets of tea.

"Um ... well now, you've given me a choice I think I might like to try something other than Earl Grey." He picked up a sachet of Darjeeling and gently placed it in my hand. Trying my best Geisha impression, I slowly pulled the bag from its sachet and placed it gently in the cup, pouring the boiling water over the fragrant tea.

"Honey?" I asked.

"Yes darling," he said jokingly, and again I blushed profusely.

"No ... I mean, would you like honey?"

"I know." He smiled.

I spooned in some honey and handed his cup to him. I hastily made my cup of tea and led the way to the leather sofa, walking as daintily as possible, playing to my audience.

"Well, this is nice." Gavin stretched his legs out and loosened his tie.

"I have to say that I think I much prefer '*Tea at Three*' rather than my coffee break at eleven." *Nigel would be devastated to hear such a thing.*

"Well, I can only hope that it has something to do with the company?"

"Maybe ..." I tried my best at a beguiling smile.

"You know, I'm pretty sure that there must be some rule against this?"

"What? Having *Tea at Three*? Surely not- it's extremely British." I looked at him sideways.

"Well, I'm not sure if *Tea at Three* is supposed to be so *enjoyable*."

"As you can tell, I like *enjoyable*. I also like all things that are comfortable, oh, and relaxing."

"Apparently so." He looked around the room. "How do you manage to stay awake in here with all the dimmed lighting?"

"I don't find it a problem, probably because I'm a *night* person."

"Is that so?"

"Absolutely." The air was thick with innuendo.

We both sipped our tea, maintaining eye contact all the time. It certainly was proving to be the best cup of tea I had had in a very long time.

"Well I can't believe this is the first time we've actually socialized together." Gavin stared at me, and it felt like his eyes were bearing through to my soul.

"I know – it's ridiculous to think that we work for the same firm, isn't it? I mean I don't think I've even seen you in the lobby."

"We must have completely different schedules," said Gavin.

"Yes that must be it. You are basically in Court every day, and I am at the beck and call of Phil every day." I grimaced.

"How do you like working with Phil?" He was on a fishing expedition.

"How well do you know him?" A lawyer is always good at answering a question with another question.

"Not very well. Actually, I've heard he's a bit of a dick."

"Yes, he can be." I put my finger across my lips pondering whether I should go on. "He's got a kind heart though - and believe it or not - a very sharp brain, although he does hide it well." I laughed.

"Well, he certainly doesn't like me." Gavin said looking down at his shoes and brushing off some lint from his very expensive suit.

"Why do you say that?"

"For one thing, I never get invited to the pub whenever he arranges drinks after work."

"Neither do I."

"I mean, when he invites the *boys* out."

"Oh, I wouldn't worry about that. In fact, I think you should take it as a compliment Gavin. I'm not sure that you would find Phil's *friends* at all intellectually stimulating."

"Really? Why do you say that?"

"Well, let me see – there's Timothy Martin also known as *"Tim-Tim-Nice but Dim"* who works for Bramstons. He's a legal executive who looks like he should be selling second-hand cars. Phil's other friend Mickey, sorry I can't remember his surname, but that's probably because I happen to think he's the most vulgar individual I've ever had the misfortune of spending time with, works at the casino and spends all his time talking about '*hot totty.*' Then of course, there is his other friend Danny Beable, the rugby player. Perfectly charming until he's had two pints, and then he spends the majority of his time groping your backside like it's a new form of a rugby ball."

"A bit rough around the edges then?"

I found myself staring at the crease lines to his eyes, which were so incredibly attractive. "Very. In fact, I'd call them highly abrasive. I can't stand the company Phil keeps. Still, at least he can hold his own at this place. I know AJ has a lot of time for Phil, and it can't be totally misplaced." It was one of life's mysteries to me how Phil managed to stay on the right side of AJ.

"Guess not."

"But seriously, I think you should really take it as a compliment that he doesn't invite you to the pub."

"Why?"

"I wouldn't be surprised if Phil thinks you are out of his league. He likes hanging around with people he feels are a little inferior to him."

"That is quite a statement – thanks."

I grabbed his cup from him. "More tea?"

"No. Thank you. I think I should get back to my desk. I have to say Penny, this has been extremely enjoyable. I do hope we can do this again sometime?"

I practically jumped all over him like a fat kid on a Smartie. "How about tomorrow? I always have *Tea at Three*, and I'd love some intelligent company." I then tried to look as nonchalant as possible.

"Sounds perfect - see you tomorrow then."

"Absolutely." I turned to my side credenza returning the cups on the tray. As I turned to face Gavin, he was standing right behind me.

"Oh Gavin - sorry I didn't see you there!"

"Don't work too hard." He kissed me on the forehead, turned, and left leaving behind a trembling fool of a woman.

Concentrating for the rest of the afternoon proved fruitless as my mind seemed trapped, like a bee in a honey jar. I was at a place where I had almost given up on love, but lust was OK. I found myself questioning his sincerity, but that was hardly surprising in view of my recent break-up.

I was woken from my reverie as my telephone rang flashing, "Val Green," on the call display. Val Green was Lord Hanley's assistant and had worked for him for years.

"Hi Val." I said with as much enthusiasm as if taking out the rubbish. In an effort to keep my overhead expenses low (making me more profitable as a lawyer), I had decided not to have an assistant. Unfortunately, some of my billable time was taken up by Val and her technological disability.

"Oh thank goodness, you are there!"

I could feel my heart sinking as I glanced at my watch. "What's the problem Val?"

"Oh Penny, I do hope you can help – Oscar wants to get this letter out before the mail goes, and I've got a dreadful problem with my computer. I don't know what to do!"

"What exactly is *wrong* with your computer?"

She whispered into the phone, "I'm getting messages."

"What do you mean *messages?*"

"My computer is sending me messages."

Like from outer space you idiot? "Sorry Val, I'm not with you. You are receiving messages from your computer? What kind of messages?" I noticed I had started to grind my teeth.

"All sorts of messages really ... some say, '*Error,*' some say something like. '*Not Found,*' but mostly something to do with errors. I keep pressing all the buttons, but they won't go away."

"OK Val. Just press Control, Alt, Delete, and then exit. You probably need to restart your computer."

"OK – can you hold on while I do it, just in case it doesn't work for me?" *A chimp could do it Val.* "Of course." I tapped my pencil repeatedly on my desk while I waited.

"Now then, let me see ... CONTROL ... ALT ... DELETE ... "

"Anything happen Val?" I needed this interruption like a hole in the head.

"Nothing."

"Nothing? Are you sure you pressed the CONTROL, ALT, and DELETE buttons?"

"Yes, yes, just as you said, 'CONTROL, then ALT, then DELETE'."

"No ... No Val ... you are supposed to press all the buttons at the *same time*, CONTROL, ALT, AND DELETE - *all together* at the same time."

She was a victim of technology. I sighed heavily. "Is any other assistant close to your desk right now?"

"No, Sylvie went to the doctor's."

"OK, I'll have to come down to your office. Don't touch anything else!"

I was always getting ridiculous calls like this from Val. She had a fear of computers and had complained vociferously when they first introduced her to the computer, clinging to her IBM golf-ball typewriter for years after the word processor had arrived. Her idea of trouble-shooting seemed to be to press any button on the keyboard until the message disappeared. The problem was that one message would disappear only to be replaced by another more sinister message. Val believed that the computer had a mind of its own and was capable of not only receiving messages from some other entity but capable perhaps of even telepathy.

I arrived at her desk further along the corridor. Her desk was littered with used tissues and a roll of toilet roll sitting on top of her filing cabinet. She suffered from allergies and had long given up the idea of using a box of tissues or a pretty cotton handkerchief. Her waste paper bin was overflowing with used tissues. This display was enough to give a germaphobe a nervous breakdown.

"OK, let's see." I peered at the message that now read:

Control error – call system administrator

"Watch this Val. I am sure you will find it really helpful." *God knows I would certainly find it helpful if you would only get this into your thick skull.* "CONTROL and ALT with your left hand and DELETE with your right hand *at the same time* … See? What it does is turns off your computer, and then you can start all over again." *And cock it all up again, no doubt.*

"Oh Penny, thank you so much! You are such a genius with the computer, you know."

Hardly Val ... the problem is that you are computer illiterate. She looked like a throwback from the sixties with black dyed hair styled in a beehive fashion. She wore a skin-tight leopard print dress with red high heels. Maybe the pipe dreams of her boss, Oscar, had fuelled her dreams of being a partner's assistant? Who knew? One thing was for sure – her attire was most definitely not that of a typical partner's assistant.

0:3 Units – Training session with Val (A COMPLETE WASTE OF TIME!!)

It seems that Val's interruption had sufficiently brought me down to Earth after my interlude with Gavin. I was able to get down to the drafting of the Anton Piller application. Placing my phone on "Do Not Disturb," I got down to business. I reviewed the Civil Rules again, this time making notes:

- Notice of application must be served on each respondent.
- Made without notice if permitted by Rule, Practice Direction or Court Order.

Great – that was exactly what I needed. I scanned the rules making further notes of what the notice must include:

- *What Order we are seeking*
- *Why we are seeking the order*
- *Verify Notice by Statement of Truth*

I then consulted a Practice Direction known by lawyers as a "PD" relating to interim injunctions and made further notes.

- *Order served personally by Supervising Solicitors*
- *Accompanied only by persons stated in the order*
- *Can only be served between 9:30 and 5:30 (Monday to Friday)*

I spent the next one-and-a-half hours typing, re-drafting, scratching my head, yawning, and stretching until I was satisfied that the application was ready for review by Phil in the morning. I printed out the document, took a deep breath, and pressed my shoulders back down to their original position. I looked at the clock – 5:30 p.m. I had missed my usual train, so I picked up the flashing voicemail message indicator that had been bothering me like a barking dog somewhere in the distance.

"Penny, it's Phil – I'm meeting some of the lads at the Ship and Anchor if you are interested in joining us. Hope to see you later."

Not likely Phil – I'd rather spend the evening with a glass of wine and a hot bath rather than listen to your mates sucking up to you. I called him. "Hi Phil, got your message. Thanks for the invite, but I just want to go home and jump in the bath."

"Hmmm, now that sounds like a *much* better idea," he teased.

"Oh, get over yourself Phil." I hung up on him. Yawning, I grabbed my trench coat and pigskin briefcase and made my way to the railway station on Queens Road. The Victorian railway station had an impressive wrought-iron glass roof and red brick exterior. Typical of most British railway buildings, it smelled of ground-in cigarette ash and musty soot. The interior was also typical with iron benches painted glossy black, overflowing rubbish bins, and the occasional burst of colour provided by bookstalls and flower vendors. Here was also the place that only the desperate would frequent – the British Rail café offering sandwiches seemingly made from cotton wool bread, cardboard sausage rolls, and tea that looked and tasted like muddy water. I bought a copy of the *Argus* and sat down on a bench to browse the newspaper.

"FOOTBALL CLUB CALLS EXTRA-ORDINARY GENERAL MEETING TONIGHT. IS OUR CLUB IN TROUBLE?"

According to our sources, Chairman Jim Bateman and the Board of Directors have called an Extra-Ordinary General Meeting to be held tonight relating to a possible sale of assets. We understand that the club is looking for alternative ways of increasing revenue other than through the turnstiles...."

Interesting ... it was obviously a busy time for the Club directors and unbeknownst to them, things were about to get a whole lot busier.

The boardroom at Seaton Athletic Football Club had large, glass windows overlooking the lush green pitch, a contrastingly peaceful place without the rowdy crowd that showed up weekly to cheer on their team.

The boardroom table had certainly seen better days. The whole room was a little shabby with fake wooden panelling and a film of sticky dust that refused to budge, much like the chairman of the club. Adorned by dusty trophies, it was a rather a sorry sight. As was customary, the Board members sat around the table cradling crystal-cut glasses with whiskey they would need to sustain them through a gruelling meeting if the agenda was anything to go by.

Jim Bateman, the chairman, was a burly man with a freckled complexion and fiery red hair, a "Ginger" as his friends would call him. He had been married for 40 years to Lillian, but had often "played away from home" with his extra-marital affairs to which Lillian had turned a blind eye. Previously, he had been a professional player - albeit for a fourth division team. But due to an injury, his promising career had ended suddenly, much like the shock of a goal hitting the back of the net.

In addition to his duties as chairman, he and his family were market traders and had been for over a century. The market that Jim and his brother, Spencer, owned was very lucrative and certainly more financially viable than the football club. Although Spencer ran the market, Jim would help out once a week to keep an eye on the family business and check that Spencer did not have his *"hand in the till."*

Peter Thompson, the Club's vice president, was a thin man with pinched features and high cheekbones. His hair was long and held back in a ponytail. He wore a pin-striped suit with a bright red tie that stood out against his white shirt like a tart's lipstick. Surprisingly, his vocabulary had expanded beyond the profanities of the world of football, but that was not to say he could not be susceptible to the occasional outburst when provoked. He sidled over to Jim, pulling him gently by the elbow away from a conversation.

"OK Jimmy, anything you want to tell me about before we get started?"

"Just need you to vote with me on the sale, Pete."

"You mean we have a choice?" Pete smiled.

"Oh, and I take it I do have your support with the ongoing court case?" Jim raised his eyebrows at Pete. "We need to ensure we have the funding so we can carry on defending ourselves against that bastard and his vicious lawyer, Tony Jarvis."

"Don't worry mate, your golden," Pete said to reassure him.

"Thanks Pete. It's at times like this that you really get to know who your friends are." Jim chuckled, the chuckle turning into a cough as if often did. He picked up his glass and took a swig, which somehow seemed to help settle him down. "Best get on with it then. Speak to yer later mate." Jim picked up a teaspoon from his coffee cup and tapped it against his whiskey glass. "OK, okay, let's 'ave some order *gentlemen. Please* take yer seats, and let's get started."

There was a scuffle as the men finished off their conversations and made their way back to their seats around the table. "Right then. Regrets, let's see now ... Mr. Steven Dixon, Mr. Christopher Ballam, and Mr. Andrew Barton."

There followed various mutterings of disapproval due to lack of attendance of said directors, which shortly settled down. "Ok, Ok, now let's get started with the agenda shall we? Item No. 1 - *Discuss purchase of new player for next season.* Attached to the agenda is a list of suggested players, and I have to say that some of these names are *very* impressive. So thanks to Frankie Marshall for putting together this list and for doing all the groundwork necessary to come up with a rough estimate of likely transfer fee. I personally feel that because of the next agenda item, it would make sense if we were to take the list away, think about it, and discuss this perhaps at our next meeting."

Jim stared down at the agenda, but heard a comment from the back of the room from one of the directors. "Oh, why's that Jim? Because we might not have any money anyway to pay for new players? *Especially* if we keep crossing the palms of transfer agents with silver!"

"Now then – I don't know who just made that comment at the end of the table," Jim said as he stared around the seated directors like a lion searching for his next meal, "But if there is anybody here that thinks I've had my hand in the till and that the allegations against me in this lawsuit are true, I'd like to know about it right now." There was silence around the table.

"How in God's name am I expected to do my job without the *full support of the Board*?!" Again there was more silence apart from a little paper shuffling at the end of the table. "We all know that Rick Montgomery has initiated this lawsuit against me and the Club because he is sore about the way he was pushed off the Board. He wants blood, more specifically, *my* blood. The only thing he could dream up was this spurious claim that there have been dirty deals going on with respect to contracts for players. I assure you gentleman that the claim is on a hiding to nowhere and that Tony Jarvis is no match for our brief, Paul Silverman. Paul's got the bit between the teeth now and won't let go until he gets the job done. Now then, does anybody have anything they want to share with the Board on this subject?"

The stony silence continued, interrupted only by the occasional nervous cough.

"Right then, let's move on to Item No 2 - *Review of proposal by Trico Superstores and purchase of the stadium grounds for redevelopment.*"

Various sub-discussions started up of varying degrees of passion. After a couple of minutes, the room had to be brought to order.

"As you can see, the offer that has been put forward is a 2.2 million pound offer for the purchase of the freehold, or there is an alternative offer for a 199-year lease of the grounds. Frankly, my opinion is that a lease of the grounds is a non-starter because we need the capital in order to purchase an alternative stadium, unless we are able to find something to lease on the outskirts of town.

We'd have to look at a more tertiary position, rather than prime retail real estate that we currently hold."

Several hands went up around the room. Jim pointed at one man seated at the table. "OK David, what do you have to say?"

Director David Peterson stood up, straightening his grey, striped tie. "I can totally see the advantages of selling the freehold and buying elsewhere in a less prominent retail position in town. But having said that, I wonder if all we are doing is downsizing and effectively not protecting the assets of the Club?"

Sarcastically, somebody with a huge smirk on his face said, "Yes, but we have to pay for the litigation *somehow*, David."

"Of course the directors could always agree that the litigation be settled and our continual costs with respect to this debacle are curtailed once and for all!" yelled another director from across the room. As if lighting a touch paper, the room exploded with various directors standing, ranting, and waving fists similar to the fans of the football club they were representing.

"Order! *Order!* I call this meeting to Order, *please* gentleman take your seats! I realize that this is a highly emotional subject, but please remind yourselves that we have responsibility as Board members to decide these matters in the *best interest of the club* and its members." Jim tried to calm things down.

There followed a mutter of grumbling and scraping of chairs as people were re-seated. "We will soon get to Item #3 on the agenda, the litigation. But in the meantime, we have to discuss this offer from Trico, which expires tomorrow at midnight." Jim sounded weary.

One of the directors, Mark Steadman, dressed very casually as if he had just walked off the golf course, put his hand up. "I really don't understand why we are under such a tight deadline. When exactly was this offer received?"

Jim Bateman stood up as if giving evidence in Court. "The offer was received a day before the notice of Extraordinary General Meeting went out."

"I just think the deadline is tight Jim, that's all," said Mark.

"You know these big stores. They are always in the best bargaining position, and they take advantage of that position. I am sure that they have a deadline for breaking ground on the new development and a number of alternative prospects lined up should the Club decline either of the offers on the table."

"Can't we request an extension of the offer, Jim? I mean, until this whole litigation thing is put to bed, I don't think it is wise to make a decision with respect to the sale of the Club. A number of directors here feel it would be better for the Club if we were to take a holding position until such time as the litigation has been finalized."

"Yes Mark, we could of course ask for an extension on the deadline, but there is no guarantee that they will agree to one. I would think they are just as likely to look further down the road and see whether the old Bingo Hall will consider their offer instead. The other thing is that we have no idea of how much longer the litigation is likely to continue. "

Noel Barrington, a grey haired director dressed in a navy blue blazer and cravat yelled, "If we settled right now, we would!"

"Settlement will require *money*. Money that we don't have," Jim said as he sighed and sat down.

"So what you are really saying is that we have no choice other than to accept this offer, downsize so that we have some funds in reserve in order to pay a judgment against us, if that is the way the litigation pans out?" Noel looked disgusted.

Jim stared at the oak table twiddling his pen. "I personally think that would be the best course of action, in order to avoid insolvency of the Club."

"Insolvency that you have brought upon us!" Andrew Barton, a tall, raven haired director wearing tortoise shell rimmed spectacles had just appeared in the doorway of the boardroom to the apparent astonishment of Jim Bateman.

"Oh Andrew, what a surprise. I thought you were unable to join us this evening?"

"I bet you did!" Andrew gloated. "I expect that that's the reason why I didn't receive notification of tonight's Board meeting in the mail, right Jim?"

"I have no idea what you are talking about. By the way, I take that as a personal slight against me." Jim looked around the room in an effort to garner support, which did not appear to be forthcoming.

"You can take it any way you want Jim, but if I hadn't talked with David yesterday, I wouldn't have known about this meeting, which no doubt you will put down to some clerical error. In any event, I am here now and will vote accordingly."

"No doubt." Jim pointed out an empty chair around the table gesturing to Andrew to sit down.

"No thanks. I don't think I could possibly sit when I am so ill at ease with the way this Club is currently headed and the underhand way in which it is being managed."

"Be very careful Andrew, I take it you are aware of the law of *defamation*?"

"Becoming quite the lawyer aren't you now that you are spending so much time with the litigators of this world."

"You seem to be implying that I am personally responsible for the lawsuit that's been filed against us?"

"Well, you are in fact being accused of fraud aren't you? I believe that this litigation could already have been settled if not for your belligerent lack of conciliation. But now that I'm in receipt of a copy of it, I see that discussion of the litigation issue has been left for Item #3 on the agenda. That in itself shows me that perhaps you are underestimating the importance of the effect this litigation is having on our football club."

Mark Steadman stood up. "I completely agree with Mr. Barton. Perhaps we should consider Item #3 of the agenda first and receive a complete update before we vote on Item #2? I move that we vote on a change of the order to the agenda."

"I second that," responded Andrew Barton while Jim Bateman stared at the two of them, trying to figure out whether this had all been pre-planned.

"OK then, all those who agree, please raise your right hand." There was an immediate show of hands. "Motion carried."

Jim sighed. "Item #3: *Update on litigation.* We are currently at a stage of the litigation called, Discovery. Some time ago, we served our List of Documents on the other side, which then led to a number of queries as the plaintiff believes we have not handed over all the documents in our possession."

"And have we disclosed all documents in our possession?" said Andrew.

"We complied with our obligations as far as my interpretation of the rules were concerned," Jim replied.

Like a dog, Andrew barked back. "And what about our lawyer? What did he think?"

"Paul Silverman did express his opinion that we might be subject to a request for specific Discovery, which did in fact transpire. Subsequently, there was an Order for Discovery made by the court for us to disclose further documents. We have now complied with that Order."

"OK Jim. In plain English, if you don't mind for those directors with no legal experience! What the fuck does that mean in layman's terms?" Andrew was glaring at Jim.

"Please keep your filthy language for the soccer field Andrew – this is a gentleman's environment, as you well know."

"Well, I had always thought so up until the point when we started to discuss whether or not we have to comply with the law."

Jim continued, "The other side did not believe we had provided them with every document in our possession, and therefore we received something called an Order for Specific Discovery. We were ordered by the court to provide copies of all computer records, emails (even those that have been archived), personal bank statements, and investment statements for various directors, including myself."

"And have we now provided *all* of those documents?" Andrew continued like a dog chewing on a bone.

"We provided *some* of those documents – those that we consider to be *relevant*." Jim shifted uneasily in his seat.

"And the reason for not providing *all* of those documents is...?" Andrew raised his eyebrows, looking over his spectacles.

"I, together with a few other directors, consider it to be extremely prejudicial to have to provide all of my personal financial accounts and bloody emails to the court. We have provided the documents we think that they are *entitled* to see."

"Entitled to see as far as *you* are concerned or as far as the *law* is concerned?"

"Same difference." Jim brushed off the retort.

"With all due respect Mr. Bateman, it is *not* the same as you well know. In fact, I am certain that Paul Silverman has advised you of it. If you want to be cavalier and play games with the court system, that is entirely your personal privilege. But when you are representing the best interests of this Club, I suggest that your *personal* privilege has no part to play in all of this."

"That's easy for you to say when you personally are not a subject to the Order for Specific Discovery."

"We are here to represent the interests of the Club, James. Surely, I don't have to remind you of that. It appears that perhaps you are conflicted between your own interests and that of the Club? What is more, I cannot believe you are putting this football club at risk because of your own shady dealings or whatever financial transactions you are trying to hide."

"Again Mr. Barton, I would ask that you restrain from making disparaging remarks about my character, which could easily lead you to court in defence of a defamation action."

"It's only defamation if untrue James. Remember that and you could save yourself from wasting your time and money in court."

"Well, we are not all blessed to work within the legal system like you, Andrew."

Visibly seething, cheekbones flaring, Peter Thompson stood up and commanded the room to silence. "OK, that is enough! I would like to ask what the next steps are with respect to the litigation and how close we are to ending it."

Jim was pleased for the reprieve from Andrew's cross-examination. "Thanks Peter. After the Discovery stage, we then start to prepare for trial, the preparation of witnesses, and gathering evidence for our case."

"Has a hearing date been scheduled yet?" Andrew asked.

"Yes, for December, next year."

"What? That is over a year from now!" said David Peterson.

"The court system is backed up, and you have to wait a long time for a trial date. That's exactly why we can't let this litigation stand in the way of consideration of such a favourable offer from Trico, which I consider to be a once-in-a-lifetime opportunity for the Club." Jim stood again, his voice trembling in an effort to control his rage. "Please remember gentleman, if we *win* this case, we stand to recoup double the costs we have paid."

"And if we lose, we stand to pay a substantial amount of money together with double costs. I'm not much into gambling Jim, at least not with this football club," said Andrew.

"We are *defendants* to this action. As such, we don't exactly have a choice other than to deal with the litigation."

"Well, there's always an opportunity for settlement!" Andrew said with exasperation.

"That's right, Andrew. Let's spend money we don't have," Jim said as he continued to spar with his nemesis.

"Or maybe sell the Club so that we do have the money to spend further on this litigation? I suggest you have your priorities completely in the wrong place," said Andrew.

"OK gentleman!" Pete Thompson shouted. "ENOUGH!! We've had an update on the litigation. Now, let's get back to Item No.2, consideration of the offer from Trico. Do we have any other questions with respect to the offer? You've all had an opportunity to read the offer in detail, as it was attached to the notice. Andrew, I take it you also have a copy of the offer?" Andrew nodded.

"Well then, are there any questions? Anybody?" Pete seemed anxious to move on. "If we accept the offer, do we already have in mind alternative premises, Jim?"

"Yes, we have located a wonderful space on Sutton Road with more land than we currently need. So there's room for expansion and at a cost of approximately

800,000 pounds for the freehold, which means an overall increase in capital of 950,000 pounds after debts if we sell to Trico." Jim was surprisingly calm at this moment.

"How certain are we that they will accept our offer of 800,000 pounds on the Sutton Road property?" David Peterson asked.

"It's in the bag, don't worry." Jim smiled.

"I bet it is," Andrew muttered while looking down at the offer.

"Right then, let's vote on the issue of whether we want to accept the offer to lease the grounds on a 199-year lease. All those in favour, please raise their hands." Two hands were gingerly raised into the air. "OK then, motion dismissed. Next motion, all those in favour of the sale to Trico for 2.2 million pounds freehold and moving to alternative premises on Sutton Road, please show your hands."

"Hold on, this is all happening too soon!" David stood up. "I think we should at least have an opportunity of visiting the alternative site before we vote on it?"

"Gentleman, at some stage there has to be trust among fellow directors as to alternative premises. We are under the gun to accept this very favourable offer by tomorrow. Trico don't care where we go to find an alternative stadium and fuck me – I'd have the guys playing on the beach if necessary if it means we can accept this one-time offer and have some capital in the bank to secure the long-term future of the Club. You all know that the turnstile figures are down and the stadium grounds are getting to the stage where substantial renovations have to be paid for. We need new talented players to bring in more money at the turnstiles. I seriously don't see that we have any alternative." Jim pleaded with his fellow directors.

"Couldn't we ask for an extension while we look at the other site?" David said.

"Yes we could, but I really don't think we are showing good faith if we ask to have the offer extended," Jim said as he was shaking his head.

"I think we should at least try." David looked around the room for support.

Pete Thomson stood up. "OK then, who votes in favour of Jim asking for an extension of the offer until Friday of this week to give us some time to view the alternative premises on Sutton Road, bearing in mind that there is a possibility that they will walk and take the offer with them?" He looked around the room, and only three hands went up around the table.

"Motion dismissed then. OK. Let's now vote on whether we are prepared to accept the offer to sell the stadium for $2.2 million. A show of hands please, gentlemen." Fifteen hands went up, including that of Jim and Peter.

"Motion carried. OK Jim, I take it you can take things from here and let the lawyers know that we will be accepting the offer. I suggest an immediate field trip for those directors who have not yet had an opportunity to visit the Sutton Road premises." Pete glanced across the table at Jim, doing his best not to smile. There was a moment of complete silence while the directors tried to comprehend what had just happened.

"Right then. Is there any other business?" Jim glanced around the stunned room, trying to conceal the sense of achievement he felt at getting his own way. *Well, that's a first,* he muttered to himself. "OK then, next meeting is scheduled for the evening of Wednesday, May 17, which should give us sufficient time to have carried out the field trip to Sutton Road."

He pushed his chair away from him, grunting while pushing himself to his feet. Small groups of men talking in hushed voices had started to form in the boardroom while Jim collected his papers from the table, sauntered toward Peter and giving him a wink as he passed by.

Eventually, the glossy blue (or was it green? I don't know because I'm among the 0.5 percent of women who are colour blind) train crept along the silver rails, expelling weary passengers onto the grey platform. I edged my way forward to the train, wary of the heavy doors that would often just spring open, catching you with their silver butterfly handles. To anybody not familiar with a British Rail train, there are number of things that you need to know in order to survive the experience:

The windows are opened by pressing the silver edge down against the rubber seal while contemporaneously sliding the bar and window down (NOT EASY).

The doors are opened from the inside by pressing the metal device across with your thumb (CAUTION: TERRIBLE NAIL BREAKING HAZARD).

When getting OFF the train, make sure that you are opening the correct door (on the left or right depending on which side the platform will appear as the train pulls into the station). (BE CAREFUL IF YOU ARE INEBRIATED AS YOU MIGHT FALL OUT OF THE TRAIN AND ON TO THE TRACKS).

Avoid all eye contact with fellow passengers unless you want them to strike up a conversation with you for an inordinate amount of time, spoiling the only "alone time" you are likely to have for that day.

If you happen to accidentally sit next to an unsavoury fellow passenger, cough like crazy and fake a terrible flu-like illness (THEY WILL MOVE AWAY FROM YOU).

In only the most desperate of situations should you endeavour to use the washroom or W.C. / toilet as it is known in England (WILL LEAVE THIS TO YOUR IMAGINATION).

I climbed the two, worn wooden steps into the carriage of the train and found myself a window seat. Most of the passengers were commuters at this time of the day, thankfully. Commuters tend to be quiet and insular. There seemed to be a code of conduct between us that required a total lack of acknowledgment of each other.

I took the same train every morning, standing with the same people, at the same place along the platform, which inevitably meant you would be in the same carriage together day after day. I had taken this commuter train at 8:30 a.m. from Hove to Brighton for two years, yet knew absolutely nothing about the people around me.

There had been an occasion when a train had been delayed for an hour because there had been a fatality (somebody had thrown themselves onto the line). In that hour, we did actually acknowledge each other's presence.

But even so, the conversation was limited to small talk about the weather and, oh how could I forget, the sarcastic remark about the inefficiency of British Rail? (Though how they were supposed to avoid somebody who had decided to end their own life was beyond me). Despite that one brief interlude, we were surprisingly quite happy to return to anonymity the following morning.

Occasionally, I would get lucky and have an empty seat beside me. Despite my little ploy of coughing profusely, unfortunately tonight I had company that refused to move. He was a middle-aged balding man wearing thick-rimmed Buddy Holly glasses. He took off his raincoat, folded it nicely, and while stretching over me to the storage rack above, I was able to get a whiff of the day's perspiration that almost made me gag. I rummaged around in my handbag for a peppermint to distract my senses and closed my eyes in an effort to block him out of my "space."

The gentle rolling of the carriage from side to side will often lull passengers into a state of semi-consciousness. Unfortunately, I was rudely pulled from this comforted state by the thud of something on my shoulder. I opened my eyes to see "Mr. Middle-Aged-Man" with his head perched at an angle on my shoulder, glasses pushed halfway across his forehead, mouth wide open, dribbling all over my Laura Ashley suit. I gently pushed my elbow into his ribcage, but to no avail. Of course, I had no choice other than to increase the force of my elbow to the point that he was startled, quickly replaced his glasses, and wiped the drool from his face with the sleeve of his jacket - while I stared out of the window trying to hide my evil, little grin.

My flat was a short walk from the station in a block of eight flats with a shared communal garden in a quiet and respectable neighbourhood. I had bought the flat a few years ago and was still in the process of making it home. A year or so after I moved in, Nigel had needed a place to live as a short-term thing, after another break-up. Somehow, Nigel just never seemed to leave. In truth, I quite liked having him around. He wasn't home all the time, usually staying either with girlfriends, one-night stands, or at his parents' country cottage in Glyndebourne on the weekends.

It had stopped raining, and I knew Nigel would not be back until quite late since he would usually go for a pint after cricket. Opening the door, I threw my trench coat on the coat stand and kicked off my shoes to rub my sore ankles. I immediately began to peel off my clothes, put on my silk robe, and headed for the bathroom to my pride and joy - a Victorian cast iron bath with clawfoot legs. I turned the brass taps. After adding a few drops of rosemary and lavender oils, I left the bath to draw while I headed to the kitchen.

Plucking a glass from the cupboard (meant for red but that did not deter me), I poured a respectable measure of ice cold Chablis while glancing at my answering machine. No messages. Thank heavens; the night was mine. Now, I could luxuriate in a fragrant bath and relive my earlier rendezvous with Gavin in blissful peace.

CHAPTER 2 - TUESDAY MAY 9, 2000

I spent the night tossing and turning in my bed and had basically given up ever trying to get to sleep after hearing Nigel come back from the pub. I couldn't decide whether my lack of sleep was because of my encounter with Gavin earlier in the day or due to the massive amount of sugar I had consumed. In any event, I had no time to stop for a coffee on my way to the office this morning and had to do with making my own in the staff kitchen. In that dimly lit galley kitchen, I found the Lord standing there with a huge canister of tea.

"Oh, good morning Penny. How are you on this fine day?" He had such a sweet smile.

"Good morning Lord Hanley. I'm fine, just a little tired."

"Oh dear, burning the candle at both ends?"

"Not at all. No, just things milling around in my head."

"An occupational hazard, my dear." I immediately changed the subject.

"My goodness, that's a huge flask of tea!"

"Oh, just my usual peppermint tea – for the digestion you know," he said as he patted his stomach.

"Oh, I see. Well, I'll pop down to see you a bit later this morning with the draft patent application for Mr. Peters."

"Smashing. See you later then Penny."

"Bye." I watched him shuffle down the corridor toward his office like a man with the weight of two ex-wives, one current and very demanding wife and the financial burden that went with it.

I decided that I needed an extra jolt of caffeine and made a strong, black coffee and then hurried along to my office. I switched on my computer and the radio - tuning it into Radio 3 for opera but caught the end of the hourly news:

"May 9th marks the capitulation of Nazi Germany to the Soviet Union in World War II, also known as 'Victory Day'."

I had just one real email on my computer (and by "real," I mean emails of any significance, after deleting the usual junk and ridiculous messages from Val asking for me to solve yet another of her computer mysteries):

From: Phil Stevens
To: Penny Banfield
Date: Tuesday, May 9, 2000 - 5:30 p.m.
Re: Draft application

Penny, I was hoping to take a look at the draft application first thing tomorrow, so please come and see me as soon as you get in.

Right away Phil.

I printed out the draft application and made my way to his office. The door to his office was open, but there was no sign of Phil. I noticed, however, that his golf clubs were missing. Sighing heavily, I headed back down the corridor to my office.

I picked up a telephone message knowing for certain that it was going to be Phil.

"Penny, it's Lisa. I'm sorry, but Phil won't be in the office today. He's feeling under the weather. He asked that you let Marjorie know. Thanks Penny."

I knew it! Lisa doing her usual bad cover-up job for Phil. Maybe he had too many drinks at the Ship and Anchor last night. Then I remembered that his golf clubs were not in his office.

Hmm ... was Phil "under the weather" or just OUT enjoying the weather?

Marjorie Brown was our human resources (HR) manager. If ever I met a person totally unsuited to her job, she just had to be that person. I had been under the misapprehension that the requisite personal qualities of an HR manager would require that they (a) liked people, (b) were approachable, and (c) should have a somewhat conciliatory nature. Unfortunately, Marjorie Brown was like a Rottweiler on heat - aggressive and highly inflammatory. I dialed her extension slowly, cursing Phil under my breath.

"Brown here."

"Oh, hi Marjorie. It's Penny Banfield."

"Yes Penny, what do you want?" She really was devoid of all social graces.

"Want? Oh nothing. I don't *want* anything Marjorie."

"How can I help you?" The word "help" seemed somehow sarcastic when she said it.

I drew in my breath. "I'm simply calling to let you know that Phil is apparently feeling under the weather and will not be in the office today." I hung up before she had another chance to impress me with her lack of charm, and I thought back to my initial interview with her. It had been the first interview that had required me to stand in the room for almost three minutes before being invited to sit down while she glanced over my CV.

"Now let me see, hmm ... Law of Contract, Tort ...all the easy subjects I see."

"Excuse me?" I remember feeling as if I was being pushed around a playground by a bully wearing bright pink lipstick.

"These subjects ... well, particularly Law of Contract, I would say is one of the easiest subjects to take in law, don't you think?" Her eyes seemed to glint, leading me to believe that she was hoping I would lose my cool.

"With the greatest respect Ms. Brown, the pass rate for that particular examination was only 40 percent, which therefore leads me to conclude that at least 60 percent of the candidates, in fact, found that subject actually quite difficult. Have you studied law yourself, Ms. Brown?" I stared at her as if examining a witness at a Moot competition.

"No, I haven't. I'm not a lawyer – so of course not." She changed the subject... "What kind of salary are you expecting? More than we are prepared to offer, I expect." I noticed that she was speaking to my CV rather than to me personally.

"Well, naturally I leave it up to you and the firm to come up with a fair and reasonable offer, should you feel I am a suitable candidate."

I was dismissed from that excruciatingly painful interview, while she stared down at her notes waiting for me to leave. After that hour or so of contemptuous mockery, I was happy to leave and never to return. So you can imagine my surprise when an offer of employment arrived three days after the interview. Had I not been desperate to find an articling position, I would have told them to stick their job where the sun did not shine, but I had been desperate to tie up a position with this particular firm.

The partnership obviously thought she had something to offer to the firm, though for the two years I had worked for the firm, I had been trying to figure out what it might be.

0.1 Unit - Calling our anti-social HR Manager for Phil (yet another drink he owes me).

An email appeared on my screen:

From: Anthony Jarvis, Q.C.
To: Penny Banfield
Date: Tuesday, May 9, 2000 - 9:30 a.m.
Re: Mr. Stevens

I understand that Philip Stevens is away from the office

---

today. It therefore falls upon you to ensure that a draft of the Anton Piller application is available for me to review at 11 a.m.

Please call me immediately if for some reason you are unable to meet this deadline.
AJ

Shit. Thanks a bunch Phil...
I picked up the phone and called Nigel.

"Hiya." I sighed. "I've just had yet another unpleasant encounter with Brown."

"Oh God, what a way to start the day. I swear to God that face of hers could turn milk sour."

"I know – she really has had a personality bypass, hasn't she?"

"I expect she just needs a good shagging. I'd say that would probably do the trick, but the problem is finding any man brave enough to venture into her particular Garden of Eden."

"Oh really Nigel, why does everything come down to sex with you for goodness sake?"

"Because everything *is* about sex, Penn. Our very survival on Earth is dependent on people having sex or hadn't you noticed?"

"Yes, I get that Nigel, but I think your idea of sexual activity is likely to lead to an out-of-control population explosion."

"Somebody's touchy today! What's up, Penn?"

"Just tired, that's all."

"Why's that?"

"Don't know – just couldn't sleep last night."

"Did I wake you up when I came in? I did try to be quiet." He sounded concerned.

"No, you're alright Nigel. I was awake. I've just got all this stuff swimming around in my head - this new litigation project we are working on and there's something going on with Phil. I can't exactly put my finger on it, but I know something is up."

"Maybe I could do some digging around and find out what it is?"

"Oh Nigel, you are such a gossip! No, that's OK. I'm sure I'll figure it out or he will tell me eventually." I stifled a yawn.

"Well, let me know if you change your mind. You know what a frantically inquisitive mind I have."

"Just another one of your many skills, my dear."

"See you at 11?"

"Actually, not today ... that's the main reason for my call. I have a meeting with AJ then. He wants to see a draft application, but Phil hasn't reviewed it yet. I'm rather nervous about handing it to him without Phil having first review."

"Jesus – I would be too. Good luck with that."

"Thanks Nigel, you are a great pillar of support – how could I ever thank you."

"I know – I would say you can pay me in kind, but you're not really my type because you don't apparently approve of sex."

"Oh, very funny – see you at home tonight?"

"Expect so, unless I get a better offer."

"Maybe I'll make us some pasta?"

"Sounds great. See you later Penn."

My shoulders had slowly crept up to my ears as if I had been pegged out on a washing line. I consciously pushed them down and rolled my head from side to side. The issue of handing something over to AJ without the safety net of a first review by Phil was tormenting me, but I simply had no choice. Phil was effectively feeding me to the lions or lion in this case. I pulled up the draft on my computer and scrutinized every word over and over, double-checking the case law as if preparing for a hearing with a judge. After one hour of scrutinizing a document of four pages, I began to feel blind to it – all the text just merged into one blur as my brain pulled up a shutter as if to say, *"Ok, that's enough."*

I printed out the document, which had been changed only once during that hour for a typing mistake, and placed it in a blue folder so I could not see it any longer. It sat on my desk for 15 minutes while I sat crossed-legged on my yoga mat, my hands over my knees, fingers lightly curled like the petals of a rose. I sat, concentrating on my breathing, which had run amok during the previous hour.

My discovery of yoga had been a saving grace. Prior to realizing the importance of breathing and being in the moment, stress had been my master and punished me frequently with epic headaches that could last for up to three days. To me, yoga was like a wise friend, there in times of trouble, gently placing a reassuring hand on my shoulder.

Placing my heels back on and bracing my body for battle, I picked up the blue folder and marched to AJ's office. His office was on the third floor and close to the boardroom, no doubt for convenience sake. His assistant, Daphne, sat directly outside his office at her pristine desk that resembled an operating table rather than a desk. She had short, dark grey hair and a round face. Her head looked like it had subsided into the folds of her neck. Her lips were pursed, and she would move them back and forth as if trying to prevent herself from saying something she would regret. Her eyes were wide open with a startled look resembling a fat barn owl sitting on watch.

"Hi Daphne. I'm here to see Mr. Jarvis."

"Hmm." She looked up and down at me with disapproval. "I'll let him know you're here."

"Thanks." I looked outside the window, which had a fabulous view of the ocean and pier. "Nice view you have up here."

"It's all for the clients' benefit, not mine - I can assure you of that. I can count on one hand the number of times I've even had time to notice the view."

Oh, I'm sure that's right Daphne. God, you are such a bloody martyr. "Oh, I'm sure. I expect you're really busy up here." I played to her martyrdom.

"Absolutely right I am." She started to work on opening the pile of mail left in her inbox ripping at it with her silver knife like a fisherman ripping the guts out of a fish. Suddenly, over the intercom, I heard AJ's voice.

"You can tell Ms. Banfield to come in now, Daphne."

"Certainly Anthony." Apart from the partners, Daphne was the only person in the firm allowed to call him "Anthony." I guess if you had worked for somebody for almost 30 years, you would at least have earned the right to be on first-name terms. Law firms were the epitome of hierarchy, unspòken rules, and behaviours.

"OK, in you go," she said as she pulled herself to her feet and opened the double French doors for me. I felt like I was walking into an amphitheatre about to get ripped to shreds.

His office was indeed cold. Some traditional oil paintings and an array of colourful antique law reports covered the walls. He sat in a high-backed leather chair and beckoned me to take a seat in front of his huge mahogany desk.

"OK then. Let's take a look at the draft application and Order shall we?"

I clutched onto the draft holding it back. "Sir, I did just want to say..." my heart was pounding.

"Come now, hand it over. Let me take a look." He sounded irritated.

"Sir ..., I just wanted to let you know that Philip Stevens has not yet had a chance to review these drafts." I was sure he could hear the panic in my voice.

"Really..." He spoke as he stared down already scanning the document "And why is that Ms. Banfield? Did he not review it last night?"

"No, unfortunately not, and as you know he is under the weather today and didn't get an opportunity to look at it first thing this morning as planned."

"Well, that is most unfortunate. Still, let me take a look. We'll see what needs to be changed."

"OK thank you, sir." I sat in silence while he nodded, grunted, and scribbled on the draft documents. Eventually, he put me out of my agony and handed the draft back to me.

"Not bad for a first attempt, Banfield." I looked down and saw that the scribbled remarks were in the world of - "Good, yes, and correct" - much like the markings of a school teacher on an essay. There were a couple of minor formatting changes.

OK so not bad then. "I'll make sure that Phil takes a look at it before it gets filed."

"Absolutely no need, you can file it with the court today."

"Today? Oh, OK then. I just need details of the addresses for the directors and the properties we are intending to raid."

"Yes, of course. I believe that your friend Mr. Wilkinson may be able to assist you there, provided he is not too busy prancing around on the fourth floor today. We should be able to get all the addresses from a company search, but we will need to have a private investigator check out the addresses prior to the raid to ensure that they are still current."

"Yes sir. Did you want me to draft some instructions to the private investigator? I presume we will be using Archie Steadman?"

"Yes, give Archie a call. He's definitely the best man for the job. Just one thing though ... because of the high level of confidentiality on this one, it's really important that we get Archie to sign a confidentiality agreement and hold his feet to the fire."

"Yes, of course. Is there anything else?"

"Hmm ... there is actually. Do you have any plans for this weekend?"

What could he possibly mean? "Sir?"

"I was hoping that you could help me out with some private investigation that is *unsuitable* for Archie?" He had a devilish smile on his face.

"Really? In what way would Archie be unsuitable?"

"Archie is too well known around town and particularly to the Chairman Jim Bateman and those guys at the football club. I hear he's been serving them with various documents for a number of years."

"I see. What do you need me to do?"

"In addition to seeking the Anton Piller Order, I want to bring a bankruptcy petition against Jim Bateman personally."

"But why do you need investigation?"

"I need some information as to his whereabouts and an address for service. He lives in a mansion out near Jevington, and there is no way that I can get anyone in to personally serve him at that address. He's too clever to pick up any registered mail, and I don't want to get an Order for Substituted Service against him. I want to serve him with the bankruptcy petition myself."

"Is that wise, sir? I've heard he's got a pretty violent past. Doesn't he have a criminal record?"

"Yes, I believe he does. In addition to his involvement with the football club, I've heard that he's involved with the ownership of various markets in the South East and in particular one out near Stevenage. I thought you might like to take a trip to Hertfordshire this weekend, all expenses paid of course, and do some digging around for me?"

"I don't think I have anything planned this weekend." *Too bad if I did anyway, as there was no way anybody could say no to AJ and get away with it.*

"Great. I'll leave the details up to you and Phil to discuss, if he ever comes off the golf course, that is."

So then, he knew Phil only too well. Nothing got past AJ; he was as sharp as a knife. "Oh no sir, I'm pretty sure he's quite unwell." I nodded trying to make it sound more convincing,

"Oh come off it Banfield, do you think I was born yesterday? His golf clubs are gone, and I saw him yesterday. He looked absolutely fine to me." He was not smiling, but I could tell from his eyes that he was amused at my attempted cover up.

I knew well enough to leave it alone, picked up the blue folder, and headed to the door, bumping into Daphne who looked extremely flustered.

"Oh, I'm ever so sorry to interrupt Anthony, but I have Laura on the phone. She said she knows that you are really busy, but if she could just have a word?" She had a pitiful look on her face reminding me of Oliver Twist about to ask for another helping.

"God damn that women – can't I get any bloody work done around here!" He exploded.

"So sorry Anthony....she said to tell you that she knows your phone is on divert and you are avoiding her, but she just had a scary call and needs to speak to you urgently."

AJ suddenly look concerned. "Put her through then Daphne." He glanced at me with a dismissive nod.

"I'll obviously keep you posted, sir."

"Thanks Banfield. Good job by the way." I had my back to him, but could not help grin as I walked back past the fat curious owl outside his door.

Lunch today consisted of an instant noodle meal pulled out of the bottom drawer of my desk, available instantly in two minutes and guaranteed to rot your stomach in five.

Eager to get started with the Anton Piller application and the opportunity of having something filed without any input from Phil, I called Nigel to get started on the process of obtaining addresses for the directors of the Club.

"AJ wants you to carry out a company search for the football club. We need all the names and addresses of the directors of the Club, ASAP."

"What, no niceties, how are you Nigel? How is your day going Nigel?"

"I don't have time for niceties right now. I'm too busy."

"And I suppose I'm just sitting here picking my nose, am I?"

"Sorry ... it's just that I have to work quickly, and I've also just lost my weekend – AJ's given me a project to work on."

"Woo hoo! Are you becoming the new 'chosen' one?"

"Oh, don't be ridiculous Nigel. Are you going to help me or not?"

"Leave it with me. I'll make the requisition and bring it down to you when it's ready."

"OK thanks. See you later." I knew I had been rude, but thankfully Nigel was very forgiving; another of his good qualities.

My next call was to Archie Steadman, a process server and investigator of many years. Archie was an ex-cop and excelled at finding those who did not want to be found. He also had a remarkable knack of being able to relate to people from all walks of life - making them feel instantly comfortable, which it turn would often lead to a wealth of forthcoming information. In another life, he would have made an excellent salesperson.

"Archie?"

"Yes my luv. Who am I speaking to?"

"Oh sorry, Archie it's Penny from Pilkington ..."

"Oh yes luv, what can I do for you? It's been quite a while since we last spoke. You must be going up in the world," he said and chuckled.

"On the contrary, I think perhaps I've been handling more crap files than interesting files lately Archie." I laughed. "It's nice to have something interesting to work on for a change. I just need you to check out some addresses for me, will that be Ok?"

"Well, that doesn't sound that interesting. Anyone I know?"

"You'll see when you get the list, but this job is really sensitive. So we'll have to get you to sign a Confidentiality Agreement."

"Blimey, must be top secret. I think I've only ever had to sign one of those twice before in my whole career!"

"It's not that *I* don't trust you Archie ..."

"Oh, you're Ok. I know it's the powers that be that have to cover their arses right?"

"Exactly."

"I expect to have the list of addresses in about an hour or so, but I don't want to fax it. So I'll leave a copy at the front desk for you to pick up. You can pick up the list, sign the Confidentiality Agreement, and leave it at the front desk, if that's Ok?"

"Yes, that's fine. So you want me to check that everybody listed on the search actually lives at the address they have provided to Companies House, is that it?"

"Yes, that's it. And if they are no longer at that address, we'll need you to carry out your extraordinary skills and find out where they are living."

"No problem luv. I'll pick up the list at around 4 p.m. and will bring my ID with me," he said and laughed.

"I know it sounds ridiculous Archie, but it really is quite delicate. It will all fall into place when you see the instruction letter, I assure you."

"Oh, I'm only joking. It's up to you what you want me to do. All I'm worried about is getting my bills paid, and your firm always pays me quickly. So no worries there."

"OK thanks Archie. Speak to you later."

"Yeah, and if for any reason the list gets held up, give just me a bell."

"Will do. Bye Archie."

Just enough time to check my email.....

From: Andrew Barker
To: Penny Banfield
Date: Tuesday, May 9, 2000
Re: Phil

Playing golf again is he?
AB

Why the hell does everybody suppose that I am Phil's keeper? I deleted the email.

It was no secret that I worked closely with Phil and had become his "go-to" person. It had started with my articling stint and basically had never stopped. As much as I liked gaining an incredible depth of experience, I hated being regarded as his caretaker.

From: Catherine Henderson
To: Penny Banfield
Date: Tuesday, May 9, 2000
Re: This weekend!
Give me a call ASAP! Looks like I am getting the keys to the cottage this weekend!!!!

Fancy a trip down to Dorset with me? We can stuff ourselves with clotted cream teas and hit the local pubs to see if the rugby team is in. xxx

Damn! A weekend in Dorset sounded perfect. I was always letting Kate down. She was going to start taking things personally if I was not careful.

From: Gavin Preston
To: Penny Banfield
Date: Tuesday, May 9, 2000
Re: Tea at Three?

Just checking that we are still on for Tea at Three?
Gavin

REPLY
From: Penny Banfield
To: Gavin Preston
Date: Tuesday, May 9, 2000
Re: Tea at Three

Tea will be ready for you at three.

Bring biscuits if you can! (Bourbon or Shortbread).
Penny

As busy as I was, I felt totally justified in having a gentleman caller at three seeing as I had now been asked to give up my entire weekend. I called Kate before I forgot to get back to her. Thank heavens for forgiving friends.

"You have reached the confidential voicemail of Catherine Henderson, personal assistant to Advertising Manager Fiona Peabody. Please leave a message after the tone ..."

"Kate, it's Penn. A weekend in Dorset would be a godsend right now. The thought of driving down there together, eating cream teas, and hunting down the local talent is so appealing. But I'm afraid I can't go. I've got to go to Stevenage this weekend. Will try and call you tonight at home." She was guaranteed to laugh at the thought of me turning down a weekend in Dorset to go to Stevenage.

I pulled out my legal pad and started to draft a "To Do" list, an activity I would often engage in when trying to procrastinate. This was my wannabe activity list, things that I should do, could do, and might do, but certainly not things that could be done NOW.

Tuesday
Company Search from Nigel
Finalize application for Anton Piller Order
Tea at Three (Gavin - biscuits?)
File application at courthouse
Check Arnie picked up list and signed agreement
Pick up pasta/meal with Nigel
Call Kate

Just before two o'clock, Nigel rushed into my office with his company search (all 22 pages). "Bloody hell Penn, I had no idea they had so many directors over at the Club." He slammed an envelope on my desk.

"Really? How many?" I picked the envelope up and started browsing through the pages.

"I'll leave it to you to count the addresses. Be careful though, some of them are duplicates or changes of addresses."

"Good God, this is going to take Archie forever."

"To figure out what exactly?" His curious face looked almost impish.

"Never mind." I just couldn't tell him – he was such a gossip.

"Why do you need this information anyway?" He was still fishing.

"I said never mind, Nigel. You know that sometimes I deal with highly sensitive and confidential matters."

"Oh I see, something top secret is it? You must have made it onto the '*A-List*'."

"Put away the green devil and go back to your office," I said and smiled.

"What? No cup of tea or any social graces?" He tried to win me over with his delightful smile.

"I told you earlier. I'm busy today."

"Not too busy to see Gavin though, I hear." He looked at me sideways.

"What? Who told you that?" God, Nigel could be annoying at times.

"The man himself."

"Let me get this straight, Gavin told you he was having tea with me?"

"Exactly. Looked quite excited at the prospect too ... and ... I think he has a surprise planned for you." Nigel looked extremely pleased with himself.

"Well, now you've spoiled it, haven't you?"

"No I haven't. I just told you it was a surprise, not *what* the surprise was."

"OK then Nigel. Thanks for this," I tried to hurry him out the door. "See you at home tonight."

"What pasta are you making for us tonight?"

"It's a *surprise*," I said, stifling a laugh.

"Touché." He blew a kiss at me as he strutted out the door.

I scrutinized the list of directors. At first sight, it looked like enough work to keep Archie busy for weeks, especially if a high percentage of them had to be traced to new addresses. Still, we had to cross that bridge when we came to it. In the meantime, we simply had to get the addresses into the application (whether they were in fact right or not did not really matter for the purpose of getting the application issued. All that was required was the address registered with the companies registry.)

I pounded away at the computer adding addresses and spell checking twice. I just had enough time to print out three copies of the application; try to put some life back into my hair; put on some lipstick; and fill up the kettle before Gavin arrived.

"Hi Gavin. Come in!" I smiled my best girly smile at him. "Earl Grey Ok?"

"Of course." My God, he looked incredibly handsome.

"I'm sorry I'm a little bit behind – just finalized the application for the Anton Piller Order. So I have to get this off to the courthouse before 4 p.m. Do you mind if I just make a telephone call while the kettle is boiling?"

"Absolutely not, please do whatever has to be done." He sat down, picked up the latest copy of *The Law Society Gazette*, and started to read an article on the value of legal executives.

I picked up the phone to call Daphne.

"Hi Daphne. It's Penny Banfield here."

"Yes Penny?"

"I've finalized the application and draft Order, and it's ready to go to the courthouse for filing, pending AJ's signature. I'll leave it at the post room to bring up to you in a second. Can you make sure it gets signed and filed with the courthouse this afternoon?"

"Of course. I'll return the papers to you when they've been filed."

"Great, thanks Daphne."

I glanced over to Gavin who seemed to be deeply engrossed by the article. "Be back in a sec - just off to the post room." I ran all the way to the post room, yelled out instructions for the post boy (ashamedly I could never remember his name) to take my envelope up to Daphne urgently. Anxious not to be seen to be too flustered on arrival back, I decided to walk calmly back to my office and found Gavin setting out the teacups.

"Oh Gavin, you don't have to do that."

"I insist. Looks like you're having a busy day."

"Yes, it's been totally crazy. I've certainly earned my tea break today."

"Well, sit down and let's catch our breath, shall we?" He gently pushed me down on the sofa, handing me a cup of Early Grey and a plate on which he'd placed a chocolate cream éclair. I was of course highly impressed.

"Oh, how wonderful! Éclairs are my absolute favourite."

"Yes, I know ... although I did have to do some investigative work to find out, but I think I went to the best possible source."

"Nigel?"

"Of course Nigel. He seems to know everything there is to know about you."

I started to feel a little defensive. "I really hope he isn't telling everybody my business?"

"No, I don't mean it like that. He doesn't gossip about you. Quite the opposite in fact. I think he really cares for you actually."

"Who, Nigel? I don't think so ... we are just friends. He just knows me well because we live together."

"I was wondering if it might be more than friendship?" He was scanning my face, searching for any tell-tale signs of awkwardness.

"Absolutely not. He is not my type. If you had seen any of his girlfriends, you would know for certain that I'm definitely not his type."

"Really? What is his type?"

"Fluff-headed debutantes, I would say. They are usually blonde, a bit on the horsey side. I think Nigel likes girls that he can impress, so anybody with half a brain simply would not do."

"Well, that rules you out doesn't it? Nobody could ever describe you as somebody with half a brain."

"Oh, you should see me first thing in the morning before that first cup of coffee. I'd say I'd be lucky to have even half a brain."

"I'd like that," he said and grinned.

"Sorry Gavin, you've lost me. What do you mean?"

"To see you first thing in the morning sometime."

I suddenly found it hard to breathe. "Well, maybe we should try and do something about that one day." I quickly changed the subject. "Guess who's going to Stevenage for the weekend?"

"You are?"

"Yep. Seems AJ wants me to do some private investigation at one of the markets – trying to locate Jim Bateman."

"Well, that sounds exciting. Will you be wearing a disguise?"

"Oh, I really hadn't thought about that, but maybe a disguise would be a good idea. I think that could be fun!"

"Hey, maybe you could dress up as a fluff-headed debutante?" He laughed.

"Now there's an idea! Hey, I wonder what car should I rent?"

Mercedes, BMW.......PORSCHE???!

"Well, it has to be a sports car doesn't it?"

"What about the Nissan 240Z?"

"Perfect choice. I'm even starting to get excited for you. Wish I could come along." He sounded genuine.

"Really?"

"Yes, I think it sounds like tons of fun."

I hesitated, but shamefully not for long. "Well, why don't you come with me then? I certainly could do with some company."

"Oh, I'm not sure AJ would approve of that." I watched him like a hawk to see if he felt uncomfortable about the idea, but could see no such indication.

"Well, I'm not suggesting that you come to the markets with me. But we certainly could have dinner and breakfast and spend some quality time together. Separate rooms, of course."

"Of course, goes without saying. It does sound *very* enticing I must say, and I don't have any plans for the weekend. Yes, I think I'd love to come to maybe offer some moral support."

"Wonderful – now my weekend doesn't sound like it's going to be a boring one at all!" I found myself animated like a child, excited at the prospect of the ice cream van arriving.

"Looks like AJ is starting to use you as his right-hand girl Penn."

"That's what Nigel said. Well kind of what he said."

"A pretty good place to be career-wise, if you ask me."

"I know. It's also very dangerous too, because one slip-up and I'm right back at the bottom of the ladder again."

"Maybe, but you don't get noticed hiding in the weeds."

"Good point. I do find it pretty nerve-wracking though. This morning I had to give AJ the draft application before Phil even had a chance of taking a look at it."

"A bit risky without the safety net of a mentor. I think I'd be nervous too."

"Still as it turned out it was Ok – he even complimented me on my work before he had a major call from his wife about some domestic disaster."

"Oh really? What kind of domestic disaster?"

"Something like receiving a *scary call to the house*."

"Wow, that sounds serious." Gavin walked over to refill his teacup.

"You don't know Laura, do you? She is known for her constant freak-outs about one thing or another. One day when I was working up on that floor during my articles, she came storming into the office demanding to see AJ with a broken barometer tucked under her arm."

"A *what?*"

"Barometer – it's one of those things people use to check the air pressure in the house."

"Do people really still use those? What on Earth for?"

"I have no idea. But anyway, she barged into his office, slammed the barometer on top of his desk moaning *it's broken.* AJ could be heard yelling at her at the opposite end of the office hallway. He practically chased her out of his office and down the stairs."

"Talk about washing your dirty linen in public," he said.

"My sentiments exactly. What was she thinking - humiliating her husband with such trivial things?"

"So, what you are saying Penn, is that this call to the house could have been anything from a paper boy reminding her that the newspaper bill was overdue to the gasman trying to get in to read the meter?"

I nodded. "To his credit though, AJ did seem to be concerned, which is a tall order considering the number of times Laura has cried wolf."

"Anyway, enough about them, let's talk about us. We're you thinking of anywhere in particular hotel-wise?" I loved that he had used the words *"US."*

"Not at all, although I've never been to Stevenage. It sounds typical of any new town, all shopping centres and nothing at all of any architectural interest."

"I've heard some of the villages on the outskirts of Hertfordshire are nice though. Would you like me to do some investigation? It looks like you are going to be pretty busy until the weekend."

"Gavin, I would absolutely love that. It would be one less thing to worry about. What an angel you are."

"Hardly, but thanks anyway," he said, as he touched my face and pulled my chin toward him with his curled forefinger. I turned my face up to him and was bestowed with a wonderful soft kiss, which in turn led to yet another burst of red to the face. I pulled away.

"I should go. I know you have to get that application filed." Gavin stood up.

I felt torn, as I didn't want Gavin to go. But I was getting a little edgy about the time. Besides, I would be seeing a lot more, and I mean a *lot more* of Gavin over the weekend. I, too, stood up. "Thanks so much for the chocolate éclair. That was really thoughtful of you."

"We aim to please."

"Seriously, it was very sweet of you Gavin. And thanks for looking at the hotel situation. I will book the car rental tomorrow. We can talk about the hotel situation tomorrow if you are free for tea?"

"It's a date. If you're sure you are not too busy?" said Gavin.

"I'm never too busy for you Gavin. I'm really beginning to value our friendship." I flashed a smile at him, then quickly looked down trying to be demure.

"Or whatever it is," he said slowly.

Now this was sounding really promising ...

"Gavin?"

"Yes?"

"Are you sure you want separate rooms?"

"I'll leave that decision up to you, I think." He seemed visibly pleased as he left the room. And this time, I think he was the one blushing.

It's not as if we had just met. I had known him a long time, but our friendship had been at arm's length before. It was like discovering a treasure that had been in the attic, after years of forgetting it was there.

Thirty minutes later, the package from the courthouse arrived in my Inbox confirming that the application had been filed. This was an *Ex-Parte* application (meaning that no advance notice of our application had to be given to the other side). *Ex Parte* applications were usually reserved for circumstances where notice might result in harm to an individual or property, or evidence being destroyed.

Our application would be heard before a judge with AJ "speaking to the application," which meant he had to appear before the judge and ask for the Order allowing us to enter the various addresses to seek and preserve evidence relating to our case. AJ had to explain to the judge why we thought the Order should be made, refer to various cases where orders had previously been granted, and show how those cases were similar to our situation (known as 'precedent case law'). All of this is important for us lawyers, but I'm sure you don't care about this lesson in law; let's just put it down to my need to explain and be understood.

My job now was to get Archie working at break-neck speed to check whether all parties were actually living at the addresses set out in the company search. If not, then he would need to find out where they were living. We needed the information before the raid. If we raided only a few addresses, it was almost certain that any evidence held at addresses we had not yet raided would be destroyed. For this reason, I concluded that Archie should be retained on an around-the-clock basis to reduce the risk of that happening. I picked up the phone and called AJ.

"Jarvis here."

"Hello, sir. It's Penny Banfield here. I just wanted to let you know that the application has been filed with the courthouse and Archie Steadman is picking up the companies search within the next few minutes to start work on checking the various addresses."

"Good work Banfield."

"Thank you, sir. But there is something I did want to ask you."

"Fire away then."

"The company search has revealed that there are a significant number of directors, in fact there are 22 pages of information. Archie is going to need a considerable amount of time to check out all of the addresses. So we should either limit the number of addresses that Archie checks out, identify the key addresses where we believe the evidence may be found, *or* we have Archie working around the clock."

"Hmm … well, I don't want the risk of missing an address. If they have any sense, they would hide the evidence with the least conspicuous director. But we can't assume that that's what they'll do. There's too much risk involved with making that assumption, so I think I'd rather have Archie work around the clock on this. Could you take care of it Banfield?"

"Absolutely sir, leave it to me."

Next call was to reception. "Hi Jean. It's Penny here. Has Archie picked up that envelope from the front desk yet?" I could hear rustling as Jean went through the various envelopes at the front desk waiting for pick up.

"No Penny – it's still here."

"Great, can you call me when Archie comes in? I'll come down and speak to him."

"Will do."

"Thanks Jean."

Later that afternoon and having successfully intercepted Archie at reception and providing him will full instructions to have a team set up to work around the clock, I left for the train station - hoping to avoid the drooling bald man who would likely be on the later train.

On the way home, I stopped off at Sainsbury's to pick up some fresh pasta, tomato, basil sauce, some chicken breasts, and a bottle of Valpolicella. Some fresh melon for dessert and the meal with Nigel was all set.

Nigel would often start work later and leave later than me, so I'd usually be home before him. After placing the chicken in the oven to bake, I called Kate but unfortunately got her answering machine again. "Hey Kate. Sorry I couldn't get hold of you. The trip to Stevenage has suddenly got more interesting. I'm going with Gavin Preston!" I hung up knowing she was going to go crazy for more information.

There was just enough time to take a bath before Nigel got home. As I turned the taps to the bath and sprinkled in some bath salts, I took stock of the day at work. Today had been a good day. Surprisingly, Phil's absence from the office had provided me with an opportunity to have direct contact with AJ who seemed so far to be quite happy with my efforts. What I couldn't understand was why Phil would take a sick day at such a crucial time. Yes, he would often take days off to play golf, but usually it did not interfere with anything important that needed to get done. Maybe he was in fact sick, but that didn't explain why his golf clubs were missing. All I knew was that Phil was acting out of character lately, and his change in behaviour could not have come at a worst time.

I heard the front door slam and keys thrown down on my precious mahogany table in the hallway, praying that Nigel had not scratched the surface. Pulling myself reluctantly out of the silky water, I wrapped myself in a huge bath sheet, patted myself dry, and stepped into a red silk kimono - another one of my prize possessions acquired from an earlier trip with my parents to Tokyo.

"Here she is ... Ms. Banfield, lawyer extraordinaire. Is she a lawyer? Is she a goddess from the heavens? Is she a gourmet chef and do I smell something almost ready to eat?"

"You know, it would be nice if sometimes you could cook for *me*," I said, barely able to hide the smile spreading across my face.

"Are you completely mad? Have you ever eaten anything cooked by these fair hands?" He stared down at his hands, which were surprisingly manly for a person who did no manual work.

"No, I can't say I have."

"Well, let's just say the last time I cooked something, it went into the oven looking magnificent, yet somehow miraculously transformed itself into a '*What-was-it?*' when it came out of the oven."

"What do you mean?"

"I had burned it beyond all recognition, to the point Jenny had to ask me what I had originally put into the oven."

"Oh, I see. So one failure and you give up?"

"Why waste everybody's time when there are so many people, you included, who are so much better at it that me." I loved the way we could banter with each other and wondered whether it was just an outcome of us both being lawyers.

"Dinner is still going to be another 15 minutes, so you can either pour a glass of wine and sit and talk to me in the kitchen or go and watch TV."

"Where's the wine?" He scoured around in the kitchen.

"In the fridge."

He stuck his red head into the fridge and finally picked out the bottle of Valpolicella.

"This?"

"Yes, what's wrong?"

"Has anybody told you what a sin it is to chill red wine?" He scolded me with a stern look on his face.

"Actually Nigel, this may come as some surprise to you, but many people are chilling their red wine. I, for one, prefer it chilled."

"You are a sinful and crazy woman."

"Tell me something I don't know." I laughed.

He uncorked the wine, pulled some large, red wine glasses from the cupboard, poured out the wine, and held them in his hands like ruby orbs. I pulled out my saucepan and started to cook the pasta.

"So Miss Penny Banfield, want to hear some goss?"

"Is there any other reason why I might have you hanging around this place?"

"I heard something about Phil today that I thought you might be interested in."

"Like he had taken a day off playing hooky to play golf while I was left holding the baby?"

"Well, not exactly. But it does involve a baby."

I stared at him intensely; curiosity had indeed at least got the cat's attention. "What do you mean *baby*?"

"I bumped into Danny Beable at the wine bar at lunchtime, and we started talking about Phil."

"Go on...."

"Seems like Phil has managed to get Lisa *pregnant!*"

"Oh my God, no!!" So that explained everything. "I thought he had been acting really strange lately. Wow, what a shocker! I was beginning to think that he was going to remain single for the rest of time."

"I think Phil had thought that, too. In fact, Danny had suggested that Phil had been thinking about leaving Lisa because she was becoming too focused on the lack of a wedding ring on her finger."

"Oops. Seems like one hell of a cock-up if you ask me."

"Literally." We both started to laugh.

"Poor Phil," Nigel said.

"Poor *Lisa* you mean. I'll never understand why she puts up with him. In fact, I've always been in admiration of her incredible tenacity."

"Maybe she got tired of waiting and took matters into her own hands?"

"Like on purpose, you mean?"

"At least that's Danny's theory."

"Oh my God. What a recipe for disaster," I donned the oven gloves, pulled out the baked chicken from the oven, and placed the pasta sauce into a small saucepan to simmer.

"Exactly what I thought. Women are so bloody manipulative."

"Excuse me? Let me correct you, Nigel ... some women *may be* manipulative in an effort of desperation." I shot him a searing look of disapproval.

"I stand corrected."

I sliced the chicken, drained the pasta, and assembled the meal.

We sat at the bistro table in the corner of the kitchen. Knowing the drill, Nigel picked up the antique candlesticks for the fireplace mantel and brought them over to the table, while I set out the cutlery and napkins.

"Every meal with you is a real occasion Penny," Nigel said and smiled.

"Oh, I wouldn't say that." I sat down placing my napkin down on my lap. "For instance, you should have seen what I had for lunch today."

"Oh yeah, what did you have?"

"I don't want to tell you for fear of evoking a strong sense of jealousy."

"Come on Penn – what was it?"

"A Pot Noodle." We both laughed.

During the meal, we speculated on whether Phil had taken the day off because he was stressed over the baby or whether he really was sick. My guess was that in complete denial, he had opted for a game of golf. Fundamentally, he was a selfish guy. I doubted that even Lisa's pregnancy would stop him from playing if he wanted. As the mother of his child, she would have to get used to the fact that Phil came first, his job second, and she was pitifully placed in third position. I felt sorry for her, my patience with Phil was running out; he was like a sponge soaking up the life force from everyone around him. Phil was a brilliant lawyer when he focused on being a lawyer. But Phil was Phil and his brilliance was always a little discounted by his group of numbskull friends. He was not ready for fatherhood, and it probably scared him shitless. He could hardly have called in "*Scared Shitless*," so instead he had Lisa call in sick for him while he trembled around the golf course in his Footjoys.

We ate primarily in silence while I mulled over Phil's situation until Nigel broke the silence.

"Well, whatever the situation he finds himself in, I have to say I feel quite sorry for him."

"Well, I don't. He is master of his own destiny just like the rest of us. In fact, Phil pisses me off. If he had more integrity, he would have put Lisa out of her misery way before she got to the stage where she felt she needed to take desperate measures."

"Whoa! What's the air like up there Penny? Have you been promoted several times overnight and suddenly become a judge now?"

I slammed down my knife and fork. "Oh, what's the point in talking to you – you men are all the same. I'm going to bed to read. I'm exhausted." I picked up my plate and threw it into the sink.

"Don't worry Penn," Nigel yelled as I left the kitchen. "I'll do the washing up."

"Well, I'm sure as hell not doing it," I slammed the door to my bedroom.

Thankfully by now, Nigel had become used to my volatility- especially when I was tired. It was one of the things I liked the most about him – his ability to shrug things off easily without holding a grudge. I had grown up with parents who were often having disagreements, which would result in days of frigid silence. With Nigel, however, I knew that every day was a new day and there would be no hard feelings. He was the perfect roommate.

CHAPTER 3 – WEDNESDAY MAY 10, 2000

This morning, I found myself travelling into work with a blonde, hazel-eyed demon aged around three years old. After leaving the station and congratulating myself on finding a seat on a packed train, I soon came to regret sitting next to the angelic face looking up at me from a pushchair in the aisle of the carriage to the train. Within seconds of pulling away from the station, the demon started to shout "cockita bitdit" (which I understood to mean "chocolate biscuit") to his frazzled mother at intervals of generally 30 seconds.

I must say, I was surprised at the incredible tenacity of the mother who stood her ground, refusing to give into the child's demands. One would have thought that after five minutes or so, the child would have grown tired. But if anything, the din increased as apparently so did the mother's absolute resolve. After 15 minutes or so, I found myself willing the mother on. *Don't give in now ... hold strong ... stand your ground with this nightmare child called, Jake.* His mother repeated his name, like her very own stress-filled mantra.

Jakey had now become more frantic with his high-pitched demands. Finally, having spoiled the journey of many commuters and their anticipated moments of solitude, he resigned himself to growling the words "cokita bitdit" to himself like a scorned bear cub until we pulled into the station,

Unable to keep my opinion to myself, I stood up and offered my hand to the mother. "I just want to say how impressed I am by your parenting – it must have taken a lot of patience to hold your ground," I said and smiled.

"Oh, no luv – on any other day, I would probably have given in. It's just that the biscuits are dirty. I dropped them in a puddle on the way to the train – can't give him them now, can I?"

I found myself to be extremely disappointed at the idea she would have relented to the demands of a tenacious spoiled demon, but then quickly realized that this was pretty much what I did every day, working with Phil.

As I ran by the reception area, the receptionist Jean smiled. "Morning Penny. If you see Phil on your travels, can you tell him that I have a client waiting for him in Reception Room 3?"

"Will do." I prayed that Phil was not absent again. It was going to be a busy day, and I really needed to get *my* work done, rather than cover for Phil. I barely had time to get to my desk, sign into my computer, and hang up my coat before the phone rang.

Caller display: PHILIP STEVENS X 102.

Well looks like my 30-year-old demon is at least in the office today. I picked up the phone.

"Phil. Jean is looking for you – apparently there's a client in Reception Room 3 waiting for you."

"No, not me. Waiting for *you*, Penny. I was calling to see if you could see this one for me. I have to go and see AJ urgently, so need you to take this one on. She's a new client, Italian I think, her name is Anna Simone ... wants to talk to you about a conveyancing issue."

"Oh God, Phil. Really? I'm so busy right now."

"Sorry Penn. You can blame AJ for this one. Thanks for taking this on." He hung up.

Like I have any choice. I picked up the phone and dialed the number for reception. "Jean - can you offer Mrs. Simone a coffee or tea. I'll be there in a couple of minutes."

"Thanks Penny. She's been waiting a while already."

"Yeah, I know. I'll be there in a sec."

I found Mrs. Simone in the reception room staring at the cup of coffee in front of her, which did not appear to have been touched. She sat on a chair clutching a huge, black shopping trolley beside her - as if it contained something extremely valuable.

"Good morning Mrs. Simone. My name is Penny Banfield, and I work with Philip Stevens. Nice to meet you." I extended my hand. She started to get up, but I gestured that she should stay seated. "No, please don't get up." She seemed to be a little confused. "I'm so sorry, but Mr. Stevens has been detained on another matter. He has asked that I see you instead, as I work very closely with him on his matters." *Unfortunately.* "He said that you have a conveyancing matter that you'd like to discuss. Is that correct?" She nodded and looked at me with Cocker Spaniel eyes.

"What seems to be the problem?"

"I want to know if my husband has stolen the deeds to my house."

"I see. Are you still married to your husband?"

"Yes," she nodded.

"Ok ... so not divorced?"

"No." She looked disgusted at the very idea.

"Do you have a mortgage on the house, Mrs. Simone?"

"No mortgage. My husband no like to borrow money"

"I see. Where had the deeds to the house been kept? With the bank?"

"Yes. In safety deposit box."

"Do you both have keys to the safety deposit box?"

"No – just me."

"So you think he stole the keys from you and took the deeds to the house?"

"Yes, in the night – he often comes to visit at night."

"Visit? I thought you said you were still married?"

"Yes, yes, still married," she said as she bore a smile of broken tombstones, some the colour of brass.

"I'm sorry, I don't quite understand. Why would he visit you if you are still married?"

"He loves me," she said as she held her hands to her heart and smiled.

"But you said he has *stolen* from you?"

"Yes, yes ... what am I going to do? I need to sell my house, but cannot because he has the deeds."

"I'm a little confused. Does your husband live with you Mrs. Simone?"

"No, he lives with God," she said and smiled looking up toward the ceiling.

"With *God*, Mrs. Simone?" She had started to look around the room seemingly disinterested.

"Mrs. Simone, what do you mean your husband lives with God?"

"My husband lives in heaven with God."

"Your husband is *dead?*"

"Yes, he died of the cancer," she counted on her fingers, "four years ago."

"Four years ago?"

"Yes, but he still come to visit me and take my deeds away from me. What can I do?" She started to cry and was rocking the shopping trolley beside her back and forth.

"Here," I handed her a paper tissue. "I'll be right back."

I went into another empty reception room and dialed Phil's extension - somehow knowing that he would be in his office and not in fact with AJ.

"Phil Stevens here."

"Oh, hello Phil. Not with AJ then?"

"Oh hi Penn. How are you getting on with your new client? My friend Tim from Bramstons referred her to us." He started to howl. "A good paying client is she, Penn?"

"How dare you waste my time like this Phil! I am so bloody busy right now, and you think this is a great time to play practical jokes! I saved your bloody arse the other day when you were playing sick or calling in not interested or whatever you'd like to call it!!"

"Oh, stop taking yourself so seriously Penn. I thought you could do with some light relief! Oh, and just one more thing - make sure you get a good retainer." He hung up, still wheezing with laughter. *Glad you can still find something to laugh about Phil Stevens, or maybe I should I call you daddy?* The birth of that child was surely going to wipe the smile right off of his smug, little face.

Back in my office, I checked my email. It revealed nothing of any relevance, a few office jokes that had already taken place due to my encounter with Mrs. Simone and that was about it. I picked up the phone and dialed Oscar's extension.

"Oh hello Lord Hanley. It's Penny Banfield here."

"Oh Penny, my dear. How are you today?"

"Fine, I'm fine thank you. I was calling because I wanted to know if you've had time to review the draft patent application?"

"Oh yes, of course. I reviewed it yesterday. Tell you what, why don't you come down to my office. We can go over things together."

"Absolutely, I'll be right there." *OK, finally some billable time*:

0.1 Unit - Legal discussion with Lord Oscar Hanley, re: draft patent application

Unfortunately, I could not charge for travel time to his office. But I thought about it, which really showed my desperate billing situation. Still the weekend would provide a great opportunity to catch up on billable time. I arrived at Oscar's office to find him rummaging around the ash covered papers on his desk until, with utter amazement, he found my draft application - holding it up in the air like a winning lottery ticket.

"Here's the blighter. Come on in Penny - do take a seat."

"Thank you."

"Now then, let's see here, yes, yes..." He nodded as he read the application, as if reading it for the first time. "Well then, I think you've managed to get it all down. Yes, I do believe that will do it!" I wondered how he could get excited at reading what must have been one of a thousand patent applications he had drafted during the lifetime of his career. I also wondered why he had called me down to his office when he said he had already reviewed the draft, and it was apparently fine - needing no amendment.

"That's great Lord Hanley." I took the draft from him and blew the ash from it.

"Oh yes, one more thing Penny." I sat down again trying not to sigh.

"I heard on good authority that you're about to make an application for an Anton Piller Order?"

"Who told you that?" I didn't have the energy to tell him the application had already been filed.

He tapped the side of his nose. "Oh, you'd be surprised. I do like to keep myself in the know. I thought you might be in need of this." He pulled from his drawer a document yellow with age, pages curling at the corners.

"Oh really, what's that?"

"An old precedent of mine from way back when. I drafted an application in 1990 for the very same thing. The rules of court have changed a bit since then, but I thought it might at least give you a good starting point and help you out a bit."

In fact, it's as helpful as a chocolate teapot, Oscar. YES the rules have changed. They've changed QUITE A BIT IN FACT. There is nothing more dangerous in law than an old precedent.

"Oh, thank you - that's really very kind of you."

"I always like to help out young lawyers that show promise. Was a young lawyer myself once you know." He clicked his top set of false teeth and looked over the top of his eyeglasses at me.

"Thanks so much." He had such a pitiful look on his face that I decided I could spare him some time. Oscar was around my father's age, but had not taken care of himself physically. He looked like a bedraggled shadow of his former self (I assumed that at some stage he had been young and healthy), but unfortunately it appeared that the three women in his life did not appear to be taking care of him.

"I expect you were quite the formidable lawyer in your younger days?"

"Oh! You have no idea. Believe it or not, I even had quite a few ladies after me in those days. I remember being a first-year associate. You know, we would push each other out of the way clambering after oath fees when we were young and hungry. Had no idea that I would still be hungry for my beer money at this stage in my life, though."

"Oath fees? Oh, you mean for witnessing an affidavit?"

"Exactly. Now, it's five pounds for an affidavit and two pounds for each exhibit, but in those days of course it was way less."

Oscar was referring to the practice that lawyers would engage in of administering an oath to an affidavit. In England, it was forbidden for a lawyer to witness an oath to an affidavit sworn by his own client. Clients would therefore have to visit independent law offices to have their affidavits sworn and would be charged a fee for it. Young lawyers (and apparently the older lawyers that struggled financially) were often very obliging when it came to administering those oaths because they were allowed to keep the fees, which were always paid in cash. I had always resented the interruption to my daily work, and therefore shied away from the money grab. However, Nigel would often run down from the third floor to reception in order to assist.

"How far off is retirement Lord Hanley? I expect it won't be too far out of sight?"

"Oh, I couldn't possibly think of retiring at this stage in my career. I have to make partner first."

"Really? Partner? Is that what you would like?" I hoped that the sheer astonishment I felt did not show on my face.

"I don't think I could possibly consider myself to be a successful lawyer until such a time as I receive an offer of partnership."

My God, he was serious. "Well, I hope ... I am sure the time will come."

"Yes, who knows - maybe even this year?" he said and winked at me.

"This year? Have you been told anything?" I imitated him and tapped the side of my nose.

"I have it on good authority," he whispered.

"Wow! That's incredible! I mean, er ... congratulations Lord Hanley. I expect it will be well worth the wait."

"Thank you, my dear," he said and beamed with pride.

Either my informer (Nigel) or Lord Hanley's informer had received different information. I found myself wanting so badly for my informer to be wrong.

"Well then, best get back to the fray." I looked down at the aging, fragile draft I held in my hands, thinking of how much it resembled its author.

At 11 a.m., Nigel called. "Hey Penn. Sorry I'm going to have to miss coffee today. I have a huge closing on a deal to finalize."

"It sure is tough at the top Mr. Wilkinson. No problem. I have so much work to do – both Phil and Oscar have managed to both waste my time today."

"It's all character building stuff, just remember that."

"Oh yeah – that makes me feel so much better."

"See you later?"

"Of course, I'm the one with no life, remember?"

"OK then, I'll be in around 9ish, I'm playing a game tonight."

"See you later then. Oh, can you bring some ice cream home? I think I ate the last of it last night."

"You don't remember?"

"Well of course I remember eating it. I'm obviously just in denial about it, that's all."

"Is that why you can't buy some on the way home?"

"Absolutely right." I smiled as I put the phone down. Seems I had another call while on the phone with Nigel. So I listened to the message:

"Hi Penn, it's me ... Simon. Er ... look, I was hoping that you might be able to spare the time and call me back. Something's happened and well I, er ... God this sounds pathetic, but I just really need to see you."

I immediately picked up the phone and started to dial. "Kate!"

"Penn? What's up girl? Change your mind about the weekend – oh God, I hope so!"

"No Kate, it's not that. I just had another telephone call from Simon." I sighed.

"Oh God, no. Really? What did he say this time?"

"Oh, just the usual – that he really needs to see me." My head was swimming.

"Well, perhaps you should hear what he has to say this time? Maybe if you give him time with you, he might get some closure."

"Closure? On what? Slamming the closet door after he has just climbed out of it?!!"

"Calm down Penn. All I'm saying is that it might just take one meeting to finally get this monkey off your back - so to speak."

"I really don't have anything to say to him that could possibly make *him* feel better. I'm still furious at him and how he treated *me!*"

"Of course you are, anybody would be. I just think that it might also provide an opportunity for you to have your say and let Simon know exactly how all this has affected *you.*"

"Yeah ... maybe. I really just can't face it right now – all the drama I mean. I have so much going on at work and what with the weekend in Stevenage, I just can't afford any emotional diversions right now."

"Listen Penn, promise me you'll think about it? I think speaking with Simon might actually be helpful for *you.*"

"Thanks Kate. I'm truly sorry about the weekend. It would have been so much fun."

"Oh, there'll be plenty more opportunities. I'll probably curl up with a couple of good books and a bottle of Bombay Sapphire."

"Well, make sure you don't forget the limes then and have one for me!"

"And you have one for me Penn - if you know what I mean!!"

God, Kate had a filthy mind at times. She had always been more promiscuous than I. "You've got it wrong this time Kate – Gavin is just coming along for the sake of my security."

"Oh yes, that's right, to make sure that nobody breaks into your bedroom at night – good one!!"

"You are incorrigible, but I love you Catherine Henderson."

"Who wouldn't?"

"You're right. Definitely 'Catch of the Day' at least."

"Like a fish you mean? Are you insinuating that I smell like a fish?"

"Oh, get off the phone, you weirdo! See you soon babe."

"Yep. Oh – and have a *fabulous* weekend."

"I will – at least I hope so. Byeee."

Restless and unable to focus on anything of importance, I decided to do some yoga. Stretching into various poses and concentrating on my balance and poise was all I needed to erase previous conversations that had taken place with Simon.

He and I split up three months earlier after dating for two years. I had believed that an engagement was imminent and had even foolishly been putting things away for "my bottom drawer." For those not familiar with this concept, this involves buying various nice things for the home to be used in marriage. It was an extremely old fashioned thing to do, but I guess at heart, I am an old fashioned girl. No doubt subconsciously I believed that every item I had been buying brought me one step closer to marriage with Simon.

Simon Allbright was everything I had wanted for a husband. He was highly educated, kind, and extremely handsome. His mother was a surgeon and his father a professor of medicine. I had met Simon through a friend of Nigel's at an incredible party at a mansion on the outskirts of Glyndebourne. He had been helping some girl who had passed out from an alcohol- or drug-induced stupor, and I fell for him instantly having seen the kindness he had shown to a total stranger.

He wore jeans and a T-shirt with a picture of the album cover, "What's the Story Morning Glory" - a kindred spirit and fan of my favourite band, Oasis. I had been so taken with their music that I had even named my goldfish (the only low-maintenance pets I could think of) after the lead singers, Noel and Liam Gallagher. His hair was so blonde it was almost white, and he had wonderful brown eyes framed by long eyelashes. Much to my annoyance, Phil often referred to him as "Pretty Boy."

The experience with Simon had left me in doubt of many things, including my own sexuality - which had unnerved me to the point that I refused to even go out with friends for a least a couple of months. During the last few months of our relationship, I remember him pulling away from me. The harder I tried to hold his interest, the more he pulled away. It was like trying to hold water in your hands. Eventually, the day I had been dreading arrived and he told me that he wanted us to break up. Although I had been half expecting it, I had not anticipated the reason for him wanting the split.

I had arranged to meet him at the Tiger Inn, a local pub in a remote but relatively close village called East

Dean. After ordering drinks from the bar, Simon joined me in the snug room.

"So what's up Si? I know there is something wrong." I put all the effort I could to muster a smile.

He shifted in his seat and looked me right in the eyes. "Yes Penn. I'm not going to deny it. There is something wrong ... but something wrong with *me*, not something wrong with you."

"Oh, please Simon, save me from the predictable 'Dear John' speech – it's me, not you? Really? That's not very original, is it?"

"No Penn, it really is *me*. You see, there is nothing that you could have said or done differently in our relationship. You are perfect in every way, but just not for me."

"Oh really, and why is that? Because you've fallen in love with someone else? You need your space, and you are not ready to settle down? Which one is it going to be?" I started to tear up.

"No Penny. This is going to be very hard to believe. So you'll have to bear with me. I think the reason why we have been struggling lately is because I am having issues with my ... er ... sexuality." His remark literally took my breath away, but I nodded for him to continue.

"I think that I might actually be gay."

I almost choked on my drink. "You what? *What* did you say? *GAY!?*"

"Yes. Gay." He looked down at the wooden table while playing with his beer mat while I struggled to breathe. He was kind and sensitive, but I had never thought for a moment that he might be gay.

"Oh my God – no! Is this a bloody joke?"

"I wish it were," he stared down at the floor.

"Well, where the hell does that leave me Simon? "

"I'm sorry Penn. I don't think there is anything you can do about it, is there? God, how I wish I could change things. I kept telling myself that it was just a passing phase and that it was impossible for me to be gay. In a way, my continued relationship with you was a way of convincing myself that I was not gay."

"You bastard!" Couples out for a romantic or relaxing evening started to stare disapprovingly or move further away from the scene.

"How *could you* Simon? Use me like a guinea pig, playing with *my* emotional well-being while you experimented on … on *not being gay!!!*"

"Penn, please let me explain." He reached for my hand, and I quickly snatched it away.

"I feel totally sick to my stomach. There is no way that you could possibly *explain* this to me. I hate you - you *selfish*, selfish, *GAY* bastard!!" I picked up my glass of Merlot and tipped it over on his head and didn't look back. I walked to the gas station nearby and ordered a cab to take me home, all the time wishing that this were just a terrible dream.

Every phone call, email, and letter that followed was unanswered. I cut Simon completely out of my life, which surprisingly was relatively easy to do. We didn't share the same circle of friends and worked in different fields. What was not easy to get over was the blow to my confidence as a woman. Had he been attracted to me because somehow he thought I emitted "butch" tendencies? Did all "strong" women run into this problem? Why had I not seen that Simon was gay? Did everybody else, but me, see it? Had they been looking at me with pity, thinking that I was so smitten that I was oblivious to the obvious? The questions stayed with me for months, and I now found myself scrutinizing anybody who had the slightest feminine qualities. Simon had been a terrible mistake that I wanted to forget.

Eventually and until now, the calls subsided and emails stopped coming. I had thought that perhaps he had found another new, but male, partner. I had no intention of stirring up old emotions that were best left alone, especially since I had become interested in Gavin. I had often wondered why Simon had been less sexually inclined than I and had even thought he might be playing "hard-to-get." How utterly ridiculous of me! The whole experience left me feeling embarrassed at my naivety.

The yoga had not really helped very much as my back still felt like a steel post. Picking myself up off the floor and muttering a rushed "Namaste," I sat back into my chair and pulled a Lion Bar from the drawer of my desk instead.

0.2 Units - Waste of bloody time, trying to forget Simon while doing yoga

0.1 Unit - Stuffing my face with a Lion Bar

I did manage to retrieve something from the afternoon, having finished the patent application for Oscar's client and sending it off to the Patent Office for registration. I diarised the file for follow up in a couple of weeks, allowing me to log the following legitimate entries:

0.6 Units - Finalize patent application

0.2 Units - Draft letter to Patent office

0.1 Unit - Report to Lord Oscar-Hanley

How I hated that every damn minute of my life had to be recorded. It was like looking after a baby who constantly needed to be fed. Most lawyers become lawyers because they want to help their clients. Unfortunately, reality hits you very soon after completing your articles that a successful lawyer is one that focuses on billable hours – confirming the old adage that *"time is, in fact, money."* I could not think of one lawyer who had made partner without being a major fee-earner for the firm.

From: Gavin Preston
To: Penny Banfield
Date: Wednesday, May 10, 2000
Re: Tea

Sorry, I couldn't make tea today – rest assured I am thinking of you. Promise to make it up to you by bringing a nice cup of tea to you in bed on Sunday morning.
G xx

I found myself blushing when suddenly the phone rang. "Penny Banfield."

"Penny, it's Raj Gosavi."

"Oh, hi Raj. How are you?"

"I'm fine, thanks. I have a landlord and tenant issue I was hoping you might be able to help me with."

"How urgent is it?"

"The hearing won't be for at least another four weeks."

"That should be OK. I have a big project that will be taking up a lot of my time."

"Oh yes, that. The project that shall not be mentioned," he said and laughed. "Anyway, if you could come and see me sometime before I leave today that would be great."

"I'll be right up."

"OK then, see you in a minute."

I was grateful for the interruption. Raj was one of the nicest lawyers I had ever had the pleasure of working with - a total gentleman, extremely sexy, but very gay. His office was always tidy. He was a lawyer who did not like clutter or to be cluttered. His assistant, Jessica, was very efficient but highly strung. Just five minutes in her company and you found yourself becoming jittery. Beautiful red and orange East Indian silk paintings on the walls provided some clue as to his ethnicity. The furniture was plain but comfortable. His office had an incredible amount of natural light.

"Hi Penny, please take a seat," he said and graciously gestured me toward a chair.

"Thank you."

"Now then, I was hoping that you could help me out with an application to the court to evict some squatters from a property in Hove. It's owned by my client as part of a huge portfolio. I think you may know of my client, Frank Turner?"

I nodded. "Yes, I think most people in Brighton know him. He's landlord to practically everybody in town."

"Yes, he did inherit an incredible number of properties. Not that they bring him any peace," he said and smiled. "I sometimes think that his life would be far simpler if he would just instruct a property management company rather than try to do everything himself."

"No doubt. So, it's a question of providing notice to the squatters of our application and then attending the court hearing?"

"Yes, that's pretty much it. No doubt the usual crowd will show up at court."

"Usual crowd?"

"These squatters typically move from one vacant property to another. They get at least four weeks' notice under the *Protection from Eviction Act*. So they have time to find their next temporary home before moving out of their present property. Usually, when they go to court, they try and get the judge's sympathy - even though there is no defence to the action. There's one woman who shows up with a baby in tow at *every* hearing for possession. I don't think she's even a squatter. I think they pay her a fee to show up in court – so more of an actress, I would say."

"Oh no – that's dreadful."

"Desperate measures for desperate folks, but I can't say I'd like to be living their kind of lifestyle and in the conditions they live in. This house, for instance, doesn't even have power or running water."

His telephone started to ring, and I got up to leave. But he waved me back. "Raj Gosavi here. Oh, hello Frank. How are you doing today?" He rolled his eyes at me. "Yes, I'm actually sitting with an associate lawyer right now, briefing her on the application. Yes, yes. Oh, I see. Well, more reason to get things started. Yes … Yes … I see … Yes … I see … Yes … I see."

At this point, Raj put the call on speakerphone. I listened to what can only be described as an excruciating telephone conversation between Raj and Mr. Turner - well, not really a conversation *with* Raj, but rather the delivery of a monologue *to* Raj. It seemed that Mr. Turner had decided at this precise moment to go over his entire portfolio, providing details of the address of each property, every tenant, and what they currently owed. He moved from one property to the next without stopping to catch his breath. Raj scribbled down a note and passed it to me:

I can't interrupt him . Otherwise he starts right from the beginning.

I wondered how long I should sit waiting for the call to end. But each time I got up to leave, Raj gestured me back. After about 20 minutes, and yes, I did say 20 minutes, I heard the sound of a vacuum cleaner and a lady complaining. *"Well, I don't have all day Frank - even if you do. I have my work to do, and I simply can't wait for you to get off the phone.*" It seemed as if his wife was vacuuming around her husband while he did his best to continue, albeit at a higher volume now.

Raj handed me another note:

OK – I need this call to finish, can you shout as loud as you can, "Fire drill" or something like that?

I looked at him with total disbelief. He nodded profusely at me. I shrugged my shoulders. Then in a gruff tone, I yelled "Fire drill – everybody out!! Fire drill! Fire drill! Hey you - young man - please get off the phone and leave the building immediately!"

"Mr. Turner, I'm sorry I have to go … no … no … we have a fire drill. No, that's OK. Don't call me back. I'll call YOU back. No, *please,* don't call me back. Please, don't call me back Mr. Turner. I will call YOU!!" He hung up emitting a huge sigh.

I had tears of laughter running down my face. "Please, tell me that you don't have to do this every time the call gets out of hand."

"It varies. Urgent client in reception; call from the hospital; judge calling from the courthouse - you know, that sort of thing. Usually, Jessica obliges me with an excuse to hang up. She's getting to be quite imaginative with her excuses," he laughed.

"Why on Earth don't you just tell him you are busy?"

"Are you kidding? Mr. Turner is my best paying client. I set a record last week for the longest call from a client - 1 hour and 12 minutes. It's all billable time, and he pays for every second of it!!" Raj had become extremely animated.

"Oh, I see." *So that's how you got your partnership.*

"Well, I had best get back to my desk. I'll draft the application tomorrow and get it to you for review."

"Thanks Penny, that would be great."

As I walked back to my office, I found myself again pondering the allure of partnership and how it could turn a perfectly even keeled mind into the mind of an addict - hungry for billable time. Oscar was praying daily for partnership, while Raj was jeopardizing his mental health for it.

Back in my office, I arrived to a voicemail message from my Dad. His voice sounded troubled, so I immediately called him.

"Hey Dad, what's up?" I started to tidy my desk while on the phone.

"Oh Penny darling, I'm so glad you called back."

"Of course, you sounded quite perturbed by something."

"Yes, your mother is sick. She told me not to bother you, but I thought you should know," he said and then sneezed loudly. "Sorry darling."

"Dad, what do you mean by *sick?*"

"Well, she hasn't been right for some time really. But she had some bad news today from Dr. Pearson."

My heart was pounding. I could not deal with this right now. "What kind of bad news?"

"I'm afraid she's been diagnosed with cervical cancer, Penn."

My heart almost stopped. "Oh no, Dad. That's terrible news. How is she taking it?"

"Stoic, I would say. You know your bloody mother, she just doesn't want any fuss, but I know she's scared."

"Of course, she must be. Who wouldn't be? What's the prognosis, Dad?"

"It could be worse, but we think she has to have a hysterectomy and pretty soon."

"Does she have a date for the surgery yet?"

"No, not yet. We should hear from the doctor soon."

"Please, give my love to Mum. Give her a hug from me."

"You could speak to her yourself, you know." He sounded hopeful.

"No, I think it's probably better that it comes from you. Are you taking care of yourself Dad?

You know you can always call me when you need to. I expect she's going to be quite difficult to handle through all this."

"Well, you know your mother Penny. Don't worry about me my love, I'll just grin and bear it."

"Yes, as always. Listen, chin up Dad and keep me posted. I will come and visit soon, I promise."

"You know we'd both love to see you." *We both know that you would love to see me, but I'd just annoy Mum, like I always do.*

"I know. I'm sorry Dad, but I have to go."

"Bye, bye darling. Don't work too hard!"

0.1 Unit - Talking on phone to Dad

0.1 Unit - Worrying about impact on Dad

0.1 Unit - Wishing I could worry more about Mum than the effect all this would have on Dad

I berated myself for having made a promise, not something I was in a habit of doing. To me, a promise was sacred and never to be broken. So consequently, I very rarely made them - at least not unless I was absolutely certain that I could deliver.

I noticed I had a second voicemail message, which turned out to be another message from Simon. Could this day get any worse? Having decided that it was quite possibly going to get worse if I stayed at work, I decided to call it a day and left for the station.

Thankfully, the train journey was uneventful. I managed to doze off for a while without encountering dribbling men or screaming demons at my side. A steaming hot bath, glass of wine, followed by a great book was all that I needed to slough off a bad day.

As I walked toward the front door to my flat, I heard pacing behind me. I turned. As I saw him, my heart took a tumble - like I had dropped 13 floors in an elevator. He looked tired but tanned and was in fabulous shape. At that moment, it was impossible to hate him as he flashed his white smile at me.

"Hi Penn." The memory of his voice washed over me.

"Si - what are you doing here? " My voice could barely be heard.

"As I said, I *really* need to talk to you. You simply must hear what I have to say," he said, sounding desperate.

"I can't think of one thing you could say that could possibly change things. But you may as well come in, seeing as you've come all this way."

We walked through the door in silence. I hung up my coat and tried to stay calm. It truly was tragic that this man was not capable of loving me - because at one time, I had wanted nothing more from life. "Why don't you take a seat in the lounge while I get the wine. I don't know about you, but I definitely could do with a drink," I said and tried to smile.

"That would be great."

Simon walked into the lounge while I pulled a bottle of Vinho Verde from the fridge - feeling a surge of rising anxiety grip my chest. *Why now? Just at the point when I'm ready to move on and trust another man.* As I pulled the cork and grabbed two glasses, it felt just like old times. Only this time, all I could count on was his friendship, that is, if I even wanted it. Maybe it was just his physical presence that I missed; the smell and feel of him. I walked into the lounge, deliberately sitting in a chair opposite from where he sat on the sofa. I didn't want him to feel too comfortable. He pulled a cushion and placed it in front of him on his lap, for some kind of protection I expect. I poured out the wine and handed the glass to him, deliberately avoiding any accidental touching of hands.

"Is that new?" He pointed to a new piece of artwork that had been given to Nigel, but I quite liked it. So we had agreed to share it while he lived in the flat.

"Oh no, that's Nigel's." I was being mean and enjoyed the look of surprise on his face.

"Nigel?" He looked concerned.

130

"Yes, surely you remember my friend Nigel Wilkinson?"

"Oh, that Nigel. I thought you meant somebody else. So you and Nigel are sharing the flat now?" He glanced around the flat as if taking an inventory of my life without him. "Like together?" He looked anxious.

I shook my head. "Only roommates, although he's very rarely here – he does have quite the social life."

"Well, he always was quite the social butterfly."

I was in no mood for small talk. "So, Simon, what did you want to talk about?"

"That's what I've always liked about you, Penn. You always get straight to the point."

"So I've been told. Listen Simon, I've had a pig of a day and actually was looking forward to an early night. I'm sorry if I appear a little impatient." I started to tap my fingernails against my wine glass.

"I thought it was time for us to air our grievances in a civilized way, preferably in a way that does not end with me dripping from head to toe with Merlot, if that's at all possible." He flashed his magnificent smile, indicating that I had at least been forgiven for my earlier outrageous lack of self-control.

Curtailing a smile from breaking out, I said, "I've been told red wine is good for your cholesterol levels."

"Ah yes … yes it is, but I understand you need to imbibe it, rather than wear it."

"Sorry about that." I looked away from him worried that I might fall too much under the spell of his charm.

"I deserved it. Anyway, I thought that there might be questions you might want to ask me. I know you didn't really get a chance to ask me at the time."

"Yes, strangely enough Simon, I *do* have some questions. The first question, I guess, is how long did you know that you were gay?"

"I had suspected it right from the beginning."

"The beginning? Do you mean just while you were with me, or prior to our relationship?!" I felt myself slipping into cross-examination mode, another occupational hazard.

"Since I was around 15, I think."

"Wow – that just blows me away! It took you that long to realize for sure?"

"Yes. At least that's what I thought at the time."

What could he possibly mean by that comment? "What kind of statement is that? What do you mean by that Simon?"

"I *thought* I was gay, but it turns out I am definitely *not* gay." I found my mind wandering, contemplating the various situations he had encountered in order to make this discovery, but thankfully had the presence of mind to push those images away.

"I don't understand. What are you saying Simon?"

He looked down at his shoes. "Look at me Si! How can that be? Are you bisexual then?"

"Nope."

"Not gay and not bisexual? Then what the hell are you?"

"Seems I am heterosexual after all."

"I don't understand this," I gulped the rest of my wine down and refilled my glass. "You *told me* that you were *GAY!*" I virtually screamed at him, sounding like the spoilt demon on the train.

"Because I *thought* I was. I've had way more time to explore my sexuality. I can say without one iota of doubt that I am *not* gay. Isn't that wonderful news, Penn?"

"Wonderful? Wonderful news for who Simon? I feel so bloody confused. I have no idea what to think. You broke my heart! You made me think there was something wrong with me!"

"I know, I know Penn. That's why I'm here. I thought you had the right to know - that you should be the first person to know. I'm really not sure what we do now?"

"We? We?? There is no '*WE*' anymore Simon. It's over. It has to be over." My heart felt like it had been kicked around the block.

"But we split up because I thought I was gay, and so did you. Now, we *know* that I'm not – surely that counts for something?"

"Yesterday you were gay and today you're not gay. Who knows what it will be tomorrow – that you are thinking of becoming a transsexual? Don't you see that we can't just pick up where we left off? I could never trust you again. I'd always be worried that at any moment, you might change your mind about your sexuality."

"I can assure you that's not going to happen." He leaned forward and held my hand.

As much as I wanted to linger, I pushed away his hand. "No Simon. I can't go through that again. I'm still raw from the experience. In fact, I thought I'd never get over it."

"I just want you to think about it Penn. I've thought of you constantly throughout my ordeal and know with every fibre of my being that I still love you. I thought you had a right to know, that's all. Please promise me that you will at least think about things." He came toward me and stroked my cheek.

I pushed him away. "How could I *not* think about things? God, I could not be more confused than I am right now!"

At that point, the front door slammed shut and Nigel appeared in the doorway to the lounge. "Hey Penn, only me! Is there any wine left? Oh, Simon. Hi. I didn't know you were going to be here. Sorry Penn, the game was called off. I'll just make myself scarce." He looked over to me and with a meaningful glance, wanting to check that I was OK - to which I nodded.

"I'd forgotten how great Nigel was," Simon said.

"Be careful Si – I'll be wondering if you mean that for all the wrong reasons."

"Ouch. That really was uncalled for Penny. Although, I can't say I blame you based on the circumstances. Anyhow, I'd best be off. I've said what I came here to say, the rest is really up to you. All I can ask is that you think long and hard. We really had incredibly strong feelings for each other, and it's not over - as far as I am concerned." He moved closer and kissed me on the forehead, evoking sweet memories of what had been before that I could not and did not want to push him away.

Being a trained advocate, it wasn't often that I would find myself speechless. But I had been silenced by the conversation that had taken place. After Simon left, I went immediately to my sanctuary, slipping into my bath robe. I refilled my glass in the lounge while the bath ran like a gurgling brook. The door to Nigel's bedroom opened slowly, and he peeked out from behind the door.

"Is the coast clear?" he whispered.

"Yes, he's gone." I must have looked shell-shocked.

"I don't like the way that boy looks at me," he said jokingly to try to pull me from my trance-like state.

"Oh, it's OK Nigel. It seems that he's back playing for the other side again."

"What do you mean, playing for the other side?"

"Simon's decided he is not, after all, gay and I'm about to stew about it in the bath." I cradled the wine glass in my hand.

"I thought you didn't get to decide about these things – they just, well … are?"

"Me too, but I guess I'm no expert on the subject." Nigel promptly picked up the glass of wine Simon had left untouched, taking down a huge slug.

"Wow! He came here to tell you that?"

"Yes, and the fact that he wants to make another go of things."

"Seriously? What a bloody fool! You *cannot possibly* be considering his offer Penny?" His face was creased with concern.

I shrugged my shoulders and clutching my glass of Vinho Verde, headed off to the bathroom. The combination of an extremely hot bath and a couple of glasses of wine sent my head spinning. *How do I feel about this?* I kept asking myself. *At least there is nothing wrong with you. Isn't that great? Simon is NOT gay. What if he changes his mind again, though? I can't go through this again – I'm too fragile. I hate him for doing this to me. Why do I feel so fragile? So raw?......................I think I am still in love with him.*

Thankfully, Nigel had the good sense to leave me alone after my bath. I climbed into bed believing that a long night would lie ahead. Surprisingly, I slept like a baby.

CHAPTER 4 – THURSDAY MAY 11, 2000

I had managed to get an early start on the day and was drafting an application for substituted service when the telephone rang. "Penny Banfield."

"Hi Penny, it's Dad."

"Hi Dad, what's up? Did you get any more news?"

"Yes, I just wanted to let you know that we've received the date for your mother's surgery – they managed to get her in for next week – the 19th."

"Wow – that was quick!" I tried my best to sound concerned.

"Well they don't tend to mess about with this kind of thing."

"Thanks for letting me know Dad. I've got a huge project coming to a head on that day so I won't be able to call until probably Saturday morning….you will call me if there are any issues though, won't you Dad?"

"Of course."

He sounded really disappointed. I expect that many daughters would have dropped everything and booked time off work. I wasn't sure if my mother even knew he was calling me with the news.

"OK Dad, I'm really sorry but I'm going to have to go I've so much to do before the weekend."

"Yes, well of course I expect you are really busy darling. I'll be in touch."

Why did I always feel guilty after a telephone call with my father? I knew he was disappointed in my behaviour and confused about the lack of relationship with my mother but it was impossible to explain it to him without breaking his heart.

An Aunt had once told me that my mother had wanted to be a doctor when she was younger before she had met my Dad. She fell pregnant with me prior to marriage and with the arrival of my birth came the death of her proposed career. I therefore grew up knowing that my existence had to be justified in her eyes and was constantly subject to criticism as my mother began to live vicariously through me.

It was never enough for me to place third or even second place on Sport's Day. Nothing but first place would put a smile on her face, although my Dad would always be there full of encouragement.

I was told to focus on my school work and grades and can't remember ever hearing anything positive about having a family or being in a loving relationship. My Dad lived out in the cold but rarely complained. He knew he was unlikely to ever please her, but that didn't stop him from trying and I loved him for that.

"Be your best, Penny. You must always strive to be the best." That's all I can remember from my conversations with her.

I was worried about her, but mainly because she might die without me getting a chance to make my peace with her.

My thoughts went back to that family holiday in Jersey one summer.

I was around 13 years old and we had been staying with friends of the family (Trevor and Mavis) just outside St. Helier. It had been a lovely day and we had spent it picnicking by the ocean. I had spent way too long in the sun and was quite red. I left everybody on the beach while I went back to the house for some calamine lotion. Mum had a migraine and had stayed behind so I tiptoed around the house trying not to wake her, fearful of her vicious tongue.

I heard laughter coming from her bedroom and thought that perhaps it might be the radio in her room but crept closer to the bedroom door so that I could hear more clearly. I heard my mother's voice, the tone of which had changed to something that could only be described as childish. She was mocking somebody.

"Oh you are such a coward! They won't be back for hours yet, come on – I'm still hungry for you."

I heard my "Uncle" Trevor's voice, "You really are impossible to resist, do you know that." I left abruptly and was halfway down the stairs when I heard the usual sounds that lovers make when they think nobody can hear.

Be your best.....Always be your best..... Are you being your BEST right now, Mother?

I ran all the way from the house back to the beach and to this day, my father had no idea why I arrived breathless and without the calamine lotion.

I had a headache brewing and decided to go down to the Pavilion to get some fresh air. I walked from Old Steyne and across to the Pavilion and began to think of Simon and days when we had walked to the Pavilion together carefree and very much in love.

I knew that deep down I was still in love with him but I also knew that I did not trust in that love anymore.

Pavilion Gardens was vibrant and in bloom – a lovely place for courting couples, picnics, ice creams and cups of tea. I very rarely had time to appreciate the gardens now that my life comprised of drafting documents, court appearances and client meetings.

I bought an ice cream and sat down at a table, people watching, noticing how my breathing had slowed and my headache had disappeared. If only it was so easy to shake off my issues with Phil, Simon and my mother.

CHAPTER 5 – FRIDAY MAY 12, 2000

It was around 10 a.m., and I sat at my desk engrossed in review of a list of addresses that had been provided to me by Archie. Thankfully, the addresses were all within the County of Sussex, which alleviated costs just a little. Not that this client was at all concerned about costs - having large coffers. There were more than 20 addresses that we needed to consider.

We had the capacity to raid many houses all at the same time, but not all of the 20 or so directors were going to be important from an evidential perspective. The raid would need to be executed with fine precision in order to be effective. If just one director got advance notice of our arrival, the possibility of capturing all the evidence would be compromised at great expense.

I found myself contemplating some of the houses that were about to be raided and wondering how our arrival would be received. It was potentially a highly inflammatory scenario. My reverie was broken by a phone call, which was not work related.

"Kate – oh my God, I'm so sorry – I did get your voicemail this morning, but I totally forgot to call you back." I felt like I was always having this conversation with Kate, but thankfully, she did not take it personally.

"Don't worry about it. Just wondered if you wanted to come over for curry and a bottle of wine tonight since you can't come to the cottage this weekend?"

"Are *you* making the curry?"

"Of course I am!"

"Oh, OK then. Twist my arm," I said and laughed.

"Cheeky bugger. We could always order in if you don't like my cooking?"

"I'm *joking* Kate. You know I can't refuse a good curry. It sounds perfect. I have so much to tell you, but the most important news is that Simon paid me a visit at the flat last night."

"What? Simon actually had the balls to show up at your place? Well, I absolutely have to see you now. I am so envious of you, Penny Banfield. My life has been pretty boring over the last couple of months."

"Oh, well in that case, I think I'll change my mind … no point coming over if you have no goss for me."

"Oh, I have goss. It's just not about *my* life."

"OK then, I'll be there at around half past six, and I'll bring the wine. Fancy anything in particular?"

"What about that lovely fizzy green wine we had last time?"

"The Vinho Verde? OK, though it's not really sweet enough to go with curry. I can bring it though if that's what you want."

"Oh yes, I'd forgotten what a wine connoisseur you've become lately. I'll leave it up to you - whatever you think would go best. I'm fine with anything, just so long as it has alcohol."

"In truth, it's probably a bottle of Liebfraumilch. But I expect you'd die of shock if I brought a bottle of Blue Nun round, so maybe I'll bring a Gewürztraminer instead."

"Whatever Penn. You know I really don't care, just so long as it's *alcohol*."

"Yeah, I know. I should probably go. I've got lots to do today and should pack for the weekend before I head over to your place."

"Oh yes, glorious Stevenage!"

"Not ordinarily a place I'd like to visit, but it's suddenly got a lot more interesting, that's for sure," I said and laughed.

"OK then. See you later Penn."

I suddenly felt quite guilty. Kate had been having a dry patch lately when it came to male attention, and I was also always the first one to end a telephone conversation because of that ticking clock reminding me of my billable hours.

Kate had been a friend since University. We had roomed together on campus, but she had been enrolled in a completely different faculty (business studies).

Our differences were obvious from the beginning. I tried to take care of my appearance, but Kate did not give a dot about how she looked (which thankfully due to her natural beauty did not matter at all). I was anal about my studies, and Kate studied whenever she had the time to devote - she had been blessed with a photographic memory, which I was in constant awe of. I had brown hair, and she was blonde; I was petite, and she was tall.

Unfortunately, Kate's first experience with men had taken place on campus, but in the most horrific way when she was raped by a drunken monster in a basement at some frat house. The identity of the rapist remains unknown to me to this day, as Kate refuses to talk about it. I remember holding her hand, wiping tears from her face in a grey and sterile clinic while samples and police statements were taken. I vowed at that time that I would work feverishly to become a lawyer and ensure that no man would escape the justice system for such a brutal crime. That had been some time ago now. Kate, thankfully, had moved on with the help of several years of counselling; and I had decided on another course of law, not involving crime.

My parents were very similar to Kate's in that they allowed me to enjoy my newly found freedom on campus and rarely visited. The support I received from them had been verging on indifferent, but at least my requests for funding were always met. At the time of my arrival on campus, I had despised my mother in any event. I can remember to this day, the relief on my father's face when I left home for University - knowing that at least there would now be a ceasefire between Mum and me.

Growing up, I had found myself willing my father to find a backbone and stand up to the bully my mother had become. I had no idea of the reason for her unhappiness, but she seemed to want to spend the rest of her life punishing my father for something. I warmed to Kate's mother the first time we met. She was highly creative and bohemian, whereas my mother was brittle and conservative.

Kate's family cottage was a constant source of joy and every opportunity we had to take a break, we would motor over to Dorset to breathe in some salty air and feel the soft touch of grass between our toes. I really did need to spend more time with Kate. It seemed that once again, work had taken over my life.

I picked up the phone, dialing the number for Archie Steadman.

"Archie? It's Penny Banfield."

"Oh, hello Penny. Did you get the stuff I sent to you?"

"Yes I did. Thanks so much for working around the clock on this. There are so many addresses Archie. I can honestly say I don't know how you managed to do all of this in time."

"It's what you pay me for luv."

"I know that. Even so, I just wanted to say thank you."

"Wish I could come with you and see some of those houses. A few of the addresses are in high-class neighbourhoods, if you know what I mean."

"Yes, I had noticed. Probably find just as much dust there as you would in my flat though," I said and laughed.

"Oh yes, and a lot more besides. You're in for a treat, I am sure."

"What do you mean?"

"Oh, you'll find out soon enough."

I hated cryptic messages and felt the urge to cross-examine him further, but decided against it. "Archie, there is one thing I was wondering about. What if nobody is home when we attempt the raid?"

"You'll have to either wait, or go back."

"Going back is not an option for us."

"Better pray they are all in then. Otherwise, you will need to take some camping gear with you," he said and laughed.

"Hmm. This is going to be way more difficult than I thought."

"Oh, I am sure Tony Jarvis has it all figured out luv. Let him worry about that side of things."

"Yes. Yes of course, you are right. Anyway thanks again Archie. I'll pass your invoice onto our accounts department for payment right away."

"Ta luv – speak to you soon. Make sure you let me know how everything goes."

"Of course." I hung up, realizing the enormity of the task we were about to undertake collectively as a firm for the first time. With so much that could go wrong, I wondered how AJ slept at night.

There was a tap at the door and there stood Nigel with two cups of deliciously sweet, steaming coffee.

"Aahh, a welcome break – come on in."

"Hey Penn." He sat down on the sofa and kicked off his shoes.

"Please do make yourself comfortable Nigel," I said and laughed. "I hope those socks were fresh on today?"

"Of course. I've never received any complaints about my personal hygiene, thank you. Are you in tonight Penn? Only because I've perhaps got somebody coming over."

"A girl?"

"Well, more of a *woman* actually and don't act so surprised."

"Oo aah – get you Nigel Wilkinson!"

"Stop teasing me. Now then, are you going to be in or not?"

"Actually, it must be your lucky day. I am going to see Kate tonight and will probably stay over now that I know you are *entertaining*. The only thing is remember that I need a lift over to the car rental place tomorrow morning. Do you think you might still be up for that?"

"Of course. I wouldn't let you down, you know that." He was such a good friend.

"Even if the mystery lady stays over?"

"It's not like that ... not yet anyway."

"Blimey. Can't believe you've already ruled out the possibility though. Are you feeling unwell?"

"Seriously, this is one hell of a lady. I have no intention of moving too quickly. I'm just cooking dinner for her, that's all."

"Good God, I hope she has a strong constitution." I chuckled.

"You can be so mean at times, do you know that Penny Banfield?"

"Yes I know. I'm sorry Nigel, I am sure she will love the meal."

He really did look nervous sitting there with his right knee bouncing up and down. I often overlooked how attractive Nigel was. In a suit, he had never had any effect on me at all. In his cricket whites however, well, that was quite a different matter. I always had a thing about men in cricket whites. Still crushing on your roommate was highly inappropriate, and I valued his friendship. So nothing was going to change in that regard. Kate had some theory about my relationship with Nigel and how it was impossible for any man to have a truly platonic relationship with a woman, but I didn't believe a word of it.

"What are you planning on cooking?"

"Well, I was rather hoping that you might be able to supply your recipe for red Thai curry."

"Does she like curry then?"

"Yes, she did mention it."

"Well, you are onto a winner then. You can't go wrong with my recipe."

"I know – you can cook it, can't you?" he joked. "Don't suppose you have it here, do you?"

"You might be in luck. I think I still have it in an email somewhere. I sent it to Kate once. Listen Nigel, I probably shouldn't be taking a coffee break today. There's still tons to be done before the weekend. I'll dig the recipe out and send it to you later by email. Will that be OK? Then if you could pick me up at Kate's tomorrow at nine and run me over to the car rental people, I can pick up the BMW."

"BMW? *BMW!*! You do realise that the firm is never going to pay for that Penn."

"I know you silly bugger. I'm paying the difference."

"Must be nice," he said.

"Yes, it is. I'm really looking forward to driving it." I grinned as I started to push him toward the door.

Before I got too bogged down and forgot about it, I forwarded the recipe to Nigel by email, took off my jacket, and got down to work. On an A4 sheet of paper, I wrote the name of each director that needed to be served, together with their address. I then laid each piece of paper out on the floor of my office, dividing the addresses into four quadrants - depending on whether the address was NW, NE, SW, or SE of the county. Thankfully, we did not have any directors living outside of Sussex. AJ would have to identify which of the 20 houses were destined for inspection. In any event, we would have to organize at least 10 cars, if not more.

In each car, we would need one lawyer with one member of support staff. Thank goodness we were a huge law firm with plenty of both. In addition to our staff, we would also need a supervising solicitor (from another law firm) to serve the Order, oversee our work, and ensure that the court rules were followed precisely.

Pulling out a new map of Sussex from its cellophane packet and tacking it to the wall in my office, I marked each address with a cross. We had a large area to cover. Some lawyers would need to leave much earlier than others with their team members. We all needed to be in place by 9 a.m. on the day of the raid and ready to leap into action at 9:30 a.m.

From: Penny Banfield
To: Anthony Jarvis
Cc: Phil Stevens
Date: Friday, May 12, 2000
Re: Service of Anton Piller Order

I have now received from Mr. Steadman details of

addresses for all directors and confirm that all addresses have been verified. Thankfully, all 20 directors are currently living within the confines of Sussex.

Please, could you review the names of the directors on the attached list and confirm that these are the directors that will receive service and ultimately be subject to the terms of the search order.

I am now drafting instruction kits for the various service teams together with a letter of instruction for our supervising solicitors for your review.

Penny Banfield

From: Phil Stevens
To: Penny Banfield
Date: Friday, May 12, 2000
Re: Service of Anton Piller Order

Fantastic! Thanks Penny. I have no time for all this bullshit right now. This is such a huge undertaking…..

I have no idea what AJ is thinking about taking on something like this during golf season.
Phil

He had to be joking. I could not imagine that even Phil would be so glib about such a huge opportunity for the firm. Had the news of a baby on the way affected his judgment and sent him off the edge? I knew Phil was selfish, but this was beyond all comprehension.

From: Anthony Jarvis
To: Penny Banfield
Date: Friday, May 12, 2000
Re: Service of Anton Piller Order

Thank you, Penny. I will take a look at the list with our client. We will identify those addresses that need to be searched.

Rest assured, I have complete confidence that you, together with Philip Stevens, will do a magnificent job of pulling everything together.

My wife, Laura, has received a long awaited hospital appointment for Friday, May 19, i.e. the proposed date for service. This unfortunately means that I will not be available on the morning of the 19th. I will of course be available by telephone.

Still, as I say, I am sure that you and Philip are perfectly capable of handling this together.
AJ

Together? Handling this together- as in a TEAM, you mean? What a complete joke. If he only knew the half of it.

I wanted to throw something at the computer. Phil had no more intention of assisting with the donkey work than I had of becoming an exotic dancer. I could see now that the whole thing was going to fall fairly and squarely on my shoulders unless I leaned very heavily on him to handle his fair share of the necessary work. My keyboard rattled from side to side as I pounded out an email to Phil:

From: Penny Banfield
To: Phil Stevens
Date: Friday, May 12, 2000
Re: Anton Piller Order

I think it might be a good idea if you and I spend at least two hours per day working on this file together. Otherwise I fear for the overall success of the operation. I trust that I can count on you being there for the team?! Penny

---

From: Phil Stevens
To: Penny Banfield
Date: Friday, May 12, 2000
Re: Anton Piller Order
Of course you can – you know you can always depend on

---

me. Just let me know what you need.
Phil

I need my bloody head examined, that's what I need Phil.

From: Penny Banfield
To: Reception
Date: Friday, May 12, 2000
Re: Going out

Jean, I'm just popping out. Need anything from Gita's?
Penny

"Hi Gita, how is everything? Business doing well?" She had dark rings under her eyes and looked exhausted. Well, I suppose anybody would look tired if they got up so early for newspaper deliveries every day.

"Oh yes, same as usual I'd say, so can't complain." She started to reorganize some magazines.

"I'll just take the Flake and a Topic bar."

"You are going to have to make a special appointment with the dentist if you keep eating so much sugar you know."

"I know, I know. Let's just call it an occupational hazard. It seems to be the best way of coping with the stress right now."

"I thought that the yoga was supposed to help with your stress?" she laughed.

"Well, it kind of works together. I eat the chocolate until I make myself feel sick, then guilt myself into doing some exercise, and work on the mat for around 15 minutes."

"Whatever works, is what I say. I shouldn't exactly complain about it – it's good for business."

"Exactly." I glanced over at the stack of newspapers and caught the following headline:

SALE OF FOOTBALL CLUB IMMINENT?

"Know anything about that?" I asked, nodding toward the newspaper.

"Oh, they are always coming up with some story or other about the football club. It sells newspapers."

"Do you think they are really selling the club?"

"There's usually an element of truth in every story. So yes, I do."

"Yes, that's what I was thinking. Can I buy a copy?"

"Of course."

I paid Gita and walked back to the office, chomping on a Flake while engrossed in the newspaper article along the way. There was talk of a sale of the Club to a local supermarket seeking prime retail space, which of course the current grounds had. Jim Bateman and his merry men were about to sell off the family silver to save their skins by the look of it. It seemed like Jim would stop at nothing to fund his litigation war.

After the customary 15 minutes of yoga to compensate for a complete lack of willpower, I got to work on compiling a table detailing the various teams involved with the raid. Then I forwarded it to AJ and Phil for their review.

Feeling a great sense of accomplishment, I decided that I would take a leaf out of Phil's book and leave work early due to having so much to do before the trip in the morning.

From: Penny Banfield
To: Gavin Preston
Date: Friday, May 12, 2000
Re: Going home

Hi Gavin,

I've decided to leave early today so I can get ready for our trip tomorrow. Will pick up the car at around 9 a.m. and come over to your place around 10 a.m.

Have to forego our Tea at Three, but I'm sure you will forgive me.

If not, I promise to make it up to you this weekend.
Penny x

I left the office and stopped off at a party store to pick up my "disguise" outfit: A blonde wig and some large sunglasses that covered half of my face. I also stopped at a cheap clothing store and picked up some "tarty" clothing; some leopard skin leggings and a low-cut top showing off as much as was possible without getting arrested for indecent exposure. *Funny how you always associate indecent exposure with men. Wonder if any women have been arrested for this offence?*

I also bought some bright red lipstick (of the variety usually associated with clowns at birthday parties). There was no way that anybody could possibly associate me with the new persona I was about to adopt. My appearance was, however, unlikely to look too out of place at a Saturday market. Yes, extremely judgmental, I know.

At home, I started packing for the weekend. Presumptuous but wanting to be prepared, I rummaged around my lingerie drawer. I didn't have anything new, which had been bought for the occasion. But I also didn't feel comfortable wearing something previously worn during my "Simon days." I decided that if anything were to happen between Gavin and me, it would have to be "Au Naturel" and my naked body would just have to do. I did, however, pack my silk dressing gown and some Gucci perfume to try and make it look as if I had at least made an effort.

Nervously excited, I chastised myself that this was supposed to be a field trip for professional purposes and that I had to stay focused. The rental car had been booked a few days earlier, and I had decided to go all out and rent a BMW sports car. We were booked into a really nice hotel just outside Stevenage, in a small village called Harpenden. Gavin had informed me it was a beautiful village with a great pub nearby if we did not feel like eating at the hotel.

He was surely going to be impressed that I'd even had time to pack a lunch of smoked salmon pate, extremely sharp cheddar and crackers, and chilled champagne. I just hoped that Kate could fit it all in her fridge. I pulled out from my bottom drawer some embroidered napkins and a tablecloth, placed them with my picnic hamper, and prayed that the weather would hold out.

Satisfied that I had everything packed, I took one last look around the place, before leaving a note for Nigel on the table.

Nigel, hope the recipe goes well – have fun! P x x

Smiling at the prospect of Nigel entertaining his lady friend, I called a cab to take me over to Kate's flat.

Kate's place was what you would call a garden suite - a flat in the basement of an old Victorian house. Kate had painstakingly spent a lot of time growing various plants that adorned the steps down to her flat from the main street and had even managed to grow a patio vegetable garden, which was the subject of much envy. Still, she always seemed to have more time than me. I guess not having a boyfriend had something to do with that, but also her job was what I'd call "fluff" – not really demanding and certainly not likely to cause any lack of sleep.

Armed with a bottle of Gewürztraminer, I rang the bell - inhaling the aromatic smell of Asian spices and feeling suddenly very hungry, which was somewhat surprising in view of all the calories I had eaten earlier that day.

"Hey babes, so lovely to see you. Oh my God, I feel like it's been ages!" I kissed her on the cheek.

"That's probably because it has," she said and took the bottle of wine from me. "Great, I'll put this in the fridge."

"It smells wonderful – did you order in?" I joked.

"Ha ha! I decided against it and thought I would wow you instead with my legendary culinary skills."

"I am impressed - well at least if it tastes as good as it smells." She brushed her hand across my head in protest.

Her flat was decorated with impeccable taste with also a little of her mother's bohemian style. I remember in the early years of moving in, she and I had had hours of fun visiting various flea markets and salvage shops buying remnants of the past, which somehow always seemed to fit together when Kate assembled them.

The only thing that was not "arranged" at her place was her cat, which seemed to move from room to room trying to figure out where it should "go." Theo was a ginger cat with cool green eyes and a temperament that could only be described as indifferent. Like most cats, he just came home to be fed and the rest of the time seemed to look like he was roughing it with company far beneath him. I really had no feelings for Theo despite having spent eight years trying to build a relationship. It was one of my life's failings, but a failing that I could live with.

Kate's kitchen was cosy, with an antique dresser and pine table that looked as if a war had been fought on it, marked with various knife marks and cracks. She had told me that it had once been her grandmother's table and that she had originally bought it from the local baker, which explained the various cross marks (as he kept track of his baker's dozen). Somehow she had also managed to find an old AGA oven that was still in working order and another item of envy. I had spent so many hours in this kitchen, laughing, crying, and just generally trying to figure out life with Kate.

"So, are you looking forward to the weekend?" She opened the wine and poured two glasses.

"Yes, I am actually. I suppose I'm a bit nervous too." I took a huge slug of wine.

"But you already know Gavin. It's not as if he's a total stranger, is it?"

"Right, but I wonder if it's going to be awkward in the car on a journey together." I played with the cork.

"Oh, I'm sure you'll be just fine. You could talk the hind legs off a donkey, Penn. So really all he has to do is nod and say the occasional word from time to time in order to let you know he hasn't fallen asleep."

"Ha ha. Very funny. So, is that what you do then? Nod at me in order to stop yourself from falling asleep?! You're probably right, I should just relax about the whole thing."

"Have you got your outfits ready?" She started to wiggle, showing off her breasts.

"Yes darling, the girls will be on display, I am sure," I said and giggled.

She started lifting lids, stirring and tasting from steaming pans while I tried to suppress the surging hunger pangs fed by waves of culinary fragrance.

"Are you sure you cooked this from scratch?"

"Of course! I just finished a night course on Thai cooking. Are you impressed?"

"I am. *Seriously* impressed. It smells divine."

"Well, the proof of the pudding is in the tasting. I'm about to serve up, so take a seat at the table."

Taking my wine with me, I did as ordered, picked up my crisp linen napkin and placed it over my lap. Kate proceeded to pile perfectly separated rice smelling vaguely of lemongrass onto my plate. She spooned out the curry arranging it on the plate, sprinkling fresh coriander on top.

"Wow, Kate! This looks wonderful." She beamed with pride at the praise bestowed upon her.

"Taste it first before you pass judgment, Penn."

I took up my spoon and tasted the curry. "Fantastic Kate. I mean *really* fantastic!"

"Thanks."

"Want to know something funny?"

"What's that?"

"Nigel is making *my* red Thai curry recipe tonight for a lady friend."

"Really? That's weird. Think he'll manage to pull it off?"

"Well, the recipe is not as good as this one, but it's probably enough to impress her."

"So, come on then?"

"What?"

"Tell me all about your conversation with Simon."

"Oh that. Yes it was quite a shocker."

I plunged into a recall of the entire episode that had taken place with Simon as Kate listened intently while eating. She grimaced and sighed at all the appropriate places as a good friend should, and on hearing myself relay the story, I noticed my heart was racing and my palms were sweaty.

"Wow, what a turn up for the books!" She looked genuinely surprised.

"Yep. Hard to really know what to say at this stage. I mean there was a time when I would have prayed for something like this to happen, but now it's just too late." I shook my head.

"Really Penn?"

"What do you mean, *really*?"

"It's just that when you were telling me about it, your voice seemed so full of emotion. Are you sure you are completely over Simon?" She searched my face for any signs of weakness.

"Of course I am. Why would I even consider getting involved with Gavin if that wasn't the case?" I averted her penetrating stare.

"Just wondering, that's all. I guess I'd always believed that you and Simon were a done deal until he came out with his great revelation. I even had dreams of being your maid of honour."

"Yes me too, only my dreams of being a bride quickly turned into my worst nightmare."

"What if he's totally figured out his sexual orientation though? Are you really prepared to walk away forever?"

"What other alternative do I have? You can't possibly have a relationship with somebody you don't trust."

"True, but then again he has always been *honest* with you, hasn't he?"

"Eventually ... I suppose, but I wish he had told me before I had fallen in love with him and had my heart broken."

"Well, you know better than anybody what's best for you. So if you say you are over Simon, then it's time to take a look at the next contender. Tell me about Gavin." This time she looked at me with an air of a psychotherapist looking quite serious and thoughtful.

"You have to meet him Kate. He's simply gorgeous. When I'm around him, it's difficult to even think straight."

"Good God woman are you losing your grip over this one?"

"I haven't felt butterflies in my stomach since, well since Simon actually, apart from of course the usual nerves I get whenever I have to go to court."

"This sounds interesting. Listen, why don't you grab your wine and go through to the lounge. I'll bring dessert, and you can tell me more."

I walked through to her lounge with its luxurious art, piano (another gift from Granny), and beautiful French doors that opened onto a back patio area. Simply painted in cream but with accents of purple and black, the room was very relaxing. More plants, one of which looked like a gigantic Triffid, were strategically placed in various corners of the room. I scanned the photos on the mantel over the black cast iron Victorian fireplace to see if I could find evidence of anybody new in Kate's life. The only thing I located was a photo of her dreadfully indifferent cat.

"Oh Kate, we really need to do something about this," I shouted.

"What?" she yelled from the kitchen.

"I can't have you putting photos of cats up on your mantelpiece. It's definitely time to go out and find you another man!"

She appeared in the lounge with two sundae glasses filled with mango ice cream.

"Oh, I don't know. I kind of like the relationship Theo and I have."

"Hardly all-encompassing though is it?" I joked.

"Beggars can't be choosers you know."

"Seriously, I think we can do better than a bloody cat, and a moody one at that!"

"Maybe. I have to say that I've yet to find any man as reliable as Theo and that's the truth."

"Reliable? Well that may be true, but perhaps you need somebody you can actually *talk* to."

"Oh, he wouldn't have to *say* anything. In any event I have *you* to talk to, don't I?"

We laughed while she refilled our glasses, and we toasted each other. As we sat on the couch with its plush damask material and comfortable suede cushions, it felt like old times, confiding in one another talking about our jobs, parents, latest fashion purchases. After a couple of glasses of wine, I obviously began to relax to the point that Kate felt comfortable to broach the subject again.

"So come on Penn, tell me the truth. You really don't have any feelings for Simon anymore?"

I was no less uncomfortable than the first time she had asked. "Why are you so interested Kate? Interested in him yourself?"

"Listen darling, I may be desperate but I don't take anybody's cast-offs and that's a fact."

I felt embarrassed at the unfounded accusation. "Of course I still have feelings for Simon. You can't spend years with somebody and feel nothing toward them."

"But are you still *attracted* to him?"

"Yes. Surprisingly, yes I am."

"As much as you are attracted to Gavin?"

"It's different. I mean I've spent years with Simon. So I know every wart and hair on his body, whereas Gavin is unknown territory."

"Which means?"

"Gavin is intriguing to me. If I am honest, I do find him more attractive than Simon but maybe that's just because of the novelty factor and Gavin has not really got to the stage of having disappointed me yet, has he?"

"Good point. So enough of the interrogation. When can I meet Gavin?"

"I'm not sure about that. I mean, we're still at the really early stage. Maybe if we are still seeing each other in a month or so, we can all get together for dinner?"

"Hmm … you *are* being careful with this one. I think you like him way more than you are admitting."

"Well, let's just say that I'm learning. Everybody thinks they've met their Prince Charming until they discover huge chinks in his armour."

"Suppose so. I just always seem to lose interest after around three months when things get beyond the mystery stage."

"You mean you don't like the smelly socks hanging around the bedroom or the farting in your company without a second thought?" *Not that Simon had ever got to that stage ... perhaps because of his gay tendencies?*

"Exactly. If truth be told, I kind of really like being single."

"Apparently you are not alone. I read an article the other day that said deliberate *'singledom'* is on the rise."

"Maybe I'll be a modern-day woman then and stay single."

"Oh, for God's sake Kate. Stop talking rubbish and settle for a life of misery like the rest of us." She poked her tongue out at me, and I pulled her in for a hug. "Anyway darling, I think I should get to bed, I've got to be up early in the morning. Nigel's picking me up so that I can go over and pick up the BMW."

"BMW! How nice. You must be going up in the world."

"Oh, I don't think so. I'm sure I'll come back down to Earth with a huge thud soon enough. Night, night." I kissed her on the cheek, took the plates into the kitchen, and made my way to the guestroom.

In bed I struggled to fall asleep. Kate was my closest friend. She had made obvious her doubts about my relationship with Simon being over and knew me more than I knew myself at times. As much as I felt a spark with Simon, I knew I had to protect myself from any further pain. Life had been almost unbearable at times, and I hated myself for having become so vulnerable to him.

CHAPTER 6 – SATURDAY MAY 13, 2000

I woke early and while in the shower began to think of Nigel and how his evening of entertainment had gone. After a quick bowl of cereal, I called him to let him know I had changed my mind about having him take me to the car rental place. Nigel seemed to be relieved but didn't seem to want to talk for long on the phone (I assumed because he still had female company). Calling a cab, I left a note on the table for Kate.

So good to catch up last night.
Will call you in the week and let you know how things go!
Love you xx

I was due to pick up Gavin at 10 and it was at least a three-hour drive from Hove to Stevenage. When I arrived at the rental place to pick up the car (and of course being paranoid about the cost of the vehicle), every nick and chip was examined at close proximity twice and marked down on a sheet before I signed off on its condition.

Driving the car was indeed a luxury. Everything about it had a quality feel, from the leather seats to the electric sunroof. As I closed the door to the car, it felt solid - almost like closing the door to a safe. I was definitely going to have to make partnership one day if I stood any chance of ever owning such a car. It was gorgeous, but I wasn't quite ready to sacrifice my life for it and join the realms of Oscar or Raj, at least not yet. On the other hand, partnership would get me away from working with Phil on a daily basis.

Since it was a lovely day, I put the sunroof down. But within seconds and not wanting to spoil my hair, I quickly put it back up. I at least wanted my hair perfect for the first impression of the day.

I arrived early at Gavin's place and parked around the corner to touch up my make-up and make sure I didn't have anything caught in my teeth. The inspection was a thorough one. I even stuck my tongue out to make sure it was perfectly pink and unstained, at which I heard a tap on the window and was horrified to see Gavin staring at me through the window. Feeling like an absolute idiot, I fumbled to find the correct control button to open the window.

"Oh Gavin, I er ..." *Shit, I'm blushing AGAIN.*

"Hi Penn. I don't live on this street you know. I'm around the corner." He was trying hard to hide his smile.

"Yes, yes, I know. I was just ... er ... just."

"Checking yourself out?" He laughed.

"Yes, I suppose that's what you could call it. Oh God, now I feel like a complete idiot."

"Aw, don't be like that. I think it's quite sweet actually. I was just picking up my newspaper and saw this very attractive woman driving this very attractive car." He still seemed highly amused.

"Oh ... thank you." *More bloody blushing.* "Wanna get in, and I'll drive you around the corner?" I laughed nervously.

"No, you're OK. Hey, how about we have some fun instead and pretend that you are curb-crawling if you like?" I caught the intense mischief in his eyes.

"Are you kidding me?" Was he really this playful? It seemed almost incongruous with a lawyer's behaviour.

Gavin opened his eyes widely and shook his head slowly from side to side. Eager to create a distraction from my earlier embarrassment, I nodded. "OK then. You're on. This should be fun!"

He started to walk along the street, playing his part, sporting his Ray Ban sunglasses, and looking extremely manly and very cool, while I drove slowly beside him leaning out the window of the car. I waited until the precise moment that we had some female company walking in the opposite direction before yelling at him in a very cockney accent. "Oy gorgeous! Fanks for the amazing time last night. I've got your number – probably call you next week sometime if I need your services again!!"

The woman pretended not to hear, although looked shocked and increased her pace. Gavin roared with laughter as soon as she passed. I quickly parked the car outside his block of flats and ran back to him in the street.

"Oh my God, that was hilarious! It's so good to know you have a wicked sense of humour." I could barely stop giggling.

"Ditto," he said as he took me by the hand leading me upstairs to his flat.

His flat was quite small but very well decorated, with a rich spicy aroma much like patchouli oil. While Gavin went to his bedroom to pick up his overnight bag, I scouted the lounge for any items that could be considered as slightly effeminate. But having found no such offending items, I started to relax. The furniture was made of birch and looked like it was of Danish design. He'd arranged some family photos on a small table; one of an older couple - presumably his parents - looking very happy and relaxed; but also another photo of a blonde sitting on a rock on a lovely white silica beach. *Hmm ... mental note to Penny - must find out more about the blonde.*

"All set then Penn? I'm sure I've forgotten something, but what the heck, let's hit the road." I smiled. Being in his company was so easy.

"OK then. I hope you are not a fearful man Gavin Preston because you are about to become a hostage to my driving skills, which can and have sometimes been described as ... well ... a little erratic!"

"Does the car have seatbelts and airbags?"

"Of course."

"OK then. Let's see if I am a man with nerves of steel."

He put his bag in the boot of the car, and we both buckled up leaving Hove behind to join the M23 motorway. Being a Saturday morning, traffic was quite heavy. Despite wanting to feast my eyes on my companion, I had to concentrate on the road. We made our way from the M23 on to the M25 circular motorway, which can often be congested.

I remembered the year before on my trip to the Dorset cottage with Kate. Traffic on the motorway had grinded to a complete standstill. Four guys from the truck in front of me had unloaded some plastic chairs from the back of the truck and were sunbathing on the side of the road, while some children from another car got out and actually started to play football.

The British are really very used to traffic jams, which is just as well. They are a daily occurrence and more often than not, will occur on a bank holiday. Today, it seemed that we were lucky. There were no traffic jams, which unfortunately meant I had to keep my eyes on the road as traffic moved at a steady speed.

The drive through Sussex to Hertfordshire by motorway is unremarkable from a landscape perspective. Although the best route would have been via the back roads, it would have taken so much longer to reach our destination. Plus, I had to get myself ready for my trip to the market that afternoon.

We decided we would try and find a nice spot for our picnic in Harpenden and walk around the village. Gavin mentioned there was a great pub on the village green called the Silver Cup, which apparently served great food if we felt like something more informal that evening rather than eating at the hotel. It was apparently only a stone's throw from the hotel. Harpenden was just a short drive to Stevenage and also close to the town of St. Albans, which we were planning to visit on the way home on Sunday.

Initially, I worried that the conversation might be a little strained. We of course started off talking about safe subjects such as the firm, our work, and the various people we worked with. By the time the beauty of the Hertfordshire countryside was whizzing by, we had reached a stage of comfort with each other. One thing that was very apparent was that we both shared relatively the same sense of humour, which in itself meant that Gavin was also quite eccentric.

It seemed that one thing we did not have in common was our parental situation. His parents were still very happy together. I said very little about my parents, but found I was quite envious of his non-toxic upbringing.

Gavin had a sister who was now living in Australia, which solved the mystery of the blonde girl in the photo. He had a great love of being outdoors and hiking, which was music to my ears - though I tried not to show it. I needed to keep him keen.

We drove along a long country lane into Harpenden that gradually led to Edwardian-style houses and then to the High Street, with its grassy borders. The hotel was close to the village green on the left. As we looked across the village green through majestic oak trees, we could see a small hotel or pub painted white, perched on the right-hand side of the green. The village was a lot bigger than I had anticipated, but had still maintained its charm.

As we pulled into the car park of the hotel and past a beautifully cultivated garden, we caught sight of the impressive Georgian-style hotel. Cream bay windows,

French doors, brass handles, and roses growing around the entrance doors - it was extremely welcoming.

I felt slightly nervous entering the hotel with Gavin. But after providing my car keys to the valet, Gavin picked up our overnight bags and we made our way in. The foyer had cream brocade wallpaper, red fleur-de-lis patterned carpets, and dark wood panelling.

The receptionist was very friendly, though efficient. She told us our room was at the back of the hotel overlooking a courtyard garden and much quieter than rooms at the front of the hotel. We took the elevators to the first floor, both excited to see our room. I had no idea how long it had been since Gavin had stayed in a hotel with a lady friend, but Simon had been the last person I had stayed with when we had been on a gliding trip in Wiltshire.

As we walked along the pristine hallway with its freshly cleaned aroma, we arrived at the door of our room. Gavin entered the card key into the slot of the door. It opened obediently, revealing a beautifully appointed room and a huge king-size bed, which looked very comfortable.

"Wow, this is great Penn!"

"I know. Well done for finding the place Gavin. It's perfect."

Gavin wandered to the back of the room and opened the French windows, a light breeze then teased the cream sheer curtains from side to side. "It's a lovely courtyard Penn. Come and see." He beckoned me over.

I put my bags on the chair and went over to the window. The courtyard was brimming with roses, camellias, hydrangeas, and peonies framed by various coloured shrubs. It was beautiful.

"So lovely," I said while smiling at the garden.

"Yes, she is," he said standing behind me. He turned me toward him, gently brushing the hair away from my face, and lifted my chin with his finger. His kiss sent a jolt of electric energy through my body, which I took as a great sign - hoping it would exorcise any lingering thoughts of Simon and blast them into the outer stratosphere.

"Thanks for coming with me this weekend Gavin. I am really happy to be spending this time with you."

"Oh, you might change your mind by the end of the weekend. We'll just have to see if I don't bore you to death. Now then, shall we take that wonderful picnic of yours and find somewhere nice to eat?"

"Great idea. I'm famished."

He grabbed the picnic basket and a couple of towels from the bathroom. "What are you going to do with the towels?" I asked.

"Thought we might need to sit on them?"

"Oh, you don't know me very well do you? I have something called a *blanket* in the hamper for us to sit on."

"Of course you have a blanket. You are a litigator extraordinaire – and preparation is the key to litigation. Penny Banfield, you are a marvel!"

"Not really, just a cold-blooded female who feels the cold." I laughed and took the towels from Gavin to throw them on the bed.

I was so glad that we were able to have a nice relaxing moment before I had to head over to the market. The weather was obliging. It was a lovely spring day with a soft, comforting breeze. We decided to eat our picnic on the village green and found a park bench nearby, which meant the blanket in the end turned out to be superfluous. I laid out the tablecloth and napkins, and we ate our luxurious feast by dappled sunlight. Occasionally, I would catch Gavin's flash of a smile and start to feel jittery at the promise it held. He was extremely good company, not only entertaining but also very intelligent. He wore a striped Ralph Lauren shirt and some chinos, looking more American than English. I noticed his hands and how gentle they looked. Gentle but absolutely *not* effeminate.

"Well, this is fantastic isn't it?" He brushed crumbs from his chinos.

"Do you think so? When is the last time you had a picnic?"

"Oh God. Way back. I think it must have been on a day trip to Cambridge with my parents."

"No picnics with girlfriends then?"

"Definitely not. I think I have probably dated more of what you might call 'high maintenance' types, up until now that is." I took that as a compliment, but just had to be sure.

"What do you mean by high maintenance?"

"The type that prefers to be taken *out* for lunch rather than provide it."

"Oh, I see," I started to chuckle. "Well, of course it's nice to be wined and dined. But sometimes I like to eat something I've made myself. Plus, I think it's a nice gesture to make an effort for the person you are with."

"It certainly is very much appreciated."

"Well thank you kind sir."

175

He stood up and wiped his mouth with a napkin. "And I can show you my appreciation later tonight." More jitters. It had been a very long time for me

"Ooh, that sounds promising." I tried not to look too eager or anxious.

"But in the meantime, we have to get you on your way. You have a job to do." He held out his hand, pulling me up from the bench.

"Oh yes, that. The actual reason for this trip." I smiled and started to pack the picnic things away.

We walked back to the car. Gavin placed his arm casually over my shoulder, which felt very comfortable. I was much more of a hand-holding kind of girl, but we were definitely not at that stage … at least not yet.

Back at the room, while Gavin read his book, I started to change into my disguise in the bathroom. "You must promise me that you won't make fun of me when you see me in all this gear!"

"Now Penny, you know I couldn't possibly keep a promise like that! All I can say is that I will *try* not to laugh."

"Well, do try not to hurt my feelings. I'm quite a delicate thing really."

"You? Delicate? I definitely do see signs of a soft underbelly, but you're also as tough as nails when you want to be – don't forget I've seen you in action. I still remember those moots. You were like a barracuda."

I was amazed at how well he knew me considering the amount of time we had spent together. I guess he must have observed me more than I thought when we were at law school.

I placed the blonde wig on my head, playing with it to make it look more realistic. I thought it made me look as if I had been struck by lightning. My "tart's outfit" of leopard skin skirt and tight black scoop necked top looked absolutely ridiculous, but I was impressed by how it showed off "the girls." As I stepped into the high-heeled shoes, I worried about how I was going to walk around a market site without breaking an ankle. I accessorized by adding large sunglasses, some gaudy gold necklaces and rings, and a slick of bright red lipstick.

"OK, are you ready?" I called out from behind the bathroom door.

"Bring it on!"

As I opened the door, I saw the shock on his face followed by a huge smile.

"Oh My God!! I cannot believe it is you! You actually look pretty fantastic, Penn."

"In a hooker kind of way you mean?"

"Well sort of, but if you wanted a disguise, you certainly have a great one. No one would ever suspect that Penny Banfield lives underneath that disguise."

"That's the general idea. Well then, I guess I should be off." I picked up my handbag covered in bling that I had borrowed from Kate, a map showing the location of the market, and my mobile phone.

"OK, you've got my number right?"

"Yep."

"I expect I'll be back at around five o'clock, all being well."

"OK then. Did you want me to make reservations in the restaurant for tonight, or would you prefer to go to the pub?"

"Why don't we try out the pub? The receptionist said that the food there is actually pretty good. I expect I sound like a cheap date now." I smiled.

"Sounds good to me, and nobody could possibly call you cheap seeing you in that outfit."

"Very funny." I leant over and kissed him on the cheek, but he pulled me closer and kissed me full on the lips. I lingered way too long, and it was so hard to pull away and get on with the real reason for the trip. I needed to get to the market, find out if Jim Bateman was there, or when he would next be available on site. As I walked through the hotel reception, I certainly turned a few heads - but I suspect, for all the wrong reasons.

The drive to Stevenage from Harpenden was quite pretty as I took some back roads, via a little village called Wheathampsted, which also had a few lovely pubs. I arrived at the A1, and it was just like any other motorway journey, tedious and claustrophobic as I would often find myself sandwiched between two trucks.

The market was on the outskirts of Stevenage at a small market town called Hitchin. I was in two minds about parking the BMW in the parking lot, which was extremely rocky. I worried it might lead to some paint chips. There was some additional parking on a less rocky area, which was obviously the better option. Although that would not keep the car from being stolen. Still looking at the worst possible outcome, I had insurance on the car.

The market was way larger than anticipated, as there seemed to be around 150 stalls selling everything from jam to electronic equipment. Most of the customers here were just looking for a bargain and not too bothered about sacrificing a degree of quality for the sake of a lower price. The waft of fried onions drifted across the market. Despite our picnic earlier, I felt hungry. It seemed like a friendly place, with families shopping together, children laughing, babies crying, and the sound of change jingling in the aprons of stall holders.

I found walking in the high-heeled shoes extremely difficult and chastised myself for not having practiced walking in them beforehand. I must have looked like a complete idiot precariously placing one foot in front of the other across the uneven ground.

My reconnaissance started by making contact with one of the aromatherapy stall holders.

"You have some lovely things here. I really wish I wasn't allergic to this stuff," I picked up the various wares, pretending to be interested.

"Thanks luv."

"How long have you been doing this?"

"Oh for years! It's me passion." The stallholder re-arranged her display.

"Yes, I can see that." I looked at the gaudy packaging thinking that there was no way that any of these items would make their way into any good quality spa.

"I was thinking of getting a market stall myself."

"Oh yeah? What are you selling?"

"High-quality clothing ... well, more like designer clothes actually."

"On a market stall?"

"Yes, that's just it you see. Not many people seem to be doing that and the overhead is way less because I don't have to pay expensive rental on a unit in a high street somewhere."

"Oh, aren't you are a smart one!"

"How much does it cost to rent a stall here?"

"Oh, you'd have to ask Spencer or Jim about that."

"Jim?" BINGO!

"Yes luv, Jim and Spencer operate the market. Well, they're the owners actually, but they're not here all the time. You'll have to go over to the office and ask."

"Oh, OK ... which way is the office?"

She pointed to the corner of the market, and I noticed a permanent wooden shack with wooden steps leading up to the door. The paint was peeling, and it looked more like an outhouse than an office.

"Thanks so much. You've been very helpful."

"My pleasure – maybe see you on site in a few weeks then? My name is Claire by the way."

"Thanks Claire." I made my way to the office very much aware of the fact that Claire was watching every ridiculous step I took along the way.

After my precarious walk, I arrived at the office and opened the door, which squeaked with age. There was a desk littered with papers and a smell of tobacco in the air. The office was dirty and a film of grime was on the floor making it sticky.

"Can I help you luv?" A woman appeared from the kitchenette with a steaming cup of tea. She had a long lean masculine look to her, her lank hair hanging either side of her face like an old pair of curtains.

"Yes, I was hoping to speak with the owner."

"Which one? Spencer or Jim?"

"I was told to ask for Jim."

"Well, what did you need to speak to him about?" She looked me up and down.

"A business proposal."

"Oh yeah, and what kind of business proposal might that be?" She looked suspiciously at me.

"Well, it is confidential actually." I tried to look confident despite feeling anxious.

"I'm the manager here. So you don't have to worry about confidentiality," she said sarcastically.

"My husband and I wanted to talk to him about a possible purchase ... a purchase of the market in fact." I could see from her expression that she was now hooked.

"Oh my word ... well yes, I expect you would want a meeting with him, Mrs ... what did you say your name was?"

"Preston. Mrs. Preston." I felt uncomfortable in the lie. "Is Jim – sorry what is his surname?"

"Bateman. The owner is called Jim Bateman. His brother, Spencer, manages the place when he is not here, but he is not here today either." Thank goodness.

"Will Jim Bateman be here later today?"

"No, he's only at the markets on Wednesdays. He prefers to be at home with his family at the weekend."

"OK, well maybe we'll come back next Wednesday then?"

"Or I could ask him to give you a call?"

"No, that's OK. My husband and I will be here next Wednesday to see him, but I'll call you before we head over. We live in Harpenden, so we don't have far to travel."

"OK then, let me write the number down here for you." She scribbled on a rough piece of paper (no need for business cards in this line of work it seemed).

Jim Bateman
Wednesdays only
01462 -816678

"Thanks. What's your name?"

"Jean."

"Thanks Jean. I'll be back on Wednesday."

"I'll let Jim know." She opened the door for me and stood at the door with her cup of tea. She looked slightly in awe of me while I walked with my back to her, grinning from ear to ear.

I had a feeling of complete euphoria driving back to the hotel. I always got an incredible rush of adrenalin every time I managed to pull something off at work. I couldn't believe how easy it had been to glean the information from Jean, but also shocked at how easy it had been to fabricate a lie. All we had to do was call on Wednesday morning to check that Jim would be there, and AJ could personally deliver the bankruptcy petition.

Nervous about the upcoming evening with Gavin, I reminded myself that each time I had worried about being with him, I needn't have. The car sped along at a comfortable 70 miles per hour, and I had the roof down - even though I was worried about losing my wig to the wind. I felt good about life and suddenly hopeful for the future.

When I arrived at the hotel room, I found Gavin lying on the bed reading his paperback. Like an obedient dog, he jumped up to his feet to greet me.

"Nice to have somebody to come home to." I smiled.

"How did it go?" He looked anxious. "I've been worried."

"Worried? Why?"

"He does have a pretty ominous reputation you know." He did look genuinely concerned.

"Oh, what's that old man going to do to me? I'm small fry compared to some of the people he must have on his hit list."

"Even so, I have been concerned."

"Well thank you. It's nice to have somebody worried about my well-being."

"Come here," he said and pulled me to him to give me another substantial kiss.

When I eventually disentangled myself, I opened the mini-bar to check out its contents.

"I feel like celebrating – what would you like? Some wine? Beer?"

"Let's have some wine." I pulled out the two mini bottles of Cotes du Rhone and some extortionately priced peanuts. We both sat on the bed propped up by plush white linen pillows.

"Well, come on. I'm all ears!"

"I managed to find out that Jim Bateman is going to be at the market next Wednesday and have virtually guaranteed that he will in fact be there."

"Really? How can you be so sure?"

"Because there is nothing more that our friend Jimmy loves than money, and I've left behind the scent of a lot of cash."

"What do you mean?"

"I basically told the lady in his office that my 'husband' and I wanted to talk to him about purchasing the market."

"Good thinking! Wow – had you been thinking that all along?"

"Not at all. When I left here this morning, I was racking my brains in the car as to how I would play things out and what I'd say if he was there. But really, it just came to me as I was walking to his office. I thought to myself, 'What is the one thing that Jim Bateman loves more than anything else? Money. So if he gets any notion that there might be an opportunity to profit from something, he'll show up."

"Were you nervous?"

"Before I got to the market, yes. I was very nervous. But as soon as I got out of the car, it all just happened naturally. I felt his assistant's eyes on my back as I left the office. So although I am dressed like a hooker, I think she would have been impressed by the car. I'm sure she'll have no idea that the car is rented."

"You know that 'hooker' look is very alluring," he said as he started to walk his fingers up my bare arm, sending an electric shock throughout my body. I put my wine down and leaned forward for a kiss, making sure that he got a full view of my cleavage.

"OK Penn, that's it – I can't hold this off any longer. I'm absolutely going to take you now, and right now!"

BINGO, I thought for the second time that day.

Any thoughts I previously had of missing Simon or still being involved with him had been truly exorcised. Our connection in the bedroom was emphatically beyond question. In fact, the best sex I'd had. Ever. There had been no need for the usual question of "How was it for you?" because we both knew the answer. If he had asked whether the Earth had moved, I think my answer would have been, "The house fell down."

We lay in bed luxuriating in each other. I tingled from head to toe when he kissed the top of my head and stroked my hair away from my face. I loved the Earthy smell of him with a hint of spicy aftershave. The only sounds were from our slow contented breath and of birdsong from the garden. Eventually, these sounds became secondary to the gurgles of empty stomachs, and reluctantly I pulled myself away.

"OK Preston, I don't know about you, but I'm totally famished. Time to get up for dinner." A pile of discarded tart's clothing lay on the floor beside the bed.

"Yes, I'm starving. But this feels soooo good," he replied.

"We could always call in room service?" I said.

"Could we? I mean, would you mind?" He looked almost relieved.

"No, I think we could both do with an early night." I giggled. "Besides, we can always have lunch tomorrow at the pub if we want."

"OK then, it's a deal. Let's look at the menu." He climbed out of bed to grab a menu as I took in the view of his pert and very muscular backside. Had I really just had sex with an Adonis? I was lost between disbelief and utter contentment.

"I feel so decadent right now," I murmured as I lay spread-eagled beneath the sheets.

"Well then, we will need some decadent food. Let's see - Smoked salmon terrine, grav lax, endive salad with goat cheese, sun dried tomatoes, and pistachio nuts. How's about some foie gras?"

"Quack, quack," I mimicked.

"I'm sorry Miss Banfield, I do not speak duck. Was that a 'Yes' or a 'No'?"

"QUACK!!" I nodded my head. He laughed. Clearly does not think I am a freak – thank God for his sense of humour.

He picked up the phone and putting on his most officious voice said, "This is Mr. Preston from Room 217. I'd like to order some room service." He proceeded to place our order, adding a bottle of Moet et Chandon and some chocolate ice cream with raspberries. After placing his order, he jumped back into bed much like a child jumps into a swimming pool.

"Where were we?" He started to kiss my neck.

"Do we have time, do you think?"

"Oh yes, most definitely." I giggled as he pulled the sheets over our heads.

After eating our luxurious room service meal, I decided to take a bath and left a thoroughly spent Gavin with the TV remote. I sprinkled bergamot and lime bath salts into the large bathtub. As I sat on the edge of the tub amidst clouds of fragrant steam, I just wanted to wallow in my bliss and relive the past 24 hours.

There were days when I hated my job and days when I loved my job and loved my life. To the eyes of many, the ratio of bad days to good were simply not worth the effort, but today I begged to differ. The good days were not just good days, they were *great* days.

I slipped into the bath, put my head back placing a towel strategically behind my neck and with my eyes closed, thanked the Gods for giving me this moment.

CHAPTER 7 – SUNDAY MAY 14, 2000

Thankfully I woke up the next morning before Gavin, which allowed me sufficient time to visit the bathroom, freshen up, apply a little light make-up, and brush my bird's nest of a hairdo back into some reasonable shape. (I defy any woman at this stage of a relationship to feel comfortable enough to allow her man to see her at her absolute worst state). Slipping back into bed, I lay my head carefully on my pillow so that my hair would be disturbed as little as possible. Then I unsuccessfully began to make small movements in the bed trying to wake him in the least intrusive way.

Eventually - and after a small dig to the ribcage - Gavin did surface. As he came to life, I began to think how unkind life was to women. Men actually looked sexier when unshaven first thing in the morning, whereas a woman just looks generally dishevelled, discounting the Naomi Campbell's of this world.

"Hey Penn. How did you sleep?"

I did my best at pretending I had just woken, stretching and yawning. "Oh morning. I slept blissfully. How about you Mr. Preston?"

"Like a baby."

"Well, that's good because we have another fun-packed day today." I jumped up out of bed and threw open the curtains with such ferocity that you could feel the draught from them across the room. "Look, it's wonderfully sunny outside. Come on Preston, I think we need to get out of this room and get some fresh air!"

"Are you insinuating that perhaps I am a little odorous?"

"Odorous – absolutely not, and also not odious." I laughed.

"I think I'll get showered up before breakfast," said Gavin.

"OK, you have a shower while I go for a quick run." I felt on top of the world having satisfied my goal yesterday of tracking down Jim Bateman and finally having exorcised the memory of Simon.

"As if you didn't get enough exercise last night," he said and winked.

"You have me there, but this is of course a different type of exercise and definitely not as enjoyable." I blew him a kiss across the room as I climbed into my workout gear and started to lace up my training shoes.

"I'll be back in around 45 minutes. I'm only going for a quick run."

"OK then. See you later. Did you want breakfast in the room when you get back?"

"No, you're alright. If we carry on like this, it'll start to look like some cheap film set where you wonder why the hell they just don't get out of the bloody room!" I laughed. I grabbed a plastic bottle of water and my key card and opened the door.

"See you later Mr. P."

I ran outside from the hotel and turned left toward the green. As I felt the sun on my face, I was sure that I sported an unusual grin for a jogger. The sunlight flickered through the oak trees. As I ran through dappled sunlight, I felt the happiest I had been for a long time. After one loop around the green, I found myself surprisingly not out of breath. So by the time I got back to the hotel, I decided on another loop - certain that Gavin would not mind.

On my final loop and as I ran back through the iron gates to the entrance to the hotel, I thought nothing of the haunting sound of an ambulance siren in the distance. I did not even notice the receptionist of the hotel foyer trying to flag me down as I raced up the staircase, energetically deciding not to take the elevator.

Breathlessly, I steadied myself as I arrived outside our room. Wiping the sweat from my brow with the back of my hand, I fumbled around for my key card while feeling a little faint. I worried about how red my face would be and how dishevelled I would look to a cleanly shaven Gavin. My worry was unwarranted because when I opened the door, Gavin was nowhere to be seen. I saw that his suitcase had been packed neatly and could see that he had been in the bathroom from all the steam on the mirrors. Presumably, he had gone down to the lobby for breakfast. So turning on the radio, I stepped into the shower to wash away the ardour of a good workout.

I always enjoyed the feeling of exhilaration and calm that came from a hot shower after a workout - your senses heightened due to the rush of adrenalin, but muscles perfectly relaxed. I languished in the shower while the telephone drilled on, unheard over the rush of water and waves of music wafting into the bathroom. I dried myself hurriedly as my stomach was audibly making its discontent known. When I finally did hear a knock at the door, I wrapped a towel around my dripping body and ran to the door.

"Just coming! Did you forget your key card?" Upon opening the door, I was met with a suited man bearing a serious expression.

"Ms. Banfield?" He looked a little embarrassed at my lack of clothing.

"Yes?" my stomach started to churn.

"I'm afraid I have some bad news. Your friend has been taken to hospital."

"What? Oh my God, what's wrong with him? Are you serious?!"

"I'm afraid that Mr. Preston was experiencing some respiratory trauma and called the front desk asking for assistance while you were out."

"What type of respiratory trauma? Oh no, I don't believe it - this is terrible - is he OK?!"

"I'm not sure exactly. The ambulance has just taken him to Luton and Dunstable General Hospital."

"I should go to him immediately … I mean I have to get dressed first, of course. Thank you for letting me know." A huge crevice appeared along my brow.

"We did try to catch you earlier when you came back from your run, but I expect you went straight into the shower and didn't hear us calling you?"

"No, I didn't."

"Anyway, I do hope it all goes well. Please let me know if you need anything further."

"Thank you. I'll be down to settle up the bill before I leave for the hospital."

"Thank you madam." He almost bowed as he left me at the door with what must have been a totally ashen face.

Adrenalin surged through my body as I threw the towel on the bed and rushed to get dressed. I hesitated to put make-up on, but realised this was no time for my vanity. I decided to just brush my hair, put it up in a wet ponytail, and hurriedly pulled on a pair of jeans, V-neck sweater, and pair of sandals. Then throwing everything into my suitcase and grabbing Gavin's neatly packed suitcase, I headed for the door - briefly scanning the room for anything that may have been left behind.

I settled the bill at the front desk and obtained directions to the hospital, which was about 10 miles away. It was a totally uninspiring drive along the motorway, not that I was interested in the view anyhow, racked with worry about Gavin. I arrived at the huge red brick hospital and parked the car haphazardly across two stalls. As I ran into the emergency department, I was greeted by a matronly figure with, thankfully, a very warm smile.

"Hi, I'm Penny Banfield. My friend Gavin Preston was brought in a little while ago."

"Are you his next-of-kin?"

"No, not at all. We were staying together at the Parkside Hotel, and I just went for a quick jog. By the time I got back to the hotel, they said he had been rushed into hospital." I must have looked completely desperate.

"You'll have to wait over there," she said and pointed to the waiting room, a typical grey but sterile room. *Why don't they ever paint waiting rooms yellow?*

"Can you at least tell me if he's alive? He is alive isn't he?" I pleaded.

"I'm sorry miss, you'll have to wait, like I said." More churning of the stomach.

So typical of the medical profession, keeping everyone in the dark worried about their liability no doubt ... worried perhaps because lawyers like you have sued the arse off them? Good point ... shut up Banfield!

I sat down again and wondered whether it would be safe to pick up the magazines or whether some deadly bacteria would be lurking between the well-worn pages. I was the only one in the waiting room, which was silent apart from mechanical sounds coming from the coffee machine. I decided to try the coffee and after plying it with various coins (most of which were accepted first time), I was provided with something that turned out to be actually not bad and quite a few grades higher than British Railway's coffee.

Taking my life into my hands, I picked up a magazine - although I could barely digest any information. Perhaps they had called his parents? What if it was *really* serious? I couldn't understand how it could possibly be serious. He looked the absolute picture of health when I left him. How would I explain this to everybody at the office? Would I get fired? Would he get fired ... if he lived to tell the tale? I shuddered.

At last, as I sat flicking through the magazine at break-neck speed, a nurse came to talk to me.

"Hi there, are you Penny by any chance?" She had a wonderfully rich Irish accent.

"Yes – yes I am. Oh please tell me Gavin is OK!"

"Yes, he's fine now. We've got his breathing stabilized, and he'll probably be ready for discharge in a couple of hours. Did you want to see him?" *Is the Pope bloody Catholic?*

"Yes, of course I do! I've been so worried."

"Why don't you come with me, and I'll show you where he is."

She had fiery red hair, pale skin, and was very pretty. I wondered whether Gavin would have noticed how attractive she was, but then realised that perhaps he had been preoccupied with his breathing rather than eyeing up the nursing staff.

"I see you are enjoying our wonderful coffee," she said as she nodded toward the steaming paper cup.

"Hmm, not exactly Starbucks, but then again not British Railway coffee either. At least it gives you something to do."

"Which is why the British always turn to making a cup of tea when there is any family crisis."

I smiled. "What was the issue with Gavin?"

"He had an extreme allergic reaction to something, which affected his breathing. We've given him some antihistamine intravenously, and he's fine now."

"Do you know what he was allergic to?"

"We're still running tests, but should have the results shortly. We can't discharge him until we've taken a look at them. It's obviously important that he avoids whatever it is, in the future." She looked serious.

"Of course." *God I hope he isn't allergic to me ...*

She took me to a smaller general ward and led me to a bed with a blue curtain drawn around it. Drawing back the curtain, I saw Gavin's alluring smile. He looked a picture of health.

"Penny! Am I ever glad to see you." I ran over to his bedside.

"Oh my God Gavin, I was terrified. The hotel gave me so little information. I was imagining all sorts of things on the way here." I took hold of his hand.

"It's just an allergy apparently. I have to say it was pretty scary not being able to breathe," he said, almost looking embarrassed.

"Of course it is! I hope they find out what the hell it is you're allergic to. I expect you'll have to carry an EpiPen (or whatever it's called) with you in future?"

"Maybe. I only hope I'm not allergic to you." He leaned forward for a kiss.

You took the words out of my mouth.

"Oh that absolutely doesn't bear thinking about. That would be a *total* tragedy!"

He laughed. "They said they are keeping me in for a couple more hours."

"Yes, the nurse said ... can I get you anything?"

"No, I'm fine. They called my parents, but I wanted to speak to you before calling them myself. Should I wait for them to get here to pick me up or will you be able to wait for me and take me home?"

"Don't be silly, of course I'll take you home. That's if they will let me?"

"I get to decide, thankfully. Thanks Penn. I'll call my parents back and tell them there's no need to come to the hospital."

"Did they know you were coming here with me?" I was so obviously fishing.

"Sort of." I decided not to be nosy, although, of course I would have killed to know more.

While Gavin called his parents from his mobile phone, I left to go to the loo - not wanting to hear what might be an awkward conversation. When I came back to the room, he was all smiles. "What an eventful weekend it's been."

"Yes it has. I've always wondered what Luton was like, and now I know." I hesitated, and we both said at the same time, "Bit of a dump."

"Still, I guess it's unfair to judge it based on one trip to a hospital," I said.

I stayed with him for a couple of hours watching TV, while we waited for the test results. Eventually, we were given the all clear. He was discharged. It turned out that he was allergic to lilacs. Unbeknownst to me, he had gone out into the garden to pick some for my return to the hotel after my run, but had developed a severe reaction. I didn't have the heart to tell him that I hadn't noticed the flowers in the room when I returned.

It was three o'clock in the afternoon by the time we left the hospital, and I had an overwhelming sense of relief driving back to Brighton.

"That's the last time I take you on a trip outside of Brighton, Preston."

"Oh, don't say that. We have to come back to visit St. Albans - seeing as we have to give it a miss today."

"But what if there are lilacs in St. Albans?"

"Then I'll just have to pick roses instead."

"Are you allergic to sunflowers?"

"Don't think so, why?"

"I was thinking that our next trip could be somewhere warmer, like perhaps the Provence - say in August?"

"Hmmmmm, I definitely like the sound of that."

"Seriously Gavin, I'm so sorry that it turned out to be a bit of an ordeal for you. The weekend was supposed to be about pleasure, with a bit of work thrown in so that we could claim expenses." I laughed.

"Well, I did have fun. I can tell everybody that I spent the entire weekend gasping for air, not only this morning but the pleasurable bit before this morning."

"Oh lovely, that's guaranteed to give me a reputation." I looked over at him, and he looked a little embarrassed and quickly changed the subject. "I'm famished. Are you hungry, too?"

"Absolutely."

"I noticed a Waitrose in Harpenden. Why don't we grab some things and have a picnic in the car on the way home? Without the wine of course?"

"Of course.

We grabbed some cold chicken, coleslaw, olives, gourmet potato salad, and sparkling water. It had started to rain, albeit it softly. So we had no choice other than to eat in the car. I drove to the park, and we devoured our food while overlooking the duck pond watching mesmerizing rings of water created by the rain

The journey home went quickly as, again, we talked of work and mutual friends we knew from law school. I briefly mentioned my break up with Simon: *"We were not sexually compatible"* but it was way too early in the relationship to talk in detail about ex-boyfriends or girlfriends, so the conversation remained relaxed.

I stopped halfway to fill up with petrol while Gavin went inside to grab some ice cream. I found myself relieved that he also had a sweet tooth and was unconventional enough to eat ice cream in the rain.

Safely back in Hove, I dropped Gavin off at his place and parked outside.

"Here, let me help you with your case," I said and took hold of it.

"Penny, there really is no need. I'm fine now. Won't you come in for a glass of wine?"

"Are you sure?"

"I wouldn't ask if I wasn't sure."

"Yes, of course, that would be lovely, but just the one glass as I'm driving."

"You know you could always stay the night here?"

"Although that sounds incredibly tempting, I should get back. I've got tons of chores to do. The flat looks like a bomb has hit it, and I have to get the car back." He looked slightly disappointed.

"I'm hoping that there will be other opportunities ahead of us though?" I tried my best not to look desperate.

"Me too." He pulled me close and kissed me holding my face in both hands. "I really like you Penny Banfield."

"That's just as well, because I've decided that I *really* like you. So I'm hoping to see more of you in the future, Mr. Preston."

"It's a deal. Come on, let's grab that bottle of Merlot." We started to walk to his flat. "I think I even have some leftover chocolate tucked in a drawer somewhere."

"Wow, a man with willpower. You must explain - what is *leftover* chocolate Gavin? It's a concept I'm not familiar with.

I stayed way much longer than I wanted to, but his company was magnetic. It had taken me a long time to trust anyone after my episode with Simon. The trust in my judgment had been shaken to the roots, and I would often find myself over-analyzing any future potential companion. This hadn't seemed necessary with Gavin. He seemed so open and free of baggage. I was sure that there had to be a chink in his armour, but I was not at all interested in finding it - at least not for a while.

CHAPTER 8 – MONDAY MAY 15, 2000

Jim Bateman sat at his desk rocking from side to side in his high-backed leather chair while staring at his computer screen and a spreadsheet showing the current state of financial play relating to the Club. *Jesus Christ, we are totally fucked.*

He stopped his rocking and picked up a pencil, drumming it against the desk. "Nothing short of a bleeding miracle is going to save this lot." *Thank God we are selling the grounds.*

He was anxiously waiting to hear from some of the directors as to how their field trip to the alternative grounds had gone. He smiled when the phone rang, hoping that this would be the news he had been waiting for.

"Bateman here."

"Jimmy?"

"Who's this?"

"It's Jean from the market."

"Oh hi, Jeannie luv. What can I do you for?" He stared out of the window over the grounds.

"It's more like what can I do for you lover." She chuckled.

"Oh, I think we are both a bit too long in the tooth for that kind of stuff Jean." Jim's laughter promptly turned into a cough.

"Seriously Jim, I had a visitor on the weekend. Said she and her husband were interested in buying the market."

"What d'ya say? Buy the bleeding market? I 'ope you told her it ain't for sale?" It was funny how his language automatically reverted to Cockney whenever he was in market mode.

"No, I didn't. She looked really well off. So I took her seriously. She said she's going to call you on Wednesday when you're here."

"Why don't you gimme her number then. I'll save her a call."

"Can't. She didn't leave a number. Apparently she lives in Harpenden and said she'll call before heading over to see you *personally*."

"Oh well, when she calls back, just tell her I'm not interested. The market's been in my family for generations. I'm not selling off the family silver quite yet."

"Are you even listening to me Jimmy?! She is going to call on Wednesday to speak to *you*. I think you should listen to her before you turn her down, don't you? Remember that everything sells at a price you know."

"Spoken like a true market trader luv." He laughs again. "Don't worry, I'm not making you redundant for a while yet."

"Oh you are too kind. Anyway, just passing on the message."

"Thanks Jean. What was her name?"

"Said her name was Preston or something. I don't think I caught her first name."

"Well, thanks for letting me know. Everything else OK?"

"Yeah, seems to be going well. Spencer seems to have it all under control. All the traders seem happy anyway."

"Maybe we should think about putting up their rent then?"

"Well, when you decide to do that, just give me some notice and I'll book myself on the next flight to Majorca - so I can avoid all the hassle. If we raise the rents on this lot, they'll all move to the new indoor market, but not before they make my life a bleeding misery. I mean who really wants to sit outside in the pissing rain when you have the option of setting up a permanent stall *inside*?"

"Calm down Jeannie my luv, I'm only joking! You make a good point though. Maybe I should seriously think about this offer after all, eh?"

"Well she's calling on Wednesday, so you'd best be here to take her call. I don't want to speak to her again. Snooty looking bitch she was."

"I've got a bloody Board meeting on Wednesday – still thankfully, it's not until the evening. Just curious - why didn't you give her my number here?"

"Because you said I'm never to give that number to anybody you don't know, remember?"

"Yeah … yeah I did, didn't I? Good girl for remembering that. Oh well, see you on Wednesday then.

Make sure you get my favourite bickies in won't ya, luv?"

"Of course, your royal highness."

Jim hesitated before placing the phone back into its receiver, deep in thought. His thoughts soon led to a smile stretched wide across his face. He always had loved the smell of money. It had been a while since he had been this excited. As Jeannie had said, *"Everything sells at a price."*

I woke early that morning eager to spill the news relating to Jim Bateman and how we might be able to serve him with the bankruptcy petition. AJ was going to be impressed, or if not impressed, at least relieved that he hadn't wasted time sending me to Stevenage for the weekend.

It had been a long night, and my appearance in the mirror, as always, showed that it had.

Unfortunately, I did not have what could be described as a resilient face. Every sleepless night, every break up, and every moment of anguish always shows up on my face, as welcome as a pork sausage at a Jewish wedding.

Rubbing in some moisturiser, I scrubbed my face back to life, trying to erase all signs of fatigue. Because I'd been reluctant to leave the warm envelope of my bed that morning, I had no time to wash my hair and instead pulled it back into a barrette and applied just a little make-up and some warm coloured lipstick.

Yet another disappointing morning exercise-wise. I had intended to start the day with a jog and therefore having failed, had probably set in motion another visit to Gita's to console myself.

The most annoying type of rainfall was falling outside, a drizzle verging on mist that appeared to fly in all directions rendering any umbrella totally useless. I dressed in a warm, navy woollen dress and cashmere sweater and pulled on my black leather boots, despite the fact it was technically almost summer. However, as any British person will know, the word summer can be somewhat confusing.

Nigel had left way earlier that morning to attend a breakfast seminar on *"How to avoid getting caught in a commercial money laundering scheme."* Sounded about as interesting as watching a documentary on the breeding habits of the common trout. He had quizzed me last night about the trip, but I was very tight-lipped. As much as I loved Nigel, he was capable of sabotaging my career in one fail swoop by breathing just one word of my relationship and sexy sojourn with Gavin Preston. Nigel joked that I treated him like a mushroom (kept him in the dark and fed him shit), and today I was inclined to keep it that way.

On the train, I tried to catch up on some sleep by cat-napping and actually managed to block out the usual morning din without too much distraction. The smell of coffee on the train, together with the rocking of the carriage, would gently bring me from my semi-conscious state to a state of morning readiness.

As I arrived at my office, I immediately noticed a bouquet of sunflowers wrapped expensively and left on my sofa. I plucked the card from the foliage:

Thanks for taking care of me. Thought sunflowers might be a safer bet rather than lilacs. G xx

How incredibly sweet of him. Gavin must have picked them up first thing this morning, though goodness only knows from where. I felt a warm glow radiate from within, rendering any thoughts of chocolate, surplus to requirements.

Spurred into action and after signing into my computer, I sent the email I had been waiting all weekend to send:

From: Penny Banfield
To: Anthony Jarvis
Date: May 15, 2000
Re: Jim Bateman

I am pleased to report that I have successfully managed to ascertain the whereabouts of Mr. Bateman for Wednesday, May 17.

Mr. Bateman will be at the Stevenage market under the miss-apprehension that he is to expect a call from a prospective buyer for the market. Please provide me with

the bankruptcy petition, and I will arrange to have it personally served by a process server on that date.
PB

Next very important email:

From: Penny Banfield
To: Gavin Preston
Date: May 15, 2000
Re: Flowers

How wonderful to arrive this morning to your beautiful bouquet of flowers. You are so totally amazing.
Penny x

As I sat at my desk, I anxiously awaited a response from either, but instead received a call from my nemesis.

"Penny my love, wondered whether you could pop down to my office?"

"Actually Phil, I'm a bit tied up at the moment. Is it anything we can deal with over the phone?"

"Not really. It's a bit personal. How's about I buy you lunch instead?

"Lunch? No thanks Phil. I have no desire to pay a visit to the Ship and Anchor surrounded by the usual dodgy characters you call friends." I glanced at my watch.

"Actually, I had in mind the Pipe of Port?"

"Wine bar? Goodness me, Mr. Stevens. You are really going up market these days!"

"Well, you know me Penn, nothing but the best for my right-hand girl."

"Now I know you want something." I sighed.

"Rest assured, it's not even work related. Anyway, you'll find out soon enough. I'll drop by your office at 12 and pick you up. We can take my car."

"Jesus, I think I might need a drink *before* I get in the car – you know how much I hate your driving Phil."

"It's way too far to walk."

"I know. I'll see if I can dig out a scarf or something to cover my eyes with. See you at 12 then.

With Phil, there was never anything like a free lunch. He definitely wanted something. It was simply not in his nature to give without the expectation of something in return. What was he going to dump on me now?

The phone rang with this on the caller display: **Anthony Jarvis.**

"Good morning Mr. Jarvis. Did you get my email?"

"Yes Penny, I did. I wanted to thank you for taking care of things."

"You are most welcome, sir." I was unashamedly brimming with self-pride.

"Quite a clever tactic to use a prospective sale to trap the rat."

"Well, I know if there is one thing that is sure to lure Mr. Bateman, it's the smell of money."

"Absolutely right."

"I was thinking I could arrange for a process server to pick up the petition this afternoon and serve it on Bateman on Wednesday, sir."

"No. That won't be necessary."

"Sorry sir? I thought you wanted to serve him with a bankruptcy petition?"

"That's right, I do. However, I've decided to take care of this *personally*. I will be the one serving Mr. Bateman. I have to say, I am going to thoroughly enjoy myself in the process."

Although I could not see him, I knew from his voice that he was smiling. "Is that wise, sir?"

"What do you mean Banfield?"

Oh-oh .. .was I speaking out of turn? "What if things get out of hand, and he starts to get violent?"

"Oh, I'm not going solo. I'll be taking a witness with me."

Oh God, no ... PLEASE don't let it be me. "Oh really sir, and who might that be?" *Please God, no.*

"I've decided the best person would be our Mr. Preston."

"Mr. Preston? Do you mean *Gavin* Preston?"

"Exactly."

"Oh, I see." My stomach started to churn.

"I understand that Mr. Preston is already familiar with the general vicinity of the market and how to get there, is that correct?"

"Um ... yes sir, I believe so." *How the bloody hell did he know about that? Was there anything that this man did NOT know?*

"Well then, I am sure we will be able to take things from here. In the meantime, I just wanted to thank you for all your hard work."

What, no snarky comments about a dirty weekend away with Gavin? Really? "You are welcome, sir."

"Oh, and Penny?"

"Yes sir?"

"Please help yourself to a bottle of wine from the firm's wine cellar, whatever takes your fancy, for a job well done."

"Thank you sir. Most grateful."

My heart was pounding and my face flushed as if I had already drank half a bottle of wine. How did he know about Gavin being involved with the trip to Stevenage over the weekend? I had deliberately not told Nigel any of the details about the weekend, but maybe he had said something about it to somebody else. Nigel was worse than any girlfriend when it came to gossip, he just simply could not keep anything confidential. I snatched the telephone receiver from its cradle.

"Nigel?"

"Hi Penn."

"Can you explain to me how it is that AJ knows that I went to Stevenage with Gavin over the weekend?"

"How the hell should I know?" Nigel sounded really irked.

"Well, I'm trying to think of who might possibly be the office gossip, and the only name I could come up with was your name."

"I take exception to that remark. No, in fact, I am utterly *offended!*"

"You *must* have told *somebody*?"

209

"Are you kidding me? Something like that could get me kicked out of my digs!"

"EXACTLY!"

"Listen, I may be many things, to many people, but I am not a stupid fool."

"Hmm ... well, who the hell did tell him?"

"Not sure and don't really care. I have work to do and so do you. Hopefully, later you will apologize for accusing me of something I have not done." He hung up on me.

Ouch. I have got to stop jumping to conclusions. As forgiving as Nigel might be, I felt bad at having hurt his feelings. Pretty sure there would be no coffee with Nigel today.

From: Daphne Porter
To: Penny Banfield
Date: May 15, 2000
Re: Court Order

Mr. Jarvis asked me to let you know we have now received the Anton Piller Order from the courthouse. I will leave it on my desk for you to pick up.
DP

God forbid you could ever get off your arse and walk it down to me Daphne. I immediately left to pick up the much anticipated Order from the fat barn owl.

The Pipe of Port was a traditional wine bar on the outskirts of town. Access was via a rickety wooden staircase into a wine cavern. Inside and dimly lit with candles, it had dusty floorboards, the original brick wall, and an air of the 18th Century about it. I could not for the life of me think why Phil wanted to bring me here, as it really was not his scene. His preference was to frequent the *"pub of the moment,"* surrounded by the young and beautiful or alternatively some scummy bar filled with loud-mouthed louts and all the weird and wonderful.

He led the way down to the cavern and to a private booth. "Well, this is very nice I must say. What's the occasion Phil?" I eyed him with suspicion.

"No occasion. Just felt it was time that I said thank you for all your help recently."

"What did you say? You want to thank me?"

"Yes I did, and don't be so bleeding cheeky. You heard me alright." He smiled.

"As nice as that may be, I get the feeling that there might be something else, too?"

"There might be." He straightened his tie.

"Knew it!"

"Oh, don't be like that Penny. I just wanted to talk to you about something more of a confidential nature and thought this place would be more appropriate."

"Oh my God Phil, this is getting scary." I pretended to laugh despite my rising anxiety.

211

We were interrupted by a tall and extremely handsome waiter with a long, brown ponytail and nut-brown eyes, which I have to say I found extremely distracting.

"OK mate?" Why did Phil insist on calling everyone mate? "I think I'll have a glass of Beaujolais Nouveau and the steak and mushroom pie. What about you Penny?"

"A glass of Sancerre and the grav lax salad, please."

"A good choice madam." He had an accent that could only be described as caramelicious.

As he left leaving us with a warm smile, I checked out the back view, which I have to say was as pleasing as the front view. Nice bottom. What I wouldn't give to get my hands on that. Jesus, I am beginning to sound like Phil!! I caught Phil watching me eye up the waiter.

"Tch, Tch." I could not believe that Phil, of all people, felt justified in criticising.

"Hey, he's not bad." I grinned.

"Not my type luv. Anyway, I thought you were already seeing somebody?"

"Oh really? And who might that person be?"

"I heard you were seeing Gavin Preston."

"And who might you have heard that from?"

"Actually, I think it was Gavin himself."

"Think or know? Gavin told you that?" Surely not? Gavin would never broadcast such a thing, would he?

"Why are you so surprised? It is supposed to be a secret or something?"

"We haven't really talked about it."

"But you can't blame him for wanting to brag about it though. A lovely girl like you ..."

"Brag?! What do you mean brag?"

"Keep your knickers on Penny. I don't mean brag, more like boast."

"I think that's even worse actually, Phil."

"He just said that he had been seeing you, that's all. No gory details if that's what you're worried about."

"I'm not worried. I just don't want my love life to be the subject of gossip in the staff room every morning." I massaged the back of my neck with my hand.

"Talking of gossip. Have you heard the gossip about me?"

"Yes, yes, I have actually." Thank goodness the conversation was drifting away from me.

The waiter brought our glasses of wine and placed a bowl of cashew nuts on the table, which I immediately began to investigate, starving as usual.

"So, you heard about Lisa being pregnant then?" He started to stare down at his beer mat, a serious band of lines appearing across his forehead.

"Yes. I did hear that. How do you feel about becoming a father?" He shifted in his chair.

"I'm scared shitless." He sounded irritated. Of course he was. No doubt he was shaking in his shoes. For once in his life, he might actually have to face some responsibility rather than running from it. He was a true anomaly. I mean, whoever heard of a lawyer who deliberately avoided responsibility?

"Maybe it won't be as bad as you think it's going to be?"

"What's your name, Polly-bleeding-Anna? Are you out of your mind? Thing is Penn, I was actually thinking of breaking up with Lisa before all this happened."

213

"Oh Jesus, this really is turning into a shit show. Listen Phil, I think you and Lisa are great together. To be honest, I don't know too many women who would put up with your antics. I know I wouldn't stand for any of it."

"I think that's half the problem. She's almost too understanding." Oh my God, he's actually blaming Lisa.

"Some men would call you a lucky bastard to have Lisa."

"I just know I can't handle being a Dad. I'm too irresponsible to handle bringing up a child." At least he was not completely delusional and knew this about himself.

"Well, maybe it's just time for you to grow up! Who do you think you are Phil, Peter-bleeding-Pan?"

"Ha ha – very funny – you just had to get me back didn't you? The thing is Penn, the thought of staying home night after night with a screaming kid fills me with absolute horror." He wasn't exaggerating. I could see that terror in his eyes as we spoke.

"Oh come on Phil, I'm sure you're not the only man in the world that has felt this way. It all usually turns out OK in the end."

"Not me, Penn." He shook his head.

I was suddenly at a loss for words and silently savoured my wine trying to formulate my argument. Yes, this was indeed an argument. To litigators almost everything becomes an argument, from the internal dialogue of "What shoes shall I wear today" to having the last word on almost every conversation.

"Phil. Can I ask you something?" He looked curious.

"Of course."

"Why are you telling me any of this?"

"Because I respect you and your opinion." He looked directly at me.

"You know I can't help you with any of this though. It's your life and your decision. I would have thought that if you really do value your freedom in a relationship, you have way more chance of making it happen with Lisa rather than without her. She's already proven that she's in it for the long run and loves you, warts and all. Yes, a baby is going to be a responsibility. But knowing how capable Lisa is, she'll have everything taken care of and you probably won't have to do anything that you have already done by donating your sperm."

"I can only do this, if it doesn't change my lifestyle though, and that's not fair to her."

"Fair? Compared to what alternative? Do you think it's fair to leave her with a child to take care of?"

"Of course not. Jesus, I'm completely torn up about this." Other than in court appearances, I had never seen Phil this serious.

"Phil, don't you think that it's just possible that sometimes in life opportunities arise when you least expect them?"

"Don't ask me. I'm clueless about all that philosophical stuff." Was he really as shallow as he made out?

"I just think that perhaps there is an opportunity for you to grow as a human being. Maybe the responsibility of having somebody to think about other than yourself will help you and perhaps even help your career."

"There is that word again – 'responsibility' – God, I hate that word."

"Then why have you chosen a profession that requires one of the highest levels of responsibility when it comes to duty to your clients?"

"Good point. See, that's exactly why you are a good litigator." I felt myself turning into more of an alligator. I wanted to rip his head off at that precise moment.

As our waiter approached with our food, I turned to Phil, staring at him intensely.

"Just make sure that you think about this one seriously. There is another life that is going to be affected by any decision you make here."

Two platefuls of steaming food were placed on the table, and my attention immediately fell from the velvety brown eyes of the waiter to the aroma of the food beckoning my olfactory system, making me salivate.

We ate in silence for a while.

I wanted him to think and think hard about this. I hated the selfish side of Phil. It really always, always, was about him. Yet fate had delivered a blow where now it was not about him, but about the life of another. I had always been in awe of Lisa and her complete and utter ability to put Phil first. She was a selfless, modern-day angel. The fact was that Phil didn't deserve the degree of love she showered upon him.

Eventually, the silence was broken by the desire for another drink. Phil ordered two more glasses of wine, which arrived promptly. Thankfully, the food had a calming effect on me. "Actually Phil, I want to thank you for confiding in me. In fact, I'm really touched."

"Truth is, apart from Lisa, I don't really have anybody real that I can talk to about this."

Real? At least he was aware of how shallow his friendships were. I guess that was at least something. "Well, I'm not really that surprised. Don't you ever get bored with that bunch of chimps at the Ship and Anchor?"

"Sometimes. Yeah, I guess I do, but I suppose in some ways I worry about the statement I am making to the world by settling down."

"What kind of statement would that be?"

"That I'm finished. An old has-been." I stared at him trying to figure out whether he was joking.

"Oh my God, you are actually serious! Finished? Really? I would say it's quite the opposite. I think that you could actually change the way that many people think about you if you were to stop all the philandering - excuse the pun, Phil!"

"So you are saying that my need to socialize is affecting the way people look at me?"

"How could it not? Do you honestly think AJ wants a partner that is going to show up at partner meetings hung over? Not to mention the fact that it is quite possible that while on a drinking binge one day, you might bring the partnership into total disrepute!"

"Hmm. You probably have a point there." He scratched his head.

"Phil, I know you say you don't want partnership, but I beg to differ. Every lawyer always wants to make partner, it's like the Holy Grail. You have to go after it. I mean, look at poor Oscar. He is desperate for something you are quite capable of doing, if only you would clean up your act." He started to look uncomfortable and would not look me in the eye. OK, so he's clearly bored now. Stop preaching Penny!

His telephone started to vibrate, at which point he glanced at the call display and turned the phone off.

"Would you like dessert?" asked the waiter. I looked at Phil and shook my head.

"No thanks mate. Just the bill, please."

I felt slightly unnerved by the fact that the Phil that I was leaving the wine bar with, was not the jovial one I had arrived with. A serious Phil? Some would say that in itself was an oxymoron. I was sure that the "lads" at the Ship and Anchor would not recognise the man beside me; a shadow of his former self.

1.3 Units - Counselling session with Phil

0.8 Units - Eating wonderful lunch

0.2 Units - Eyeing up beautiful waiter

Back at the office, while admiring the wonderful flowers from Gavin, I couldn't help feeling sorry for Phil, for just a minute that is. He really had seemed terrified at the prospect of losing his bachelor status, yet did not seem to realize that in reality his freedom had disappeared the moment he decided to move in with Lisa and become accountable to somebody else.

It was an interesting fact that men seemed to project an image of being happy to continue being single for as long as they could. Yet the oddest thing was that statistics seemed to show that more men than women actually wanted to get married. In itself, it did of course prove that either men were liars when questioned by market researchers, or alternatively that market research was totally worthless.

For the rest of the afternoon, I picked up from where I had left off on Friday - putting together an instruction kit for each team. AJ had now informed me of those directors who would be raided.

In each kit was a map highlighting the exact location of the address for which they were responsible, a checklist of all the court rules which needed to be observed, and in particular, the legal rights of the director when served with the Order. The directors were within their rights to refuse entry to their house; it would, however, be viewed as contempt of court if they did. The instructions also reminded each lawyer of the duties of the supervising solicitor who would be overseeing the search and making decisions on any issues of privilege or relevance.

I telephoned the team leaders, obtaining their mobile phone numbers for the contact telephone list and added them to the instructions - a reminder for each leader to ensure that their mobile phones were fully charged the night before the raid.

It was decided that each team would be in place at 9 a.m. with the "raid" taking place at exactly 9:30 a.m. at each address. Since the majority of the directors were now off work, as the football season was at an end, they were likely to be home. Many of them were retired anyway, and their responsibility to the Club was the only working responsibility they had.

0.1 Unit - Pondering the mystery of the male psyche

2.5 hours - Drafting instruction kits for teams in readiness for service of Anton Piller Order

CHAPTER 9 – TUESDAY MAY 16, 2000

The raid was now only three days away, and I found myself hyperventilating with such frequency that neither the yoga exercises nor the chocolate-fests worked. I had spent the previous night wrestling with my sheets until the point of exhaustion and every bone in my back creaked with discontent. While pacing the kitchen floor waiting for some milk to warm up, I felt so alone that I almost called Gavin at 1:15 a.m., but thankfully thought better of it.

In any case, it was simply not in my nature to ask for help. I'd learned to be self-sufficient at an early age; not wanting to ask my mother for anything, or burden my father with any more than he already had to contend with.

I felt as if the responsibility of the raid had now been placed firmly on my shoulders, with Phil appearing to hold the reins, though in reality hiding behind me. I had well and truly been left holding the baby, and it looked like Lisa was also going to be left the same way, only literally. If everything were to go well, he would receive a resounding pat on the back. But if there was any failure associated with the raid, it would fall under my auspice, potentially ruining my career forever.

Nigel was going to have to make my coffee a double espresso this morning. I barely had the energy to pick up the phone.

"Nigel?"

"Yes my ladyship?"

"Can you get a double espresso for me this morning?"

He laughed. "Oh, I thought I heard you in the kitchen last night."

"Yes, sorry about that. My God, I thought I'd never sleep again."

"What's wrong, Penn? Trouble in the love department?"

"No, not at all. At least I don't think so, unless you have heard something I am not aware of?"

"Relax Penn. Believe me, I am sure I would be the last person to know. I know you view me as some sort of sponge for office gossip, but I can assure you I've been hard at work the past couple of days, what with everything going on at the football club."

"Oh, and what commercial stuff might that be Mr. Wilkinson? Are you handling the purchase of the Club by any chance? Maybe you have a new client called Trico Superstores?"

"Well, I'm not really supposed to say ..."

I laughed at the irony. "God, how ridiculous. It's like one department is doing something the other department is not supposed to know about, but in reality everything is related, what a joke!"

"What do you mean?"

"I'm not at liberty to say."

This time he was the one to laugh. "Sorry Penn, have to go. See you at 11 a.m."

Corporate lawyers were either incredibly busy, or totally laid back doing the usual corporate secretarial work, while waiting for their next urgent job. My job on the other hand was simply busy, all the bloody time.

I scanned my calendar and saw that Mr. Peters was due to come in this morning. Oscar had wanted me to meet with him. Why? I could not say. I personally had no interest in somebody whose major claim to fame was the solution to a wobbly table. Rocket science it definitely was not. Besides, it had been so long since I had been in contact with a wobbly table that I wondered seriously about the feasibility of the product. Still, ours "is not to question why," as Oscar would say.

Mr. Peters was intending to bring in a prototype of the gadget and "give me a demonstration" of how it worked. I had imagined that it was a wedge of some sort that basically you just shoved under the table. However, Oscar seemed to be expecting something quite technical. So I was somewhat intrigued as to how complicated it possibly could be.

The telephone rang with a shrillness I hadn't noticed before, possibly because I am not usually in the habit of staying up all night.

Call display: Daphne Porter

"Oh hello Daphne, how are you?"

"Oh, I'm run off my feet, as usual. Mr. Jarvis wants you to pop down to the courthouse to get something filed urgently for service tomorrow. I think it's a bankruptcy petition. Will you be free later this morning?"

"It will have to be late this morning. But can I ask why is he not giving this to the court runner to file?"

"Oh, it's way too confidential to put into the hands of the court runner. I'm not even allowed to see the name of the debtor. He's going to add that himself just before he signs the petition."

"Well, OK then. I'll come and pick it up before lunch, if that's OK?"

"I'll let him know." She slammed the phone down. *Oh you're welcome Daphne, oh and by the way Daphne, perhaps you could work a bit more on your social graces?*

So AJ was preparing his bankruptcy petition for service on Jim. I found it surprising, however, that he would keep details from even his personal assistant. I called Oscar's assistant, Val.

"Hi Val. It's Penny Banfield."

"Oh Penny, your timing couldn't be more perfect. I was just going to call you." I think it was just possible that she might have been able to hear me sighing loudly.

"Oh, it's OK. No, don't worry. It's not a computer issue, at least not for now," she said and laughed nervously.

"Oscar wanted to know if you were free to join him for lunch. He's taking Mr. Peters over to his club and thought you might want to join them?"

"Well, I don't currently have plans for lunch. So that should be OK."

"Perfect. Oscar will be delighted." *Why would Oscar possibly be delighted? I know I was definitely NOT delighted to be going to lunch, especially not with his weirdo client.*

"I wanted an update on the patent application. So I'll speak to him at lunchtime about it. Thanks Val. "

From: Reception
To: All
Date: May 16, 2000
Re: PHIL?

Anybody seen Phil?

I could only imagine the responses our receptionist Joan was getting.

Try the pub!

How about the golf course?

Is he at the casino again?

My advice would have been that she try anywhere other than his office.

A knock at the door and there he was. I felt like a bounty hunter, just knowing his whereabouts.

"Oh, here he is - the man of the moment."

"What are you talking about?"

"Just got an email from reception. Everybody is looking for you, *again*."

"Well, that can wait. I need to talk to you." He looked serious again for the second time in days.

"Does it have to be now Phil?" I pleaded.

"Yes. Now."

"Phil, I am so busy. You of all people should know that." I slammed down a file on my desk.

"Yes, but this really is important." He closed the door, and I began to get a little anxious.

"Is everything alright?"

"Yes. I think it is. I just wanted to bring you up to date on things."

"What things? Something to do with the raid?" My heart was racing.

"Me, Lisa, and the baby." My God, I could hardly believe my ears.

"Oh, I see. So, what's up?"

"I did a lot of thinking after our lunch yesterday and basically began to feel like a prick. I mean, you really did put everything in context when you said that there was a life in the balance with this decision. I felt so selfish and, if truth be told, felt like a spoiled child." He looked down at the floor.

"Go on." This was really getting interesting.

"I decided not to go for drinks with Mickey and the boys after work and went for a walk in the park instead, thinking things through. I kept asking myself what I wanted my life to be about and the answers that came back were not as shallow as you might think."

"Please Phil, you don't have to tell me any of this." I had started to feel very uncomfortable in my new role as family counselor.

"I know I don't have to tell you. I want to. I told you, I really don't have anybody other than Lisa that I can talk to about this kind of stuff."

"I'm not exactly the firm's agony aunt though, am I Phil? In all honesty, I can't really claim to have a good bedside manner. You know all you are ever going to get is straight-talking from me?"

"Yes, I know that, and that's exactly the reason why I trust you."

"OK then, keep going."

"I decided in the park that I was going to go home, tell Lisa how much I loved her, and ask her to marry me."

"What? Did you? I mean ask her to marry you?"

"Yes. Yes, I did. She said yes, but only after bursting into tears."

"Wow! That is excellent news. Congratulations!"

"Thanks. I have to say that I really don't think I would have got there without our chat yesterday. So thanks Penny for all your help."

"Oh Phil, we could hardly call it help. I just basically told you what I think anybody in their right mind would have said."

"Well, let's just say I didn't hear it from any of my friends."

"Why am I not surprised about that. Guess Mickey is not the sort of guy to give good advice, eh Phil?"

"Exactly. Anyway, I better report in to reception before they send out a search party."

"Good idea. The last thing you want is another woman hunting you down." I laughed.

"Let's touch base later today so that you can bring me up to date on what's going on with the Anton Piller Order. I can't really say I'm on top of it. I've had my head up my ..."

"Yes," I interrupted him. "Yes you have. So I'll drop by around four?"

"OK, great." He left my office, and I felt surprisingly relieved.

I felt quite satisfied with myself. If all else failed with my career in litigation, maybe I could make a name for myself in family mediation?

I picked up my yellow legal pad and two pencils and headed off to see the Lord and his crazy client with a table-related issue. Nodding politely at the senior lawyers along the way and smiling empathetically to those assistants who I knew had to endure the unreasonable expectations of intolerant bosses on a daily basis.

I found Oscar in his office with a client who surprisingly did not resemble some crazy scientist, but looked actually quite attractive. Blonde, blue eyed, and very well dressed in a navy blazer and cravat. This man was definitely from money.

"Oh, there you are Penny. Jeremy, this is Penny. She's our associate lawyer who has been helping with your patent application."

"Pleased to meet you Penny." Peters leaned forward and offered his hand to me.

"Good morning Mr. Peters. How are you today?"

"Absolutely fine. It seems that we are quite close to making the 'Table Tamer' a reality. It's always good when dreams take shape. Would you like to see how it works?"

"Absolutely." I tried my very best to sound excited while he pulled from his pocket a white plastic bracket (a souped-up kind of wedge as anticipated) and placed it under the foot of a small table in Oscar's office. The gadget had a knob that could be twisted so the wedge would expand as desired.

"Wow. I expect you must be really excited about this." *I was becoming great at bullshitting.* Phil had obviously made more of an impression on me than I had realised.

"How long have you had the idea in mind Mr. Peters, if you don't mind me asking?"

"Oh, probably five years or so. It's taken quite a while to get the design finalized." *Five bloody years! For something that a couple of napkins stuffed under a table leg can solve in an instant? Jesus, you just don't get that time back. Somebody needs to tell this guy to get a life.*

"Goodness, that is a long time! You must be a very tenacious man."

"Oh, you can count on that." He smiled at me, and his eyes lingered on me a little longer than felt comfortable.

"So Lord Hanley, I take it that the application has now been approved by Mr. Peters?"

"Absolutely. Yes, it has my dear. So if you wouldn't mind seeing that it gets filed, that would be wonderful."

"Of course." I took the application from Oscar and turned to leave.

"Mr. Peters and I have some other matters to attend to and then I understand that you will be joining us for lunch?"

"Yes, that's right. Thank you for the invitation. I'm looking forward to it." *My God, I was turning into a complete liar.*

"What a pleasure to meet you." Jeremy Peters flashed his charming smile at me again.

"Who knows, we may even get an opportunity for you to show me how your design works again if there is a wobbly table at the Windsor Club."

"Exactly."

I started toward the door, very aware of piercing blue eyes watching me leave the room with interest.

Back in my office, I started to finalize the application forms and cover letter to the Patent Office. The application would be sent in the mail today. After diarising the file for follow up in two weeks, I moved on to my next task of drafting the application I had promised Raj regarding the eviction of squatters.

The Protection from Eviction Act required at least four weeks' notice be given to tenants and the provisions of that Act, also applied to squatters. In Brighton, there were a number of empty properties, which meant that squatters were able to live rent free for up to six weeks, if not longer. Sometimes it would take at least two weeks to even know that squatters had taken occupation of a property.

Squatters would often attend the court hearing (although not always) and then move onto the next unoccupied property for another four to six weeks of rent-free living.

It was necessary to serve the squatters with a "*Notice to Quit*" either personally or by affixing it to the front door. The very first time I served squatters, I had naively affixed the notice to the front door using my high-heeled shoe as a hammer to nail it to the door. Unfortunately, it had sounded very foreboding, resulting in one of the squatters opening the door to me and inviting me inside. I was, however, able to effect personal service on him, albeit with some embarrassment.

I was surprised to see how caring the squatters had been toward each other and found myself impressed by the general civility in the house, when compared with the lack of civility sometimes encountered in a law firm. Why anybody would want to live in a property without running water or electricity was beyond me, but beggars cannot be choosers, and rent-free living was rent-free living.

The application was pretty standard, and I was able to use a precedent that I had used before. Therefore, it took very little time to draft, meaning that I had dealt with both Oscar's application and the application for Raj by the time Nigel showed up at 11 with our coffee.

"Hi Penn. How's it going so far? Still knackered?"

"Yes, I am tired. But surprisingly, I've managed to be quite productive this morning."

"How was Mr. Wobbly table man?"

"Actually, he's really quite attractive and not quite as wacky as I had imagined."

"Really?"

"Yes, but I still can't quite imagine how a person would spend five years of his life working on such a thing. He seems pretty excited about it though. So who am I to burst his bubble?"

"Five bloody years! You have *got* to be joking!"

"No, sadly not joking, Nigel. Did you get a double espresso?"

"Of course, I did. I know how to take orders. You've trained me pretty well." *Yes I had.*

"So then. What gossip do you have for me today?"

"Nothing much. It seems that the only thing people think is worth talking about is that you and Gavin are seeing each other." He looked nervous at delivering the news.

"I wondered how long it would be before it became common knowledge."

"It wasn't me Penn, I swear."

"I know it wasn't. I'm sorry I jumped to conclusions earlier on. Turns out it was *Gavin* that spilled the beans."

"So how do you feel about *that*? Well, hang on a minute ... I don't actually think it's a bad thing. It means that he's actually pretty proud of the relationship to make it common knowledge, don't you think?"

"Suppose so. I'm trying not to read too much into it if the truth be told."

"Quite sensible, if I do say so myself."

"How about you? How did your curry evening go on Friday night? We haven't really talked about it."

"Actually, it went well. The recipe worked like a treat."

"Well, enough for her to stay over at least?" He looked very uncomfortable. "Oh my God, yes she did!"

"Nigel Wilkinson you old dog! What's her name anyway?"

"Emma. Emma Bradley."

"Hang on a minute. Isn't she an assistant?"

"Yes, she is." He could obviously see some fleeting look of disapproval on my face. "And what exactly would be wrong with that?"

"Nothing ... absolutely nothing."

"Nigel, I feel like we should celebrate this incredible time in our lives. We are both dating sane, straight people at the same time!"

"It is pretty incredible, isn't it?! Here's to us!" Nigel raised his paper cup, and we pressed our coffee cups together.

After Nigel left the office, I picked up my coat and went up to collect the bankruptcy petition from Daphne. The petition was in a plain, brown envelope and had been sealed - but had a Post-it note attached:

FOR FILING BY PENNY BANFIELD

It was highly likely to raise a few eyebrows at the courthouse when it was filed, as Jim Bateman had a very high profile locally. Thankfully, Daphne was not at her desk when I picked it up so there was no need to engage in any social niceties with her (even if she were capable of such things).

The courthouse was just a few streets away from our office - a fifties-style white concrete building with wide steps leading to the large, wooden front doors embellished with a golden coat of arms.

As I got to the second floor, I was surprised to see that since my last visit, the courts had installed a ticket system. You basically had to take a number and wait until your number was called. By all accounts, the system was not working too well. There were at least 12 people waiting in line, one of which was a beached-whale-of- a-man leaning back in his chair, eyes closed with his ticket held between his closed lips. It seemed like he had been waiting for some time. Still, if I were to be held up for a long time, it would provide me with a wonderful excuse to miss lunch with Oscar and Mr. Peters.

Unfortunately, it turned out that my filing did not take as long as anticipated. I did however have to go straight from the courthouse to the Windsor Club for lunch.

The Windsor Club was an old, red brick building with a glossy black door and traditional brass plate. Large potted topiaries framed the entrance and a security commissionaire met me at the door wearing full regalia. He pointed to the cloakroom situated by the front door and asked me to sign in. Reviewing my entry, he seemed surprised that I was a guest of Lord Hanley.

"Oh, it makes a change for Oscar to have somebody interesting for lunch."

"I'll take that as a compliment. Thank you. What about his other guest? Is Mr. Peters not interesting?"

"Is he a friend of yours?" he asked carefully.

"Oh no, not at all. I barely know him."

"Well, in that case. I'd say he looks a bit wet behind the ears, but you didn't hear that from me," he said and winked.

I laughed. "I think I would probably agree with you there. Which floor is the restaurant on?"

"Just up these stairs here, and then turn left."

As I climbed the stairs, I wondered why on Earth Oscar would be having lunch with Mr. Peters. If indeed he "could not stand" him? In the restaurant, I found Oscar with his client sharing a joke while reviewing the menu. Either Oscar was faking it completely, or he had told me he didn't like Jeremy Peters just to get the file off of his desk and onto mine. *Was he just like Phil?*

"Sorry I'm late, I'm afraid I had to file something urgently at the courthouse, and the wait was horrendously long." I brushed my hair away from my face.

"Oh, it's absolutely no problem, my dear. I am sure Mr. Peters will agree with me, the wait was well worth it." He looked over the brim of his glasses at Jeremy Peters.

"Most definitely worth waiting for." Mr. Peters pulled out a chair for me. I started to feel uncomfortable.

"Here Penny. Take a look at my menu. I'll ask the waiter for another."

"Oh, thank you, Mr. Peters."

"Please, do call me Jeremy." I smiled at him warily.

"Penny my dear, I was just telling Jeremy all about you," said Oscar. *Well Oscar, that is interesting isn't it, seeing as you practically know nothing about me.*

"Oh really? And what would you possibly have to say about me that might be of interest to Mr ... sorry, I mean, Jeremy?"

"Well, I told him that you are a successful and ambitious young lawyer, very bright and also as I understand it, *single.*"

I started to blush. "Well, thank you, Oscar. I am not sure about the single bit though." They both looked surprisingly concerned at the revelation.

"Oh, really? I had no idea you were spoken for. I am sorry Jeremy, it seems that my information about Penny here may be a little outdated." He looked embarrassed. *What the hell? He obviously had been discussing my marital status with his client ... was he trying to pimp me out?*

"Well, I have to say I am rather disappointed. I had been telling Oscar here how difficult it's been meeting suitable young ladies, and I think he rather thought that you might be an appropriate match for me," said Jeremy, with no apparent hint of embarrassment.

I gulped my water down, almost choking. "Oh, I can't believe an attractive man like you would find it difficult to meet women. There must be plenty of suitable young ladies at the yacht club or tennis club?"

"Sadly not. I am quite shy actually. The sort of guy who finds it hard to make the first move." *Yes, the sort of guy who resorts to having Lord Hanley pimp out the young associates of his firm to find a suitable date.* Maybe Oscar felt that his efforts to emotionally tie-up Jeremy Peters might keep him away from his ex-wife? I really had no idea why Oscar would take an interest in the personal life of his wife's ex-husband.

"Sorry, but I recently became spoken for. It is, however, to be fair to Oscar, a very recent change in my circumstances."

"Well, maybe if circumstances change, perhaps you could let me know?" He handed me his business card. It all felt wrong, so very wrong. Thank goodness, the conversation changed.

He started to rub his chin looking around for the waiter. "Anyway, enough of this. I'm famished. Let's order something to eat."

I found myself praying that the lunch would be exceptionally good to make up for the exceptionally dull company. This was going to be a very long lunch.

As it turned out, lunch was extremely good (well almost anything is bearable with a good glass of Chablis). But underneath my professional exterior was a seething lioness, wanting to rip the head off Oscar. How dare he treat me like a commodity to be traded? Despite the occasional glare, Oscar seemed totally unperturbed at his faux pas.

Just before dessert, Jeremy turned to me, moving his chair closer. "I feel like I have something in my eye, Penny?"

"Really?" Looking down at the table, I started to brush crumbs away from the tablecloth.

"Yes, it's really painful." He moved even closer. I moved my chair away.

"Maybe you should go to the bathroom and take a look?"

"Perhaps you could take a look for me?" He leaned forward.

I laughed at his ridiculous ploy and stood up to leave. "I'm sorry Oscar, I'm going to have to get back to the office. I have such a heavy workload right now."

"Oh, really? That is such a shame. You are going to miss dessert."

"Yes, I know, such a shame. But I really must get back." *There simply isn't enough sugar left in the world to make me want to stay in the company of "Mr. Jeremy-Wobbly-Table-Fix-It-Peters" any longer than was absolutely necessary.* I stood up. "Thanks Oscar for lunch. It's been interesting." I couldn't bring myself to even look at Jeremy, let alone say goodbye. I picked up my handbag and started to leave.

"Oh, Penny. Wait a minute!"

What now you ridiculous creep? I turned to face Jeremy.

"You seem to be forgetting something."

"Oh really, and what might that be?" I could barely keep the sarcastic tone out of my voice.

"This." He leaned over the table and picked up the brown envelope containing the bankruptcy petition, which I had filed earlier with the court.

"Oh my God. Yes, yes of course. Er, thank you, Jeremy." I grabbed the envelope and briskly walked away from the table. This ridiculous situation had almost led me to a place where I could have left behind one of the most confidential documents in Brighton. Well, at least confidential for now.

I was genuinely relieved to get back to the confines of my office and headed straight along the corridor to AJ. Thankfully, Daphne was still at lunch and I was able to deliver the petition straight to him. His door was open, and by all accounts, he was on the phone to his opponent, Paul Silverman - lawyer for the football club.

"Paul, I've told you before, you and your client can either choose to comply with the rules of court, or not. You need to know that I will, however, be holding your feet to the fire to ensure compliance with those rules. Evidently, your client feels that the rules do not apply to him or the Club, but it's my job to remind him that he *must.*"

He glanced up and saw me standing in the doorway with the brown envelope. He beckoned me in and pointed to a chair. "If your client continues to drag this litigation on, I'll have no option but to apply for an Order for Security of Costs, as I have serious doubts about the liquidity of the Club. Anyway, I've said what I had to say, the rest is for you to discuss with your client. I await hearing from you after you have taken your client's instructions." He placed the phone back into the receiver very deliberately and took a deep breath.

"Miss Banfield, I see you've brought the petition back. Everything went well at the courthouse I take it?"

"Absolutely, sir." I handed the envelope over, feeling like a cat laying down a dead bird at its owner's feet.

"Splendid. Thank you. I'm going to have fun delivering this. I will, however, need your continued involvement tomorrow."

"Yes sir. I had been thinking of that. I will, of course, be calling ahead to make sure Jim is going to be there and continue the ploy at least until you arrive."

"Spot on. That's exactly what I had in mind."

"What time do you anticipate being at the market?"

"I thought 11 would be a good time."

"OK, I'll call now to make sure he is going to be there and let you know the outcome."

"Excellent. Thank you, Penny."

Back in my office, I made the call (making sure that the call was not traceable).

"Bateman here."

"Good afternoon Mr. Bateman. I was given your number by Jean at the market. My name is Mrs. Preston."

"Oh yes luv, Jeannie did call me and tell me you would be in touch." He sounded anxious.

"I was hoping that my husband and I might be able to meet with you tomorrow if you are going to be at the market." *Please God ...*

"As it happens, I will be at the market tomorrow, but only until around 2 p.m. I have to get back for a Board meeting."

"Oh, I see. Would ... say 11 a.m. work for you?"

"Yes, I could do that. Can I ask if you have any previous experience with running a market?"

"Not personally, but my husband has some experience. He wants to discuss some new ideas with you."

"Is that right? Well then, let's meet and see if we can do business together."

"Look forward to it. See you tomorrow James." *IT'S IN THE BAG!*

From: Penny Banfield
To: Anthony Jarvis
Date: May 16, 2000
Re: Service of Bankruptcy Petition

Jim Bateman is anticipating a meeting with you at 11 a.m. tomorrow at the Stevenage Market.

Penny Banfield

CHAPTER 10 – WEDNESDAY MAY 17, 2000

Another sleepless night. This time for all the right reasons. As Gavin cluttered around in an unfamiliar kitchen to make morning coffee, I stretched out in the bed like a cat languishing in the sun. The evening before, and indeed any time spent with Gavin, was time mentally away from the pressures of work. God knows there was enough to think about right now.

The sound of the coffee percolating told me that Gavin had been successful in his quest. He came back to bed and slid next to me.

"Hey." He snuggled behind me, kissing my neck.

"Oh, hello. Are you still here?" I smiled.

"Yes, afraid so. I'll just make your coffee, and then I will be out of your way," he said stroking my back.

"Well, we certainly have an interesting day ahead of us, don't we?"

"Looks like it. I have to say I'm a bit wary of spending the best part of a day with AJ. "

"Oh don't worry, I'm sure you will just shine."

"Wish you were coming too." *He was so intuitive, or was I just so obvious?*

"Just a little bit, but I'm a big girl, I'll get over it." I laughed.

"You know, I think AJ holds you in very high esteem."

"Oh, he doesn't even know I exist. I'm just a background kind of-girl. Phil will get all the recognition for any work I am doing on this project."

"No, I don't agree actually. In fact, I think AJ has a good measure of Phil, he's certainly no fool."

"Well, it remains to be seen if Phil is fooling AJ or not. It certainly feels like he's making a fool out of me most of the time. I guess we should be getting up. What time are you meeting AJ at the office?"

"Eight."

I jumped out of bed. "Let's be having you then Mr. Preston. Last into the kitchen gets to make breakfast!"

He started to run, and I deliberately held back and smiled. "Why don't you get into the shower while I get started? Eggs and toast OK?"

"Sounds great. How do you like your eggs?"

"Scrambled, please."

"OK. Scrambled it is."

It felt good to be in the kitchen making something for somebody other than Nigel. It had been some time since I had taken care of anybody in this way. Simon had always been the one cooking for me. By the time Gavin had made it out of the shower, I had creamy scrambled eggs with cheese, granary toast with raspberry jam, and fresh coffee lay out on the table.

"Wow, what a spread! I must say this feels very domesticated." He poured out some coffee.

"Yes, sorry about that." I was blushing.

"Oh, don't be sorry. I quite like it, actually."

"Let's eat before it gets cold." Almost inevitably, we started to talk shop as we ate.

"I would give anything to see the look on Jim's face when he gets served with that petition today," I said.

"I'm more interested to see AJ's face. I don't think I've ever seen him so fired up about a case before. I think this vendetta goes back quite a long way."

"Yes, I think so, too. AJ used to be on the Board at the football club, and I guess he feels quite strongly at the way Jim is mismanaging things. You do realize that I'll be expecting a full summary of the day's events when you get back, Mr. Preston?"

"Absolutely. Want to come over to my place tonight?"

"Won't you be tired?"

"Expect so. But it would be nice to be exhausted in your arms tonight rather than the confines of my lonely flat."

"Well, if you are sure?"

"Absolutely. I'll call or see you when I get back. If it's later in the evening, I'll send over a cab to pick you up." Since neither of us had cars, we resorted to cabs. The independent side of me flinched at the idea of being picked up in a cab, but I let it slide - allowing Gavin his moment of chivalry.

"Sounds great." I could hardly contain the grin spreading across my entire face.

"Anyway, I really shouldn't keep you any longer. You have a hard day ahead of you."

He pushed back his chair to stand up. "Yes, I should be making tracks." He leaned down and kissed me on the forehead. Oh my, how I loved that! I tried to play it cool, but it was impossible. I jumped up and hugged him close.

"Be careful at the market today. Jim has a very nasty temper by all accounts. Make sure you don't get caught in any crossfire today. Oh, and Gavin ..." he looked quite serious by this time, "make sure you don't run into any lilacs at the market."

Three telephone messages were waiting at the office, one from Kate (I had forgotten to fill her in on the weekend and it was now Wednesday), another from Archie Steadman, and the third from Raj Gosavi.

I started with a call back to Archie. "Archie, it's Penny Banfield here, just returning your call. What can I do for you?"

"Just wanted to give you the heads up that I heard through the grapevine that one of the directors has moved from the address I provided to you recently. Apparently, he moved yesterday."

"Goodness, that's quite impressive."

"Well, we want to make sure that the information you have is current, don't we luv?"

"And that's exactly why we come to you Archie. You are the best."

"Thanks, but I can't take credit for this. It was one of the lads in the office that got word of it."

"OK, fire away. Which director are we talking about?"

"Steve Dixon. Seems he's moved to a rather nice address in Rottingdean."

"What's the new address?" He read the address, while I scribbled away.

"Thanks Archie. I'll be in touch after Friday to let you know how things went. Wish me luck."

"Oh, a bright girl like you won't need luck, Penny." Archie certainly knew how to placate my nerves.

My next call was to Raj. "Mr. Gosavi, Penny Banfield reporting for duty."

"Oh, hi Penny. Thanks for getting back to me so quickly. I have a new client I thought I might pass on to you."

"Great. What's the issue?"

"Personal injury claim, but the client is fee sensitive. So I really can't take this one on."

"Fee sensitive? As in can't pay her bills, or as in may require a contingency agreement?"

"The second option. I can't carry that overhead anymore when my charging rate is 250 pounds an hour."

"Of course not, I understand. What's the name of the client?"

"Petra Borgensen."

"Sounds Scandinavian."

"Yes, she is Scandinavian. She is from Denmark."

"OK, thanks Raj. Email me her contact information, and I'll set up a meeting with her."

"Great. Thanks for taking this one on."

"No problem. I'm happy to help." *Fee-sensitive clients are always welcome. At least while I am busy building my practice and inching my way up my legal ladder of success.*

Nigel and I often joked about the ladder of success and how you had to be careful of hurting people on your way up the ladder because you might just meet them again on the way down.

I called Kate and unfortunately got her voicemail again. Did she ever pick up her phone cold-turkey? Sometimes I hated voicemail.

"Hey Kate. I am so incredibly sorry. I cannot believe it's already Wednesday, and I haven't been in touch. There is a lot going on right now, but unfortunately a lot of it is confidential, so I can't spill the beans. I can, however, tell you that the weekend with Gavin went really well. In fact, so well that he has told practically the entire office that we are an item. So that can't be bad. Listen, I am going to be over at his place tonight, so I won't have a chance for a talk. But maybe we could meet after work one day next week, have something to eat in the Lanes, and catch up? Let me know. Love you babes."

I looked at my watch, 9:15 a.m. I could not help thinking how things were going in the car with AJ and Gavin. If the company was uncomfortable, at least the ride in AJ's Daimler Jaguar would not be. Gavin was likely enjoying the rather luxurious form of transport to Stevenage. My phone started ringing.

"Penny Banfield."

"Hi Penny, it's Jean. I have a call for you, from, well sorry, it's Simon. He says it's important."

"Did he say anything other than that?" My heart was pounding.

"No, I'm afraid not. I did try to tell him that you were really busy. He was rather insistent I'm afraid."

"OK. Put him through."

"Penny?"

"Hi Simon. What can I do for you?"

"Wow, why so formal?"

"Well, you are calling me at work, and I am extremely busy right now. Jean said it was important?"

"It is important. Listen, it's really hard to do this over the phone, so I wondered if you could meet me for lunch today? Even if you could spare half an hour, I'd be grateful."

"I have got to eat *something* at lunchtime I suppose. Where do you want to meet?"

"I thought we could meet at The Ruby?"

"OK, see you at 1p.m." I hung up.

What was going on? I hope he did not have something dreadful to tell me, like he had AIDS or something awful like that. Why couldn't he tell me over the phone? Despite being wary, I found myself also looking forward to lunch. Looking forward to it, why? Because of my inquisitive mind? Because I still found him incredibly attractive, or because I was as usual, just being a hungry little piglet?

I decided to create a diversion (well, it also could be described as "work") and called the new client Raj had passed on to me - the *"Fee-Sensitive Client."* What this usually meant was that the client could not afford to pay for work on an hourly basis, but instead the client agreed to pay a high level of commission on the amount of damages awarded by the court. Often this meant that a third of the funds awarded by the court would be paid by the client to their lawyer upon settlement or judgment. Not a bad rate of pay and certainly more than your run-of-the-mill 10 per cent commission in other industries.

I invited Petra Borgensen into the office. Luckily she was available right away. I spent an hour or so interviewing and cross-examining her to see how she would hold up in court, trying to find potential holes in her case.

The diversion proved to be very effective because by the time Nigel had left from our morning coffee, I barely had time to type up a statement from my new client before it was time to meet Simon at the Ruby.

Simon was extremely versatile in the world of choosing a place for lunch. Although he was OK with eating at the local pub, he also enjoyed wine bars and eclectic places like the Ruby. I suppose you could describe the place as a bistro/wine bar. Decorated in a contemporary way with glass tiles, silver light fittings, suede sofas, and leather chairs, it was comfortable but also a little pretentious. As I passed by the window, I noticed Simon sitting in a chair looking decidedly uncomfortable. I always knew when he was nervous. He would rake his hand through his blonde hair three or four times in succession. He looked up and barely smiled. I felt my heart jump much to my annoyance. I opened the door and was met with a wall of cool air, which almost made me laugh. *Air conditioning in Brighton? In May?* I had been right, this place was totally pretentious.

"Si ... how are you? God, you look nervous. Do I need to worry about this conversation?"

"No, I'm OK Penny. Please, sit down." He pulled a chair out for me.

"What made you choose this place?" Immediately, I felt mean because he then looked a little defensive.

"Well it's new, and I thought it might be nice?"

249

"Oh, I see ... like neutral ground. Do you like it here?"

"Not really. To be honest, I find it a bit ... pretentious. I'd probably prefer a glass of wine at the Crooked Billet."

I laughed. "Me too. Can you believe they have bloody air conditioning?"

"I think the owner is American," he said and smiled.

"Well, I have no issue with that per se ... the issue is more with the weather in Brighton at this time of the year."

Simon laughed at my comment, and I found myself drawn to his beautiful mouth and perfect white teeth. I picked up a menu. "Have you ordered yet?"

"Yes, I did order. I hope you don't mind, but I saw the lamb curry on the menu and ordered it for you. I take it you still like curry?"

"Yes, of course I still like curry. Good choice, Si." I started to relax and sat back into my chair, pushing against an overstuffed cushion that was almost too plump for comfort.

"Well then, what's this all about?"

"I just want to impress upon you that I meant every word I said to you last week. I can't stop thinking about you, about us, and how wonderful we were together before I had my little, well, let's call it an *'episode.'* I can't sleep thinking at how the best thing that ever happened to me has slipped through my fingers, and there's nothing I can do about it."

"I'm sorry, Simon. I have been thinking about things, I really have. I think you should know that I'm in the middle of dealing with a huge project at work, but also I've started seeing somebody else."

Simon stared at the floor, then started to rake his hair again. "OK, so what you're saying is that it's too late then." He shook his head. "How long have you been seeing this new guy ... what's his name?"

"Gavin. Not long, although I've known him for some time. We went to law school together."

"Oh, I see. A lawyer ... that must be nice ... I mean having somebody who has so much in common with you." My heart was breaking, he seemed to be doing his best at putting on a brave face.

"That was never our problem was it? In fact, we had very few problems I would say - that is until you did have your *'episode'*."

"I can see I'm going to regret this for the rest of my life. I can't imagine I'm ever going to get over the fact that this happened with us. The best thing that ever came into my life is gone because of my lack of judgment or understanding about myself."

"Si, please don't. There's nothing we can do about it now, is there? I mean it's happened."

"But it's like this huge part of my life is missing. We know everything about each other, and now it's all gone ... it's all wasted."

Simon leaned closer to me, grabbing my hand. Surprisingly, it felt right. I mean holding his hand. I had held his hand multiple times in the past, but holding his hand at that moment, it felt like coming home after a terrible rainstorm, into a warm dry home. I struggled within myself to remove my hand because it felt so good, so comforting.

"Simon. I can't. It's not because I don't have feelings for you. Please, understand that's not the reason. I'm just scared, so very scared to trust you."

"You have to know that I'm never going to hurt you again, Penn. I think I'd rather kill myself first."

"But Simon, how can I possible *trust* you again? It's virtually impossible to have a meaningful relationship without trust."

"In time, you will learn to trust me again. I know it. Please Penn, don't walk away from this ... from us."

The waiter arrived with our food, looking quite uncomfortable at having interrupted our conversation.

"Let me think about it, Si. It's complicated. I do still have strong feelings for you, but as I say, I'm not sure I can ever make myself vulnerable again to you."

He turned to me and took both of my hands in his hands. "I know that in the circumstances, it's the best I could hope for. I'll wait forever if I have to. I just can't imagine a future without you, Penn."

I nodded, surprised at the tears forming in the corners of my eyes. I hadn't realized that my feelings for Simon were, in fact, still so raw. I picked up my knife and fork and started to shift the food on my plate. It seemed my appetite had been affected almost as much as it had in the early days of Simon's gay discovery. Despite the wonderful aroma and exceptionally good lamb curry that had been placed before me, my mouth felt like dried chamois leather. It was difficult to swallow. I pushed the plate away.

"I'm sorry Simon. I really have to get back to work. There is so much happening right now. I feel guilty taking a lunch hour."

"I totally understand. Why don't you get back to work? Maybe we could talk on the weekend after you've had time to think things over."

I picked up my handbag, opened my purse, and left some cash for my meal.

"No, that's OK. You don't have to ..."

"I insist. Anyway, best be going." I hesitated and then leaned forward to kiss him as I would kiss any European friend. He looked surprised, but pleased. I realized instantly that he had misread the situation.

"Bye Penn. Be in touch then?"

"Yes."

I practically ran from the restaurant all the way back to the office. With each step, I berated myself for my weakness in not holding my ground. In the safe confines of my office, I closed the door, threw my coat over the sofa, and did some deep breathing exercises while standing, before getting back at it. My phone was flashing with a voicemail message, and I was still feeling guilty for having taken lunch.

"Hi Penn. It's Gavin. Just thought I'd let you know that the deed has been done. I really wish you could have seen Jim's face. I seriously thought he was going to have a heart attack. AJ, of course, is smiling like a Cheshire cat right now. Anyway, I'll tell you all about it later tonight when I get back. Take care."

So the visit to the market in Stevenage had not been wasted, and AJ had achieved his goal of serving the bankruptcy petition. If Gavin had wondered where I might be for lunch, he did not let on. Well, I was forgetting that we were not really at that stage yet. I wondered if I should tell him about meeting Simon for lunch.

"I told you already, you stupid cow, I need to speak with Paul Silverman now. It's bloody urgent, and no, he can't get back to me. I don't care where he is or whether he is with clients. I need him right now!! You can tell him that when he can actually spare me the time to call, there's no bleeding guarantee that I'll still be a client of his!" He slammed the phone down leaving it shaking in its cradle.

"FUCK!" Jim stormed around the room with his hands on his hips, then picked up the phone again and called another of his directors, David Peterson.

"Davie Boy? You will never guess what's happened. That fucking Tony Jarvis has gone beyond taking the piss. Served me with a bleeding bankruptcy petition. I can't bloody believe it! No, no, he didn't want to serve me at the Club, he came all the way up to the fucking market and humiliated me in front of everyone ... well, I mean Jeannie was there. Personally, I think he just wanted to see me squirm. He knew if he turned up at the Club that he wouldn't get anywhere near me. I am wondering if he intends to serve all the directors with a petition? You'd better lie low just in case mate. I've tried to get hold of Paul, but he's too fucking busy to get off his arse and pick up the phone. Gawd, when I think about all the bloody bills of his that I've paid, he should be on call 24/7. Bloody lawyers, they are all the same. Money sucking bastards. Yeah, I'll call you when I eventually hear from him. God, I need a drink. I don't even remember driving back to Brighton, I was so riled up ... probably racked up all sorts of speeding tickets on the M25. Yeah, yeah, I know. I'll have calmed down by the time of our Board meeting. Jesus Christ, he even fooled *Jeannie!* Sent some bloody, high-class bitch up there pretending to be a buyer for the market. He's got it coming to him - that fucking Tony Jarvis. I swear to God, I am going to have the last word on him, even if it kills me. Yeah, yeah, I know. Anyway, I'd better get off the phone just in case that good-for-nothing lawyer does condescend to call me. See you later tonight. What a fucking awful day. See ya, Davie Boy."

He picked up a crystal tumbler, poured some amber liquid from a glass decanter, and sat in his chair rocking from side to side as if trying to soothe his inner, crying baby.

At around 3 p.m., I was disturbed from my reverie having heard a light tap on my door. Gavin was at the door with a wide smile. I jumped up to greet him, making space for him on the leather sofa. "Oh my God, Penn. I wished I could have filmed it for you."

"Don't rub it in Preston."

"No seriously, you should have been there. But I am glad you weren't. Jim was so angry. I swear to God, I was worried that he was going to turn violent."

"Really?"

"Thankfully, AJ kept his cool. The sheer joy of having served Jim was almost oozing out of every pore. He was still smiling about it as we drew into the car park just now."

"What did he say ... I mean Jim. What did he say when you served him?"

"Well, first of all, I went in to his office, pretending to be interested in the market. As originally thought, he was of course enthralled about the idea of making some money. Anyway, he invited me to sit down and when I declined, he looked at me with a quizzical look on his face. I opened my briefcase, pulled out the brown envelope containing the petition. His mouth dropped open as I walked to the door, passed the envelope to AJ - who had been waiting outside. AJ walked up to Jim's desk, pulled the petition from the envelope, and touched Jim on the arm with it saying, 'Consider yourself served, Bateman.' 'You bastard!' Jim yelled at him, thumping the desk with his fists. AJ said, 'I'm totally aware of my heritage, and you are quite mistaken on that front. You probably want some time to read the petition, so I'll leave you to it. No doubt you will want to speak with Mr. Silverman about it.' Then AJ walked toward the door, and I followed - seriously worried about the prospect of some flying missile being thrown at us. Thankfully, he didn't throw anything at us. But after we closed the door, I did hear him bashing things around in the office."

"Oh my God, Gavin. Anything could have happened. He really does have a violent past, you know."

"I know, and that's exactly why AJ didn't want to put you in a position of danger. I think he actually holds you in very high regard." *Hmmmm, had they been talking about me?*

"Tell me more …"

"Oh, I can tell you all about that later tonight. Anyway, how's your day been? Anything interesting happen?"

I hesitated and sighed. "Nothing very exciting, I'm afraid. Oh, hold on a minute, there was something … I did have breakfast with a fascinating man this morning."

"Really? How fascinating?"

"Oh, I think I can tell you about that later tonight."

So later that evening while Gavin and I were curled up on the sofa having shared a fabulous seafood lasagne, a bottle of Viognier, and stories of the day, it seemed that Jim Bateman and his bad day continued …

Jim had arrived for the Board meeting. The boardroom had the appearance of a war room, and the directors looked as if they had been working through the night. Chairs were pushed aside, the surface of the boardroom table covered with various maps, plans, and file folders. Various cups and saucers had long since been replaced by crystal cut glasses with amber liquid either with or without ice. Small groups had formed while various factions discussed in low voices the alternatives being placed before them.

Jim sat at the middle of one side of the table leaning back in his wide backed chair and smoked a cigar. His sleeves were rolled up to the elbow, and his necktie loosened almost to the middle of his chest. He looked as if he had been in a fist fight. He held his head to one side supported by one hand leaning against the table. From time to time, his face would twitch slightly with frustration. Still, he said nothing while those around him schemed and plotted.

It is a good deal ... they say the real estate market is going to turn ... I can't for the life of me decide ... I'll just go with the majority I think ...

The carriage clock on the mantel in the boardroom chimed 8:30 p.m., indicating it was time to bring the meeting back to order. Jim stood up, went to the sideboard, and helped himself to another scotch, not bothering to refresh his ice. He took a large swig, wiped his mouth with the back of his hand, announcing:

"Okay gentlemen, let's be having you. Time to vote on our motion."

The various men suited in shades of navy, grey, and black shuffled their way back to their seats around the boardroom.

"On the motion to go ahead with the purchase of the freehold of the site on Sutton Road - please, raise your hands." Jim surveyed the various hands in the air, noting studiously where the votes were coming from.

"Those against the motion - please, now raise your hands." Noticeably, more hands than the previous vote. "OK, well it appears the motion has been rejected, which in turn means that finding alternative premises on Sutton Road has now fallen by the wayside. We will have to keep looking for alternative premises." Fucking idiots –

have they any idea what a good deal was when it was staring them in the face?

"Any other business?"

"Yes, I have something I would like to raise." Jim turned to his nemesis, Andrew Barton.

"Go ahead Mr. Barton."

"Since the Board has decided to sell off the family silver, I would like to discuss at our next meeting some restrictions on the future funding of this fiasco of a lawsuit that you have entangled us all with."

"We can certainly discuss that at the next meeting. In fact, I would highly advise that we do because I have no intention of being the fall guy on this issue any longer." Jim glared at his fellow directors. "OK then, if that's all. Meeting is now closed."

Jim sat in his seat, rocking his head from side to side, and waited for the clan to dissolve until his ally, Pete Thompson, sidled over. "What a fucking awful day, eh Jimmy?"

"You can say that again. I even got served with a bloody bankruptcy petition this morning by Tony Jarvis."

"Send a 'gofer' from the office, did he?"

"Oh no ... he wanted to watch me squirm in person. So he came and delivered it himself."

"What a bleeding nerve. He's asking for a kneecap job one of these days."

"Settle down now, Pete – no need to go that far." Jim managed a slight smile.

"I can't believe they didn't take up that offer. It took me ages to negotiate that deal for Sutton Road," said Peter.

"I know. They are such a bunch of wankers. You could almost see them shaking in their shoes. These bloody directors have no balls whatsoever – scared of their own shadows, this lot."

"I don't know what we're going to do now. We may have to play outside the Brighton area, Jim?"

"I'm past caring at this stage." Jim sighed. He offered Peter a cigar, and they both lit up in an effort to relax. The old friends, surrounded by fragrant circles of smoke, sat looking over the grounds, wondering how much longer the Club was going to survive.

CHAPTER 11 – THURSDAY MAY 18, 2000

Yesterday had been really busy, and I'd barely had time to mull over my lunch date with Simon. I had not discussed it with Gavin. I didn't want to spoil what had been a wonderful evening. In any event, I'm not sure if it was too early to bring up "Ghosts of the romantic past," or even entanglements of the present. Until I had sorted things out in my own mind, it was probably best left alone. I knew, however, that Simon was waiting to hear from me and at some stage would want an involved and lengthy conversation, but hoped that he would leave me alone until after the raid.

AJ had called a meeting at 9:30 to go over the planned raid. I would be presenting the game plan to the team. As I sat on the train playing with a loose thread on the sleeve on my dress and clearing my throat constantly, I wondered what it would be like to do my job without anxiety – I'd probably turn into Phil.

It was a wonderful morning, puffy clouds across a powder blue sky - in fact, the sort of morning that would be perfect for a walk along the seafront. The waves looked perky, but there was nothing menacing out there today. A middle-aged, tall man walked through the carriage carrying his Starbucks coffee, which had a wonderful aroma, reminding me that I hadn't had my morning coffee in the rush to get out the door. It would have to wait until I got to the main station, as the idea of drinking British Rail coffee was repellent. Hmmm ... a nice cup of medium roast and perhaps a KitKat to go with it? I had, after all, worked off a few calories the night before. In any event, I would need to eat something in order to avoid having my stomach rumbling throughout the meeting.

As the train pulled into the terminus station, I was already pulling together small change for a coffee from the Starbucks on the corner of Queens Road. Standing in line, I was thankful I had not ordered a complicated latte as the queue seemed enormous. I practically inhaled the coffee before I drank it. *Why does coffee always smell better than it tastes?*

From Starbucks, I headed across the road to Gita's to pick up the KitKat. "Good morning, haven't seen you for a while!" Gita looked up from the newspapers she had been re-organizing on the counter.

"No ... er, really? I thought my sugar consumption had gone through the roof lately."

"Maybe my husband has been serving you at the counter then," Gita had a light girlish laugh.

"Highly possible. I certainly haven't noticed myself wasting away, so I'm still being a good customer I'd say." I handed her exact change. *It's utterly shameful that I know the exact price of almost all my favourite items of confectionery.*

"Anyway, best be off – have a really busy one today."

"Oh, before you go - I hear Phil is getting married, is that right?" She looked at me in disbelief.

"Yes, unbelievable isn't it? Anyway, have to go Gita - will speak more next time." *Wow good news travels fast. Phil must have told her.*

I left the shop as the front doorbell clanged behind me. It was so lovely outside. A light breeze played with a few of the newspapers on a stand outside the shop. That walk along the seafront would have been lovely, but being the responsible employee that I am, I continued on to the office.

I threw my coat on the sofa, switched on the computer, and picked up my messages while drinking coffee and consuming the KitKat in a break-neck fashion. A quick check in the mirror to make sure there was nothing "astray," and I headed out the door. I quickly did a U-turn back to my office, grabbed my folder with transparent slides from my desk, and made my way up to the boardroom.

The vibration of excited voices grew louder as I reached the boardroom. A projector was set up with a screen waiting for my presentation. I grabbed a glass of water, a tissue, placed the first slide in place in the projector, and sat down - waiting for AJ, who had not yet arrived.

Across the room, Phil was talking loudly to a group of articling students doing a very good impression of a modern-day Pied Piper, enchanting them with his stories. I noticed a very pretty brunette with piercing blue eyes, blushing and laughing way too loudly. He was clearly trying to impress. I wondered if I'd ever been like that as an articled clerk. Right now, I really didn't feel like talking to anybody, as was often the case whenever I had to do a stint of public speaking or at court. Call it nerves if you like, but I preferred to call it focus.

Phil turned around and saw that I was sitting down, nodded but carried on his performance. It was probably a good thing he was not going to the Annual General Meeting tonight at the Vintage Lodge Hotel. Each year, the firm would report on how it had fared financially and announce any partnerships that had been granted. I assumed that - confident that he was – he was not on the list of new partners. Phil had made his own surprising announcement that he was going to have to miss the event for a pre-wedding family dinner with Lisa's parents.

I was quite taken with how seriously Phil had been taking his new responsibility in life. It was an incredible turnaround. The shotgun wedding was planned for the weekend immediately after the raid. He and Lisa were headed to the States to get married, and I was genuinely happy for them both.

Head down, I began to read my materials until an instant hush came over the room indicating that AJ had arrived. Holding his tie as he sat down, he cleared his throat and began.

"OK everybody. Let's get to it, shall we? As you know, tomorrow is the execution date for the Anton Piller Order. Penny Banfield has been working on the finer details as to how we will be organised, so I will hand you over to her. If you have any questions, we will both do our best to answer them at the end of the presentation."

My stomach started to feel acidic, but I managed to push the anxiety down and held it in place while I got started. The first part of public speaking is always the hardest. I identified the various locations that we would be attending and divided the lawyers and staff into teams; a slide was shown with an organizational chart for each team. Each team had a leader, each leader would have a mobile number. The leaders would communicate with AJ, myself, and each other by phone. Each team would also have at least another team member with a mobile phone, just as a precautionary measure.

I handed out the kits to each team leader, explaining that they contained a location map, names of team members, contact mobile numbers for other teams, and three copies of the Order to be served. One copy was for service on the named director by the Supervising Solicitor from the other law firm that would be attending to ensure that the Order was executed according to court rules. The second copy was for the Supervising Solicitor to retain, and the third copy was an additional copy. Just in case.

All teams were to be in place at precisely 9 a.m. and were to park in an inconspicuous place near to each location. At 9:30 a.m., upon receiving a confirmation call from AJ or myself, the teams would simultaneously execute the Order. The Supervising Solicitor would be travelling in the car with each team and there would be a maximum of five people per car.

After service of the Order by the Supervising Solicitor, they were to proceed to search the entire house for evidence. We understood this to mean everything, including items in lofts, basements, kitchen cupboards, and even lingerie drawers. It was likely to take them all day at each location to carry out a thorough search. Team leaders needed to satisfy themselves that no evidence remained behind. Any evidence found would be tagged, identified, and given to the Supervising Solicitor for retention. The Supervising Solicitor would keep an inventory of all evidence found, provide each team leader with a copy of the inventory, and prepare his report for the court.

If there were any calls about whether items were relevant evidentially, they were to defer to the Supervising Solicitor who would retain the items. Ultimately, it would be open to us to make a court application regarding the relevancy of the item as evidence. If they encountered any violent behaviour, they were to call the police immediately. I turned toward AJ indicating that I had covered everything I had to say.

"Thank you, Penny. Now then, any questions? Oh, perhaps I should first clarify that overtime will be paid if necessary," he said as he stared directly at Andrew Barker who immediately stared down at the boardroom table, beet red. I thought it was cruel behaviour on the part of AJ, although some people in the room found it highly amusing.

Raj Gosavi stood up. "I was just wondering what we do, if there is nobody home when we arrive?"

"Yes, that's a great question," AJ replied. "You are instructed to wait until somebody returns to the home.

The order allows us to carry out the raid only between the hours of 9:30 a.m. and 5:30 p.m. If we have to go back, we will. But of course, it means that we run the risk of the householders hearing about the raids from the other directors destroying or hiding evidence, before we make our next visit."

"Could be a long day then?" Phil said.

"That's right. I understand, Mr. Stevens, that you will be leaving on Saturday for a very important family event. Perhaps we could talk about that after the meeting to ensure that contingency plans are in place, to take account of your family requirements?"

"Thank you, sir." Phil looked embarrassed. The pretty brunette looked disappointed.

"Anybody else?" AJ scanned the room with intense focus.

"OK then. If you do think of anything from now until tomorrow, please let either myself or Penny Banfield know. So, that's it. Good luck everyone! Let's make our client absolutely happy about his decision to instruct Pilkington, Isley & Simeon to carry out this very important task." AJ picked up his file and left the boardroom, leaving a vacuum of energy behind him. The shuffling and mumbling quickly turned into a hum.

Gavin sidled over to me and said very quietly in my left ear, "Hello sexy." I smiled trying not to make it too obvious that I clearly was under the influence of his charm.

"Did I do OK? I was so nervous. I'm surprised you didn't hear my knees knocking together."

"You did great. My God, Penn, you're a natural-born speaker and litigator."

"Thanks, but it doesn't seem to get better. I still get nervous."

Gavin looked at his watch. "I'm sorry, I have to go. I'm in court in half an hour," he said as he brushed his hand very gingerly across my backside as he left. I prayed that nobody had seen that as he ran out the door.

Glancing around the room, I noticed somebody had left a pack behind. The name on the kit was Andrew Barker. *Typical.* I picked up the kit and headed up to his office. When I arrived, he was on the phone. The door to his office was closed so I waited by his assistant's desk.

Anita was a pretty red head around 20 years old and known for her efficiency. Impatiently, I found myself looking around until my eyes focused on the screen to her computer. An email message was open and visible. I saw my name in the heading of the email. Of course, I found it impossible to ignore. Abandoning all sense of honour in favour of curiosity, I leaned in to read more, just as the screen went blank. I quickly brought the email back to the screen:

From: Joanna Fletcher
To: Anita Brightman
Date: Thursday, May 18, 2000
Re: Penny Banfield

OMG. I saw her on her way to the meeting. What a mess! I can't believe that she has managed to get her grips on Gorgeous Gav. Is he crazy? I hate her. Why her

---

of all people?

I'd practically give my right arm to experience just one night with him ... can you imagine what that would be like?
Jo

I stared at the screen in disbelief. A Mess. A MESS?! So that's what the secretarial staff thought of me. I should have felt crushed, but instead I felt a surge of anger. I glanced up to see if Andrew was now off the phone and noticed Anita walking back to her desk. I walked around the desk and handed Andrew's kit to her.

"Oh, hello Anita. I wonder, could you give this to Andrew? He left it behind at the meeting today." I handed her the package, she barely even acknowledged it.

"Of course." She glanced at her screen and noticed the email, moved around the desk, trying to block the screen with her body.

"Will you be at the AGM tonight Penny?" She was so obviously trying to distract me.

"Absolutely. I'm taking *Gavin* as my date." I smiled a knowing smile to her, hesitating as long as possible wanting her to feel uncomfortable. She fidgeted with the ring on her finger.

"Oh, really? That's great. I had no idea you were seeing each other. Well, I'll see you tonight then." She stared back at me, daring me to say something. I give it to her, she was a good actress.

"Yes, *we* will see you tonight." I smiled at her. "Oh Anita, I was wondering if you could do something for me?" I deliberately paused.

"Yes, of course ... absolutely." She looked at me with eager eyes. "Penny?" she said breathlessly.

"Could you do me a favour and send an e-mail to Joanna Fletcher?"

"Joanna Fletcher?" She blushed so hard I thought she was going to break out in hives.

"Yes, that's right – Joanna. I gather she's a friend of yours? I was wondering if you could send her an email telling her that the *experience* is way better than anybody, even her, could imagine. I mean, we are talking HOT!"

I tried to suppress my laughter as I walked away knowing that this would probably be the last time Anita ever left her desk without safely locking her computer.

It had been a busy day, my train of thought having been constantly interrupted by telephone calls from various members of the team, asking frankly ridiculous questions that really needed no help from me other than in the world of "hand-holding." To his credit, Phil had got more involved the past day or so, but the majority of the work with respect to the raid, still fell on me.

I started work on the squatters file, arranging service of the documents with an articled clerk (relieved that I no longer had to do this, having previously served my time). I also called a couple of witnesses and interviewed them regarding the new personal injury file. Then glancing at my wristwatch, I saw it was 4:30 p.m.

In view of the email earlier that afternoon sent by Joanna Fletcher, I felt I really ought to make an effort with my appearance and spend more time than usual getting ready for the AGM. I felt like every pair of single, young female eyes was going to be on me, judging whether I was worthy of Gavin's attention. Picking up the phone, I ordered a cab back to the flat. There would be no time to take the train if I was going to arrive looking less of a *"mess"* than usual.

Back at the flat I noticed my answering machine flashing, but had no time to pick it up as I headed directly to the bathroom. I scraped my hair back and scrubbed my face profusely with apricot exfoliant. I washed my hair with coconut and lime shampoo, conditioned it with kiwi and avocado conditioner, and scrubbed my body down with a pomegranate and rice scrub. By the time I had finished, I smelled like a tropical fruit salad.

I decided to wear a black, velvet dress cut just above the knee with a scoop neck and play it up with some glitzy shoes and silver jewellery. I had worn this outfit once to a party with Simon and had received numerous compliments. I had no idea why I had allowed the remark to get to me. This type of thing usually washed off my back, but somehow I found myself ruminating, wondering if I was going to be capable of holding on to Gavin's attention long term.

I decided to wear my hair down and used my curling tongs to make soft curls. I finished off with some smoky grey eye shadow and a plum coloured lipstick, which I didn't normally wear. The end result was quite different from how I had arrived at my flat and most likely the very best I could do without professional assistance.

I called a cab to take me to the AGM. While waiting, I picked up the message that was waiting.

"Hey Penn. It's me. I just wanted to let you know that I am still waiting for your answer. I really don't care how long it takes for you to make your mind up. I want you to be sure about the decision you make because at the end of the day, I am 100 percent certain that you are what I want for the rest ... for the rest of my life. Hope you are OK. Love you." He sounded almost desperate. *Oh Simon ... it would be so much easier to let you go if I felt nothing, but I can't go there yet.*

I had found myself thinking of him as I had been getting ready, rather than Gavin. Maybe that had more to do with the fact that I was associating my outfit with Simon, but what if that wasn't the case? What would life be like if I never heard from or saw Simon again? Would I be sad? The answer was that I would be sad. He had looked so inviting when we had met for lunch. I wonder what would have happened if *he* had leaned forward and kissed me at that lunch – would I have responded? What about Gavin? How could I possibly consider walking away from a guy that made me feel ridiculously jittery with just a smile? I decided to park these thoughts until after the raid. This was definitely not the time to make any serious decisions about my future.

The cab sounded the horn outside, and I ran downstairs, wondering where Nigel had got to? Presumably he was getting ready at the office for the AGM. Men had it so much easier than women when it came to time spent getting ready for events. It was so unfair.

I slid into the back seat of the cab and was met with a brilliant smile. "Good evening Miss Banfield. Very pleased to see you again."

Again? I stared at the cab driver, totally not recognising him. "Sorry? Have we met?"

"Yes, miss, of course we have met. I have met you at the newsagents. I am the brother of Gita, don't you remember?"

"Err, Yes, I think so. I'm sorry, but I have forgotten your name. I really am dreadful with names, I'm afraid."

"Anil! It's Anil." He flashed another majestic smile at me.

"Oh yes, that's right, I remember now. Hello Anil. Could you take me to the Vintage Lodge Hotel?"

"Yes, of course ... special event tonight - Mr. Phil told me about it."

"Phil? Phil Stevens, you mean?" *Seems like Phil was also a good customer ... of course he would be, probably as a result of his drunken escapades.*

"Yes, Mr. Phil. I think he is a fellow colleague of yours?" I suddenly became a little uncomfortable knowing that this man apparently knew quite a lot about my life, yet I knew nothing about him.

"Yes, that's right. Phil's my colleague, but he's not going to be there tonight." I checked my lipstick in my pocket mirror and teased my hair back into place.

"Oh, this I know already. I had the good fortune to take him to his party tonight."

"Yes. The dinner party you mean?"

"No, I don't think so, actually. He says he is trying not to drink tonight because the lads will try to get him '*Pissing at the Big Booze Up,*' and he doesn't want to get bad neckache from the lady indoors."

"Pissed, I think you mean? Anil, are you sure? He told you he was going to a *party?*"

"Oh yes - very big party, Miss Penny! I take him to Embassy Club just before I pick you up."

"Oh, I see. Well, I must be mistaken then." I caught sight of the furrow on my brow, which had appeared very suddenly, interfering with the sophisticated diva look I had been trying to achieve.

We arrived at the Vintage Lodge Hotel just as it started to rain. Desperate not to mess up my hair, I thrust banknotes into the hands of Anil, not caring about the change and ran from the cab to the protection of the red and cream awning of the hotel.

A couple of articling students stood under the awning smoking and greeted me with over-enthusiastic smiles. I grinned back knowing how stressful this evening was going to be for them, on show, trying to be noticed but not overly noticed in a very competitive environment.

Fidgeting with my dress, I headed straight for the bathroom heavily scented with gardenia. I was incredibly nervous, aware that as soon as I headed over to Gavin's side, whispers of bitchery would encircle the room.

Glancing in the mirror, I settled down some stray hairs and headed for the toilet stall.

I just knew I could not face a room full of witches without having some kind of alcoholic sustenance. So, having been a Girl Guide as a young girl, I had come prepared. I definitely needed something to calm my nerves and dissolve the appearance of parenthesis in between my eyes. I pulled out a cooler from my handbag, screwed off the top and sat on the toilet seat, sipping away until I felt the alcohol settling in my empty stomach, anaesthetising my nerves. *How absolutely completely un-bloody-dignified Banfield.*

When I felt sufficiently numbed by the alcohol, I dropped the bottle into the plastic bin in the cubicle and went to the sink to wash my hands. One last glance in the mirror, and I headed off to the ballroom.

I immediately spotted Gavin in a black dinner suit leaning against the bar talking to an assistant. She was a blonde with a milky complexion and almond-shaped eyes. Her hair was quite short, emphasizing her pretty elfin face. I straightened my back and sauntered over to Gavin to interrupt the cosy tete-a-tete.

"Talk of the devil," Gavin said and smiled, putting his arm around me. "Here is my girl. Wow, you look stunning, Penn." I smiled first at the elf and then to Gavin.

"Thanks. How long have you been here?" I barely glanced at Gavin but continued to stare at the assistant, noticing that not only was she pretty, she had the figure of a stick insect.

"Oh, about 10 minutes ... sorry ... do you know Emma? Emma Bradley – Penny Banfield."

I held out my hand. "I don't think we've worked together Emma? Pleased to meet you." *Another lie.*

"You too. You do look fabulous, Penny! Gavin was just entertaining me while I wait for my date."

"Oh?" *I didn't know that partners were invited ...*

"Yes. I think you know him really well, in fact." She smiled. "I'm dating Nigel!"

"Oh ... Nigel - of course!!" *So this was the assistant he had been seeing.* I was relieved that she was already spoken for, but hoped that my relief didn't show too easily on my face. She was really pretty. Nigel had done well for himself.

Gavin ordered more drinks (#2 for me, unbeknownst to him, but who was counting?) just as Nigel arrived, looking extremely flustered. "Sorry I'm late! Hi Penn ... Gav. I see you've met Emma."

"Yes, Nigel. We've *finally* met." Nigel looked at me in an odd way as if to say *"What is wrong with you"* and to be perfectly honest, I don't know what was wrong with me.

"Did you get dressed at the office Nigel? I have to confess it was nice having the bathroom to myself."

Nigel laughed. "No, I got ready at the gym. I didn't have time to get back home and then catch a cab here in time." He looked around the room. "Good turnout. Has AJ arrived yet?"

"Not yet. Think we should find our tables before the stampede starts?" Gavin said.

Eager to get off the high heels, I smiled gratefully as Gavin led us to the table, and we left Nigel and Emma at the bar. Gavin whispered in my ear, "I want to take you home right now. I *really* don't want to sit here listening to a boring old speech. I want to go back to my place and stay up all night with you."

"Oh, but you are forgetting one very important detail Mr. Preston ... I have a huge responsibility to fulfil tomorrow. I'm totally unable to stay up all night. You can, however, accompany me home to *my* place and ensure that I get a good night's *sleep* if you want?"

"OK, it's a deal." He looked disappointed.

"Hey something funny happened in the cab on the way over here."

"Really? A randy cab driver?"

"No, nothing like that. I actually knew the cab driver, well at least, kind of. He told me that he'd dropped Phil off at the *Embassy Club*. I thought Phil said he had a pre-wedding dinner with his future in-laws tonight?"

"He does ... well, at least that was the excuse for not being here tonight." Gavin looked equally puzzled.

"Thought so. Wow, wonder what's up with that?"

"Oh, probably Phil just being Phil. If it wasn't dark, I'd place a bet on him being on a golf course somewhere."

"Poor Phil. He really struggles with self-discipline doesn't he?" I picked up the menu and started to salivate. "Well, this is costing someone a pretty penny ... guinea fowl, truffles, lobster?! Maybe our fee structure is going up again this year? Still it could be my last supper if things go haywire tomorrow, so I probably shouldn't complain about the cost."

"It'll be just fine. Try not to think about it for a few hours at least." Gavin held my hand.

I glanced across the ballroom and saw that AJ had arrived, looking immaculate in his dinner suit and ready for the "big show." A short, red-headed waiter arrived at the table with wine, and I thought better of it, cognizant of the fact that a clear head would probably be needed for the raid tomorrow. Nigel and Emma then joined us at the table together with another six members of staff, including, unfortunately, Daphne, the fat barn owl.

Within minutes of AJ's arrival, and after being seated, the first course was served – a delicately arranged salad with multi-coloured beets, Roquefort cheese, and a sprinkling of pine nuts. There was a gentle buzz of conversation and the clattering of cutlery and crockery. Occasionally, Gavin would stroke my hair, which made me feel both good and uncomfortable, bearing in mind that this was a work function. Although there was no firm policy about office romances, I was almost certain that flouting our connection too flagrantly would not be received too well.

Despite the alcohol, I had started to get quite anxious thinking about the following day but kept trying to push the thoughts away, much like shoving dirty laundry away under the bed when visitors arrive unexpectedly. I wondered about Phil. What could he possibly be doing that was more important than attending the AGM? Typically, he revelled at the opportunity of any social interaction, particularly with the up-and-coming female articled students. I assured myself that Anil must have misunderstood the situation and visualized Phil sitting around a dining table on his best behaviour with Lisa's parents.

I glanced over to the table just opposite ours, until my eyes settled on Joanna Fletcher. I smiled and placing my arm on Gavin's arm, winked over to her who immediately averted my eyes. Sometimes I really disappointed myself with my lack of maturity, but decided to allow myself this one indulgence tonight.

The evening progressed slowly, and I for one was excited to hear the names of the newly announced partners. Of course, a couple were already known to me, but there was sure to be a name or even two that would come as a surprise. Oscar was seated at his table, brushing crumbs from his dinner shirt and smiling with pitiful anticipation. How I felt for him, aching for something that had been held from his reach for so long.

At last and while coffee was being served, AJ rose from his chair and made his way to the stage area and the podium set out with various documents. A hush fell over the room, aside from the occasional cough and tinkling of coffee spoons.

"Now, I'm sure you are all anxiously awaiting the announcement of the latest additions to the partnership. So, without further delay, it gives me great pleasure to inform you that the partners are happy to welcome the following lawyers as partners: Rajesh Gosavi would you please take a stand?"

Raj graciously stood looking appropriately humble and embarrassed at the rapture of applause that ensured. He sat down quickly, allowing AJ to make the next announcement.

"Tim Fairhurst."

The applause began again and a few cat calls from several female admirers who by now had consumed more than just a few glasses of wine. Less humble, Fairhurst demonstrated the actor in him (always very handy in court) and started to bow.

"And last, but definitely not least. Philip Stevens." I heard a couple of gasps and then complete silence for a least a couple of seconds. AJ didn't look the slightest surprised at their surprise, but instead seemed rather amused by it.

"What? Gavin - what did he say? Phil? Phil? Jesus, I don't believe it! What the heck is going on?"

Gavin laughed so loudly that it sounded almost unnatural. "Well, well, well. What a dark horse he is." I found myself getting irritated by Gavin and the fact that he found this funny.

"Now then, it's incumbent upon me to inform those of you who are unaware that, unfortunately, Mr. Stevens is unable to be with us because he is to be married this weekend and is attending a family dinner tonight with his future in-laws. I am sure that you will, however, join with me in welcoming our three partners to the firm and wish them the very best. Please, raise your glasses everybody and drink to the partnership!"

Everybody complied with the exception of Lord Hanley, who remained in his seat, removed his glasses, and began to rub them with his dinner napkin. My heart felt so heavy. Poor Oscar. How I wish his fairy tale would come true.

How was it possible that Phil could have known about his partnership announcement and not be present tonight? Maybe he had not been told yet? No, that was impossible – there was no way the firm would announce a partnership without it being known by the lawyer concerned. How, or more to the point, *why* had Phil kept this from me? I felt a twinge of betrayal. He had thought enough of our relationship to confide in me about Lisa and the baby, yet did not see fit to tell me about the partnership? It now seemed absolutely impossible that he would be at a nightclub as the cab driver said, but equally inexplicable that he would be spending the night with his future in-laws at the very moment that his partnership had been announced.

I felt an impulse to leave the room, track down Phil, and ask why he hadn't told me about his partnership. But the compliant side of me stayed, knowing that any departure from the room prior to the announcement of the profits and future plans for the firm, would be viewed as highly inappropriate.

AJ proceeded to go through the annual task of announcing how the business plan from last year had been implemented, its successes, and some adjustments that would be required for the coming year. After around 40 minutes, a slight and gentle snore could be heard from a table at the back of the room. It seemed that the harder we tried to ignore it, the louder it became. I wondered if AJ could hear it from his vantage point, but he seemed undeterred.

Eventually, his speech began to wind down. "And for those of you who are still *awake*, I would like to thank you for coming tonight and particularly want to thank the litigation team for all their hard work on a recent project they have been working on. I wish you the very best success tomorrow and raise my glass to you." There was a huge round of applause again, and I noticed that AJ was looking directly at me.

AJ left the stage, allowing the DJ to set up on the stage for the final part of the evening.

Gavin whispered in my ear, "Do you want to stay for the dancing, or would you prefer to leave now?"

I whispered back, "Let's go. It's going to be a hard slog tomorrow, and I need a clear head."

"That's my girl," he said, taking me by the arm and leading me toward the door.

In the cab on the way home, I was full of questions. What was Phil playing at? Why didn't he come to the meeting? Didn't he know that this was one of the most important evenings of his career? What was going on? Gavin patiently dealt with the interrogation, allowing me to wear myself out much like a puppy chasing its tail. By the time we reached my place, I had tired of the subject and my attention had turned to preparing for the day ahead. This comprised of setting several alarms, calling British Telecom for an early morning call, and setting the alarm on my mobile phone. Gavin again watched patiently, before settling me down with the comment, "That should do it."

While Gavin made me a nightcap of brandy and milk, I arranged my clothes for the following day and packed my briefcase. All set for the morning, I sat on the sofa next to him, my head resting on his shoulder from time to time and taking sips from the steaming cup. We both knew there was no chance that sleep would come easily, but one could only hope.

CHAPTER 12 – FRIDAY MAY 19, 2000

As anticipated, most of the night had been spent tossing and turning. Gavin had tried to settle me down by rubbing my spine, which was so comforting. Eventually, I decided to stop torturing him and got up at 5 a.m. to make myself a very strong espresso. I started to review the itinerary for the day at the kitchen table. Unplugging my mobile phone, now fully charged, I noticed three missed calls from last night, which on further investigation appeared to be from Simon.

I was going to have to turn my mind to dealing with the Simon situation immediately after today. There was a voicemail, too. It was Phil, I think, although it was extremely hard to make out as all I could hear was the sound of rapturous laughter and drunken men. No message as such was left and no caller ID, but I knew it just had to be Phil. *Great. Phil's going to be working with a hangover today of all days.*

So it had been true – Anil *had* dropped him off at a nightclub. What the heck was going on? Why would he choose to go to a nightclub rather than hear the announcement of his partnership? More to the question, why the hell would he go out drinking the night before an incredibly important day at work? It was too early to call and give him shit about it, but as soon as it was a decent time to call, I intended to call Lisa, tell her to yank his sorry arse out of bed, dose him up with *Nurofen*, and kick him out the door to work. There was no way I was going to allow him to bail on me on this incredibly important day.

My neck grew increasingly stiff, so I decided to have a hot shower in an effort to get rid of the tension. I could usually calm myself down this way, but it was futile today, as I couldn't stop thinking about Phil and the prospect of him letting me down. Picking up a soft towel, I started to pat myself dry when suddenly my stomach lurched and my heart started to race. *Oh just terrific, a panic attack ... now? Of course now - why on Earth would it NOT be now?* Sitting on the side of the bath, I tried to control my breathing before the room started spinning. There had to be an easier way to earn a living ... was this level of stress truly worth it? I had spent years cramming for exams, more years in training, only to be rendered a nervous wreck whose very life depended on how many billable hours she could bank each year.

After a couple of minutes, the pounding in my chest started to abate. I stood up, wiped the steam from the bathroom mirror, and scrutinized my face. Was this job beginning to age me? I had heard that aging slowly crept up on a woman until she was suddenly "old," much like a frog sitting in a pot of simmering water unwittingly boiling to death. Oh, what the heck, it would all be over at the end of today, and I could then relax and get on with the rest of my life.

I crept back to the kitchen and this time brewed some herbal tea. In view of the panic attack, it was probably not a good idea to hit the caffeine again. As I sipped my tea, I reviewed copies of the documents that had been passed to the Supervising Solicitor and reviewed the Rules of Court again. Just one slip could render the entire project illegal and therefore useless. Ultimately, the responsibility was Phil's, even more so now he was a partner. But in reality, it would be my head on the chopping block if there were any "cock-ups," as Phil would say.

Having now run through everything in my mind, I felt sleepy and decided to crawl back into bed beside Gavin to see if I could at least rest my body, if not my mind.

The next thing I knew, multiple alarms were going off and the telephone was ringing. Barely conscious, I could hear, *"Good morning madam, this is your early morning call from British Telecom."*

"Thank you." I replaced the receiver and ran to the various alarms - turning them off and resetting one for Gavin.

Gavin moaned from his side of the bed. "Oh God, what time is it?"

"Are you being funny?" I laughed. "We set every alarm to 6:30 a.m. last night, remember?"

"Oh yeah, I remember." He yawned.

I kissed the top of his head. "Go back to sleep. There's no need to get up. I'll leave you some fresh coffee before I leave. You have another hour before the alarm goes off again."

"I hope everything goes well. I know you are just going to shine, Penny Banfield."

In the bathroom, I carefully applied my make-up, tied my hair back in a ponytail, got dressed, and spritzed some Gucci on my hair. I started to brew some fresh coffee for Gavin, picked up my phone, keys and briefcase, and headed quietly out the door and on my way to the railway station.

The train was surprisingly busy at this early hour, but I still managed to find a window seat. Surveying the various unfamiliar faces around me until I got bored, I closed my eyes, taking the opportunity to breathe. I could hear the announcement of the various stations in the distance while being rocked from side to side by the train. The early morning trains, although busy, were more subdued – there being no signs of children at this time of the day. *Hmmm. That was something to think about.* Who was I kidding? There was no way I could ever be described as an early riser, despite the obvious attraction of having no demon riders on my way into the office.

Letting myself into the back door of the main office, I climbed the concrete stairs from the basement car park to the ground floor turning lights on as I made my way through to my office. I noticed no lights on in Phil's office and no sign of activity. There were already some people making preparations for their day (early risers!), but sadly I knew Phil would be in dire need of an early morning wake-up call if he had indeed been out partying the night before.

My phone was flashing indicating voicemail, which was probably Simon trying to get me at the office yesterday. He was becoming a pest. Yet, I wonder why I had not simply told him I was not interested in getting back together? Was I avoiding the final closure or was there more to it than that? It was almost like I wanted to keep him in reserve like a secret insurance policy, but I really wasn't the sort of person who keeps somebody hanging on just because I couldn't cope with the possibility of being alone.

I dialed Phil's number, glancing at the clock – it was now 7 a.m., a totally reasonable time to call him in view of the responsibilities that had been placed on us today. The phone was picked up almost instantly, which I found quite odd. I had resigned myself to calling at least five or six times to wake up the household.

"Phil?"

"Who is this?" Lisa sounded frantic.

"It's Penny Banfield, Lisa. I was just trying to get hold of Phil."

"He's not in the office then?"

"No. He's not. Is he not at home?"

"Penny, I am out of my mind with worry. He didn't come home last night. I don't know where he is!!" I felt my heart sink like I had been going down in a fast elevator.

"What? I thought he was at an anniversary dinner with your parents last night?" *Of course I had to play along with his story.*

"Not exactly. They are coming over tonight. He was out with the guys last night. They wanted to take him out for a drink to celebrate the wedding."

"What? The night *before the raid*!? I assume he's told you that we have a major project today?"

"Well, not exactly. He just said there was something huge going down today work-wise."

"Is he completely *insane?!* Why the hell did he go out drinking last night? Jesus, when you say drink to celebrate, do you mean some kind of *STAG NIGHT?!*"

"It wasn't supposed to be. He said he'd just go for a few drinks, nothing too excessive because of the work thing."

"I'm speechless. Totally bloody speechless! What am I going to do today? He is supposed to be a key player with today's operation!"

She became totally silent until thankfully, good sense got a hold of me. I was thinking only of myself, of course. I was sure she had more than enough worries of her own to care about other than my issues with Phil's disappearance. "I'm sorry Lisa. That must have sounded terribly selfish of me. Goodness only knows how worried you must be. Have you called all of his friends?"

"Yes, of course I have, but nobody's had the decency to call me back. I've left messages all over the place. I gave up waiting for him at two this morning and then must have fallen asleep until I woke up at six and couldn't believe that he wasn't in bed beside me."

"I hate to say it, but ..."

"Yes, I have called the hospitals ... and the police. They have no reported incidents or information."

"Well, at least that's something. He is at least *somewhere*. Listen, I am going to start calling everybody I know to see if they've heard from Phil. If I receive any news whatsoever, I'll call you immediately. In the meantime, I know it's hard, but please try not to worry. You have to think about the baby. If ... sorry, I mean *when* we do find Phil, I am going to kick him from here to kingdom come."

"Not if I see him first. I'm carrying more weight than you these days what with being pregnant and all."

Good to see that her sense of humour was still intact, of course it would be. She lived with Phil; it was a prerequisite. "OK. Take it easy, Lisa. I'll be in touch."

I spent the next 30 minutes leaving messages with every possible person that might have some information, with the exception of AJ. Don't ask me why I didn't drop Phil's sorry arse into the shit, but that's just me. Even now, I still had his back. The first call was of course to Nigel, who had been staying with Emma because if the *"King of Gossip"* didn't have any information, then it was unlikely anybody would.

Unfortunately, Nigel had heard nothing. Having already devoted enough of my time trying to track down Phil, I had to focus my attention on getting the teams together and in place for the raid. Somehow, we would just have to manage without Phil being at the start of our raid.

I called the various team leaders checking that they and their teams were ready, had mobile phones, and everything they needed. Having everybody other than Phil's team secured and in place (including my own team), I called each member of Phil's team informing them that there had been a *"slight hitch in the arrangements"* and that they were to report to me rather than Phil, unless they received a call otherwise.

Thankfully, they were on schedule to be in place and ready to go without him.

My phone rang. It was Gavin.

"Penny, has Phil showed up yet?"

"Nope. I feel so sorry for Lisa. I can't believe that she'd even consider marrying him after this. Where the hell do you suppose he is?"

"I hate to say it Penn, but you don't think he stayed with some other woman last night?"

"Of course it's crossed my mind. I don't know anybody as unpredictable as Phil, so who knows where he is?"

"Anyway, I just called to wish my girl the best of luck. It's your show, Penn – what with Phil going AWOL. I just know you're going to do a tremendous job."

"Thanks. It's good to know I have at least one ally on the team." I laughed. "I'd best be on my way to get in place. I'll check in with you when I get to the location."

"OK. I'm on my way to my location. Just think that by tonight it will all be over, and we can celebrate your success."

Despite my protestations, in reality, I had already planned to take the whole operation on myself. Plan B was always one that did not involve Phil being there. Let's put that one down to a woman's intuition. Phil was never one to be relied on when it came down to doing hard graft. Whether he was present at the raid, in all likelihood, it would have been me that would take the lion's share of the work. That is probably why I had spent days and sleepless nights going over and over every step of the operation.

7:45 a.m. I had Andrew Barker and Jessica Millership from the office on my team. Mark Stanley, our Supervising Solicitor for the day, was also in the car looking almost bored. Andrew, as instructed, was outside the office, sitting in his Ford Fiesta fidgeting. This was probably the most excitement he had experienced in his entire life. The thrill of the operation was lost on me at this moment; all I cared about was the ultimate success of the project.

I climbed into the front seat next to Andrew, checking one last time that I had all the necessary documents, phone, snacks, and bottled water. "OK everyone, do you have your kits?" They nodded. "All right then. Let's get on with it, shall we?"

We started on our way to our address just outside Crawley. During the journey, I found myself not really paying attention to the talk in the car, which largely comprised of Andrew trying to impress Jessica with his weird sense of humour. Mark would chip in from time to time but mainly stayed quiet as was his general nature if I remembered him correctly from law school. Quiet was good. My neck was like a steel post and from time to time I tried to loosen it up by rocking my head from side to side. *Where the hell was Phil? How could he do this? Were things about to get even worse now that he was a partner?*

There was only one way out of this nightmare and that was to work my arse off until I became a partner myself. That way, he could no longer use me as his "go-to" person. It seemed like I had now joined the world of Lord Oscar Hanley: *"A career in law is only worthwhile if partnership is attained."*

As an experienced litigator, I would have suggested adding the following words: ***"and the sooner the better."***

Ethel stands on a bench by the dryers, anticipating the imminent escape of a wild animal. After some desperate motion, the bag is ripped open revealing a pale and naked man, hands tied behind his back, mouth covered with duct tape, and a pink feather boa wrapped around his head. He pleads with his eyes for freedom, while Ethel averts her eyes to save embarrassment.

Mr. Singh unties the boa while reassuring the captive. Finally free from restraint, the naked man runs immediately to the door of the launderette, covers his genitals with his hands and runs down the street. A wild animal? How could Ethel have known? This was indeed a wild animal and difficult to tame.

Phil Stevens ran awkwardly in the direction of Surrey Street. His head was pounding and felt thick from the night before. He had no phone, no change, and no way of making contact with anybody - but could at least tell the time from the clock over the railway station. 7:15 A.M.

He still had time to get to the raid if he acted quickly. He tried to hail the odd car or taxi, but soon realised as they kept driving past, nobody in their right mind would pick up a naked man unless they were extremely trusting. It seemed that it was a little too early for the trusting people of the world to be up and around.

As embarrassing as it was, he would just have to turn up on the doorstep of an old acquaintance who lived a short distance away from the railway station - hoping he would be home. The odd person that did pass him in the street would surprisingly do nothing to help. Although they would stare at first, it was if he became invisible to them after a very short while as they pretended not to notice. Most would cross the street to avoid him. Eventually, he stopped running and made his way gingerly along the street having embedded a few tiny shards of glass into his bare feet from pavements sticky with dirt.

He hobbled along until he arrived at #7 Compton Avenue and rang the bell. The bell didn't appear to be working, so he started knocking on the door loudly with all the force he could muster. The door was eventually opened after a number of chains and locks from inside had been opened.

"What the heck????? Phil? What are you doing here … naked?"

"Hello mate." Phil rolled his eyes, pushed the door aside and stepped inside. "I need a humungous favour."

8 a.m. I picked up the newspaper, which had been brought along by Andrew.

POSSIBLE BANKRUPTY FOR DIRECTOR OF FOOTBALL CLUB

News certainly got around quickly in this town. I wondered who had spilled the beans? Certainly nobody from our office would have leaked this to the press. It *had* to be somebody from the Club. I could not imagine that Jim, himself, would have informed them as bankruptcy was not exactly something a person would like to broadcast. I smiled. If everything went well today, Jim's days at making headlines had only just begun.

My phone rang. It was AJ.

"Good morning, Penny."

"Morning, sir."

"Just thought I'd check in with you. How is everything going? I tried to call Phil earlier, but was unable to get hold of him. Perhaps he's in transit in an area with bad reception?"

"Yes sir, I expect that's it. Things are going well. Everybody is on their way to getting into position, and all teams are expected to be in position at approximately 8:45 a.m."

"Excellent. Well, good luck, my dear. I'm sure we will speak later in the day."

"Yes, sir." I hung up and sighed heavily. I was full of complete loathing for Phil at that precise moment.

Andrew laughed. "Does he have any idea that Phil is missing?"

"No, he doesn't, and I am not going to be the one to tell him. Are you?" I stared him down.

"Of course not." He looked away.

The phone rang again. My call display indicated it was Simon.

"Penny ..."

"Not now Simon. I'm really busy, and I can't talk." I hung up on him. He called back a couple of times, but I did not pick up.

"Simon still out of favour then?" Andrew chuckled.

"Shut up Andrew, and keep your eyes on the goddamn road, will you?" *Andrew could be a complete buffoon at times.*

I started to call the team leaders, checking that they were almost at their locations. Phil's team was also in place. We were all OK and on time. In a couple of hours, we would know whether the raid had been executed or not. It would be so nice to be able to breathe freely again, but the day ahead was going to be long.

8:45 a.m. We were at our location in Crawley and had parked as close to our address as possible: 26 Bevington Close was home to Peter Thompson, vice president of the football club. It was a large house in a very upmarket neighbourhood with perfect lawns and clipped hedges. The garden was fully stocked with large hydrangeas, rose bushes, and rhododendrons. The house was painted cream with blue trim. It had a huge gabled porch with seats either side of the entrance - much like the entrance to an old church. Two cars were parked in the driveway, a silver Jaguar and a red mini, which looked promising.

We stayed on the other side of the road, just out of eyesight from the inhabitants. The Order was effective from 9:30 a.m., which meant that we could not enter the property until after that time. Otherwise, the Order would have been rendered illegal. It was torturous knowing that they were inside, could leave at any time, and we had no option other than to wait. If both cars and all occupants left before 9:30 a.m. and there was no one left inside the building, we were toast. At around 8:50 a.m., my phone rang. It was AJ.

"Penny, I still haven't been able to get hold of Phil. Is everything OK?"

"Yes sir, everything's under control. Just as soon as he is available, I'll be certain to have him call you. Everybody is in place at their locations, just waiting now until 9:30 before we leap into action."

"OK, OK, that's great. If you could tell Phil to call me if you hear from him, I would appreciate it." *Not half as much as me, AJ, believe me.*

"I told you Phil. She thinks it is me calling her, so she won't pick up."

"Of course she does. That's because it *is* you calling her. She obviously doesn't even think for one second that it might be *me* calling from *your* number. Why would she? I have to get hold of her Simon! I don't have my kit and can't for the life of me remember the address that I was supposed to be at. I don't even have the list, so I can't call anybody else either."

"Can't you call the office Phil? There must be *someone* there who will know or at least be able to find the information for you?"

"Are you kidding me? They just made me a *partner* for Christ's sake! Do you have any idea how bad this is? I could lose my job over this whole escapade!" Phil looked extremely red in the face, and his volatility was increasing.

"Listen, calm down. For heavens' sake Phil, let's get you dressed."

"Anything you have in your wardrobe is going to swamp me. Next to you, I already look like a short-arse. I don't need to accentuate that, do I?"

"I'm frankly surprised that at a time like this, you are actually concerned about your appearance. But I do, I suppose, get your point. What do you want to do then?"

"You'll have to drive me over to my place. I would have Lisa drive over here, but since she's found out that I am in fact alive, she's refusing to pick up the phone."

"OK then, in the meantime, will you do me a favour and for Christ's sake throw that bathrobe on. I'm finding it a little off- putting seeing your kit jiggle around when you get agitated."

They both left in Simon's car and headed over to Phil's place. Phil lived in a large Victorian house with steps leading up to the wide front door. The house had been divided into four large flats. Phil and Lisa lived in a top-floor flat. He had no keys, so would have to humiliate himself publicly and plead with her using the intercom to beg forgiveness.

As they approached the house, still sitting in Simon's car, Phil became acutely aware of the true extent of Lisa's anger. The small, alder tree outside the house was unusually colourful having been littered from branch to branch with various items of clothing ... to be more exact

... Phil's clothing. The bottom of the tree and surrounding grounds were littered with various pairs of shoes, underwear, ties, and a couple of other stray items.

Phil ran from the car like a man on fire, only wearing the bathrobe. "Jesus Christ, I don't believe it!! Has she gone completely stark raving mad? Lisa!! Lisa!!" He called up to the top flat and like a man possessed, he alternated between the buzzer and yelling up to the top-floor flat Lisa! Lisa! For God's sake Lisa, let me in!!!!

Eventually, after about 10 minutes, various occupants from both sides of the street were opening windows in an effort to rid themselves of the nuisance.

"What's all the fuss about?"

"Shut up would you mate, I'm trying to bloody sleep."

"Piss off you moron!!"

"Get lost you freak!!"

Not one person recognised him or even thought it might just be possible he could have a legitimate reason for wanting to enter the building. Simon watched from the car, looking concerned when it appeared that Lisa was refusing to let Phil into the building. At that moment, Phil resembled a beaten down vagrant rather than a partner from an eminent law firm as he trampled around the front lawn, examining various items of clothing. Thankfully, Phil found some underwear, which he picked up together with a mismatched pair of shoes and something very colourful.

He stormed back to the car. "I can't believe it! Can you believe it? She's not even answering the intercom!"

"She must still be pretty mad, mate. Guess she doesn't think it's appropriate you getting completely wasted and staying out all night just before your wedding?" Simon said trying his best not to laugh.

"Ha ha, very funny. You heard me explain everything to her earlier, well before she hung up on me. She knows I have an important day ahead of me!"

"She's obviously not feeling very sympathetic at the moment, Phil. Maybe you should give her some time to calm down. We *really* need to find you something to wear."

"I don't have time. I've no choice other than to wear this." Phil looked down at a couple of items pulled from the fashion show taking place on his front lawn.

"Shame she didn't throw a suit and shirt down at your feet, eh mate? At least something a bit more subdued than that." Simon laughed raucously.

"I'm so desperate, I'd wear a bloody thong right now. I just *have* to get over to Gatwick. I'll call Julie, my assistant, as we head out. She'll be in the office by now and can get the address from my computer."

"OK then, Gatwick it is." Simon started the car, and they sped along as Phil dialed the number to the office.

9:30 a.m. After spending 45 minutes in the car, we rushed out like greyhounds released from their cage, eager to get our teeth into that little, wooden rabbit. Mark, our Supervising Solicitor, seemed a little less enthusiastic, sauntering his way over to the front door. He knocked on the polished brass knocker. We heard someone yell inside, "*I'll get it.*" The door was opened by a strikingly attractive long-haired man wearing a pinstriped grey suit and red paisley tie.

"Can I help you?" He stared at the three of us as if we were a posse from Jehovah's Witness.

"Are you Mr. Thompson?" Mark asked.

"Depends on who is asking?" the man with the paisley tie said evasively.

"Her Majesty's Court is asking, sir." Mark sounded irritated.

"You what? What Court?"

"Why don't you let us in, and I can explain." Mark pushed the door aside, and we all followed behind. "This is a Civil Search Warrant issued by the court on May 15, 2000, allowing us access to the premises to search and gather evidence with respect to Action No. 2000786 – Montgomery v. Seaton Football Club Limited."

"A search warrant? Are you fucking kidding me?"

"Most certainly not. I have been appointed by the court as Supervising Solicitor to ensure that everything is carried out according to the strict Rules of Court. If you have any questions relating to relevance, you must refer the matter to me. I will make the necessary decision."

"Search? Search for what?"

"*Evidence,* sir. Evidence that may assist the applicant in pursuing their civil claim against Seaton Football Club, of which you are a director, is that not correct?"

"Correct, I'm the vice president ... but what does *my home* have to do with this? You are invading my privacy and upsetting my family." He looked toward his wife who looked distraught.

"It's called an Anton Piller Order, and I know it does seem rather draconian, but it's a form of mandatory injunction allowing the lawyer for Mr. Montgomery to search the premises. They brought the application due to a failure on the part of the football club to properly disclose all documents relating to the case in their List of Documents."

"Listen, I don't know anything about that and you are not going to find anything here, I assure you."

"Well, that is for us to find out. Now, I must ask you stand aside so that I may allow the applicants to perform their search."

Mr. Thompson became extremely agitated and red in the face. He immediately started stabbing various numbers on his phone and would swear at regular intervals. While he became immersed in his exercise of profanity, we got started, inspecting computers, and asking his wife for passwords, which surprisingly she knew. Andrew undertook the laborious exercise of examining every file on the system, checking various discs, and asking for any further discs that might exist. In the meantime, I got started in the lounge, checking through the desk for folders, papers, and anything remotely relevant to the contract for the purchase of the player and the litigation. I was about to move into the dining room when I received a call from AJ.

"Penny. AJ here. Listen, I've just received an anonymous call from somebody saying they are aware of the raids that are going on and informing me that we will find all the information we need at 3 Pine Close, the address in Gatwick - the address for David Peterson. I'm not really sure how reliable the information is, but I believe that's the address that Phil and his team are checking out. Is that correct?"

"Yes sir, that is correct."

"Well, no doubt that's why Phil hasn't been able to return my calls. He's obviously collecting evidence."

"I expect so, sir. Listen, I don't mean to interrupt, but I think they need me in another room."

"Of course. Just wanted to keep you informed. Carry on the good work!"

"Thank you, sir". My heart was pounding. *Trust Phil to get the address with all the booty.*

I had been under the impression that my address would be the most fruitful, knowing that there was no way Jim would be keeping the documents at his residence, but had no idea that David Peterson's address would prove to be so valuable.

I ran up to Mark, whispering, "Mark, something's cropped up, and I need to go to another address in Gatwick. I'll arrange for somebody to drive over here to relieve me, but I'm going to have to leave. Will that be OK? I mean to just have Andy here with you?"

"Yes, that's fine."

"OK, I'm on my mobile if anything crops up here."

Andrew was pretty engrossed in what he was doing, but I needed his car. So I interrupted him. "Andy, I'm sorry something has cropped up, I need to go across town. But I'll be back to pick you guys up. I need the car."

"Are you insured?"

"Well, more to the point, are you? I mean if other drivers want to drive your car?"

"Yes, I think so. But be careful!"

"Of course. Thanks Andy."

I called Colin Davidson, a first-year associate on Phil's team, informing him of my arrival, pulled out my kit, located the address on the map, and was on my way.

I arrived at the address for David Peterson in Gatwick amidst a flurry of activity. There were a couple of cars parked outside, and I could hear arguing from inside the house. I walked through the open door and saw three men standing over Brian Evans, the Supervising Solicitor for this address, and Colin who was rooting through files and placing them in various piles on the floor.

One pile comprised of a variety of discs, so I presumed this was the evidence pile. Within a short time, I realized that there was one director, and he was flanked with two other directors who had driven over to his place (no doubt the moment word about the raid got out). Seems that the tip AJ had received had not been a prank.

"Excuse me please gentleman." I tried to brush by the group of men, who then looked my way, some of them looked incredibly hostile.

"Hi Penny," said Colin.

"Colin, I'm so sorry that you've been without Phil. We'll have to send Drew over to the address in Crawley to help out over there".

Colin turned to Drew Fletcher, an articled clerk on the team. "Drew!" he shouted. "Can you make your way over to the address for Penny's team in Crawley? They need an extra hand over there."

Drew nodded quietly, seemingly annoyed that he had been pulled from his treasure trove of evidence. Colin looked back at me and whispered, "Well, it's going quite well. We're finding tons of stuff."

"That's great Colin. What can I do to help?"

"OK, take a seat – go through the filing cabinet over there," He pointed to another cabinet across the room, "while I continue with this one."

Upon seeing my arrival, a man who was obviously David Peterson, turned to his fellow directors standing around with their arms crossed. "Oh great, another fucking lawyer - just what we need." Of course, I had to reply.

"Well gentleman, we would have preferred it, if you had listed all these records in your List of Documents, but at the end of the day, it is nice to see you in your natural habitat."

"Wow, what do we have here fellas - a clever tart!" David said thinking that his mocking would get under my skin.

There was very little he could say that I had not already heard; I had spent some of my training at the law centre and as part of my training had taken statements from hardened criminals in jail.

"Listen love, why don't you shut your pretty mouth and just get on with it," said David.

"Oh I will, don't worry. I'm pretty good at *getting on with it*. Perhaps you could make us a cup of tea in the meantime?"

"More chance of winning the bloody lottery, luv." David chuckled.

"Well, I'm glad that you're finding this amusing because I, too, find this very funny – we obviously must share the same sense of humour, David."

"OK Penny," said Brian, the Supervising Solicitor frowning at me.

"Yes, of course Brian, sorry about that. I think I am enjoying myself way too much."

We carried on from cabinet to cabinet, the pile of evidence growing visibly. We were just about to move from the study to the bedroom next door when David became very agitated.

"What the fuck do you think you are doing?" This time I decided to stay quiet and let the Supervising Solicitor answer the question.

"We are just continuing with our process Mr. Peterson, that's all."

"In my *bedroom*?!"

"Yes, that's right. The Order covers the contents of the entire house, garage, and loft."

"Jesus Christ, you're going to be here all day and all night!"

"I wouldn't expect so … in all probability, we'll be done by around 5:30 p.m."

"What the hell do you think you are going to find in my *bedroom?!*"

"One never knows. You'd be quite surprised where the juiciest of evidence has turned up in the past."

David looked disgusted while Colin and I got to work. There was a video player and TV in the bedroom, so I started to look at the labels on some of the videos and immediately David started to protest.

"No, No, *Absolutely not!* I can tell you that they have absolutely nothing to do with the lawsuit!"

"Well, that's for us to decide, not you," I said, pushing the video into the player and turning on the TV.

"Wait! Wait! Er Brian, can I have a word with you in private please?"

"Absolutely. Penny could you hold off for a minute?" said Brian.

"Of course."

I browsed around the bedroom tastefully decorated, no doubt by his wife, while the two men talked outside. When Brian came back to the room, he loosened the collar of his shirt.

"Listen Penny, it seems that the materials you're about to sift through are irrelevant. You are also likely to find them somewhat offensive since they are of a highly explicit sexual nature. Unfortunately, it falls upon me to determine whether in fact the materials are indeed irrelevant. So if you wouldn't mind leaving me here, I'll go through the video materials to make my determination."

"What and miss the sex show? What a spoilsport." I glared at David. "OK then Brian, I'll be in the kitchen if you need me." I brushed my way past David, looked at him in a very disapproving manner, muttering, "Tch, Tch."

To my utter dismay, it seemed that while I had been discussing possible items of a sexual nature, we had received an unexpected visitor to the house in my absence ... a very colourful one at that. It seemed that somebody had shown up in a shocking pink and yellow jockey suit, and as I entered the lounge, the jockey slowly turned around to face me.

"Phil? Oh my God, what the hell are you playing at!? Have you completely lost your mind? Why the hell are you wearing a *jockey suit* for Christ's sake and where on Earth have you been this morning?"

Just behind me I heard a very familiar voice. "Hi Penny." I turned to see Simon standing there, and my heart skipped a beat. His hair was a little untidy and as he stood there in his faded jeans and rugby shirt. I couldn't help but stare at him with total lust.

"Simon? What are you doing here?"

"Seems that Phil needed a friend he could rely on, and I turned out to be the nearest one." Simon smiled that kind-hearted smile of his, and I found myself longing for the time when we had been together.

"Yes Penn, that's absolutely right. I've just been through the nightmare of a lifetime, and Si is the only one who would come to my rescue." Phil looked genuinely grateful, which was quite unnerving.

As touching as it was, I just could not stop myself from staring. "Jesus Christ Phil, what's with the jockey outfit?" I stifled a laugh. Despite being extremely angry with Phil, I had never seen him look so ridiculous.

"Long story Penn ... one I would prefer to tell in private."

"Oh, in private? Oh yes, of course Phil … no doubt. I'm sure that you do want to keep the whole bloody ridiculous story *private!*"

"Penn, it will all be explained later, but in the meantime try not to be too hard on him." Simon placed his hand on my shoulder, and I felt an electric shock run through my body.

"Oh …" It happens so infrequently to me that I am always shocked when it happens. I had now been rendered speechless. For here before me is a scene almost unimaginable. Phil is standing there looking like a reject from Goodwood Park - having nothing meaningful to offer as everything has been handled by his team in his absence. He resembles a vibrant court jester trying to look as professional as he possibly can for a lawyer dressed in a jockey suit and just look who has shown up to enjoy the show … the ringmaster himself … "Anthony *Fucking* Jarvis," as Jim Bateman would say.

Step up … step up. Our first act, newly appointed partner of Pilkington, Isley & Simeon, a real "PISS artist" in his own right, Phil Stevens, standing unbeknownst to him in the presence of the eminent ringmaster, Mr. Anthony Jarvis, also known to many by the name of "AJ."

AJ had not seen Phil, and Phil had not yet seen AJ, as he had his back to him. Only I had the pleasure of witnessing the scene; realizing that in all probability that this spectacle might turn out to be the most ridiculous event in the history of the firm.

"Miss Banfield, what are you doing here?" Phil immediately turned around at the sound of AJ's voice.

"Sir!" Phil looked completely terrified.

"Philip? Is that really you? Why on Earth are you dressed that way? What the hell is going on here?" AJ looked around at us. "This isn't a bloody circus for crying out loud!"

I decided to sit back and enjoy the show. What were the lyrics of that song? Something like, *Clowns to the left of me, jokers to the right, here I am stuck in the middle with you.*

"Well, it's quite a long story, sir," said Phil.

"Well, come on then. I'm all ears." The silence was excruciating.

"I'd prefer to discuss it in private, sir."

"Well, I'm sure you would and maybe in the circumstances it would be more appropriate, but it's hard to imagine why on Earth you would be dressed as if you have just fallen off a *horse*; why you have not been returning my calls; and *why*, it would also appear, that Penny Banfield here is so clearly covering for you! Why she would feel any loyalty toward you is beyond me. I wasn't born yesterday Philip, and I certainly will not have the firm made the laughing stock of East Sussex. Please, just remove yourself from the premises and report to me immediately after the wedding."

If there is to be a wedding AJ, which at this moment seems highly debatable I'd say...

AJ continued, "It is just possible I may have calmed down by then, but I cannot guarantee that. Penny, I assume that you can carry on with the job you have already been doing?"

"Yes sir, of course." I was trying so hard not to smile, as I didn't want to eradicate any credibility I now had with AJ.

"Sir, if I could just explain myself," Phil protested.

"No Philip, at this precise moment in time, I could not be any *less interested* in anything you have to say." Thankfully, due to his training as an advocate before a judge, Phil knew exactly when to stop speaking.

"Come on mate, I'll drive you home." Simon placed his hand on Phil's shoulder and steered him toward the front door.

"Thank you, Simon" I said, full of gratitude and admiration for the kindness that lived inside his heart. Phil shuffled along slowly with my modern-day knight in shining armour.

"Sir, can I have a word with you in private?"

"Certainly Penny, perhaps we should go outside."

We moved into the garden, a very peaceful respite from the ridiculous activity that had been taking place inside.

"What can I do for you?" He still looked angry from his earlier exchange with Phil.

"I just wanted some information about the tip that you got? This house does seem to be the main repository for evidence. I've checked in with the other team leaders, and so far nothing has been found of any real significance at the other locations. I know it's early in the day though. Can you tell me anymore about the call you received?"

"Yes, of course. I received an anonymous call - although I immediately recognised the voice. I have a very strong suspicion that the person that called me was Andrew Barton. He said that he'd heard about the search warrant and that I could save myself a lot of time by visiting just one house and provided me with this address."

"But why would he just hand over that kind of information? I don't understand?"

"Most people in town know that Andrew does not see eye-to-eye with Jim Bateman. In fact, he's been very vocal about his disapproval of the litigation involving the Club. Andrew probably wants the litigation over as soon as possible so that they can try and dig themselves out of the financial mess they're in. He feels Jim is entirely responsible for what's befallen the Club, and Andrew takes his fiduciary duties to the Board very seriously. Did you see the headline in the newspaper today by any chance?"

"Yes, I did actually. Oh no, do you think that Andrew is responsible for leaking news of the bankruptcy to the press?"

"It did cross my mind." His eyes seemed almost gleeful.

"Looks like Jim's days are numbered in more ways than one, doesn't it sir?"

"Certainly does. Anyway, have I answered all your questions?"

"Yes, sir. I should get back to work."

"Of course. Thank you for stepping up and taking control of a potentially disastrous situation, Penny. I certainly won't forget this and what you have done for the firm."

"Thank you, sir." I started to blush. *A partnership would do nicely. In fact, **the sooner the better, sir**.*

"I'll report to you as the day progresses."

"Excellent. I have total faith in you." He started to turn back to the house.

"Sir, I do just have one more question?"

311

He looked quizzically at me and nodded.

"What made you come over here?"

"I was worried because I couldn't make contact with Phil. He's never failed to return my calls before. Let's just call it a hunch. Was he out drinking last night?"

"I'm sorry, sir. I don't know anything about that." I stared down at the lawn.

"Probably wouldn't say even if you did know, no doubt. Your loyalty is a very admirable quality, I must say."

"Thank you, sir."

We made our way back into the house through the French doors – to this really beautiful house, unfortunately disturbed by our activity. AJ made his way to the front door. "Keep up the good work everybody!"

I started to rummage around in the kitchen looking for further evidence, and Brian came down from upstairs looking quite pale. "Is everything OK, Brian?"

"Um, I just came down to get a glass of water." He cleared his throat.

"Find anything relevant?"

"Relevant? Oh no, absolutely *not* relevant, no, not relevant at all." He seemed to be avoiding eye contact with me.

"Are you OK, I must say you look a bit peaky?"

"No, I'm all right ... just a little shocked at what I have just witnessed. I'm so glad that you didn't have to watch those videos. I can't say I've ever seen anything like it before in all my life." My imagination had started to run wild.

"Well, I feel like I've had a very lucky escape. Thanks for checking that out for me."

"Just doing my job. I've seen many things doing this job, but nothing quite like that." He loosened his tie.

"This is proving to be one of the most interesting days of my life, *so far* that is." I smiled.

"Oh well, best get on with things, time is marching on." Brian and I made our way back upstairs.

11 a.m. The first call I made was to Gavin. He was team leader for the Jim Bateman address in Jevington. I had tried before, but it had been busy. This time he picked up.

"Hi Gavin. It's Penny."

"Penn, how are things going on over there?"

"You wouldn't believe it if I told you, but the short answer is things are going well – I think we have the main address for evidence. You find anything?"

"A few odds and sods, but nothing of any real substance. Jim is blowing a gasket here – he's so angry I'm worried he's going to have a heart attack."

"I guess the leak to the newspaper didn't help either?"

"He's been on the phone all morning, pacing up and down, swearing incessantly."

"No doubt."

"Any word from Phil?"

"Yes, he eventually showed up, but wearing a jockey's outfit - if you can believe that!"

"What? Did you say a *jockey's outfit?!* Are you having me on? Was he hung over?"

"Most definitely hung over, although he's probably gone back home to sleep it off."

"What do you mean? Isn't he with his team?"

"No, I am."

"Where's Phil?"

"Sent home by AJ. Anyway, I have to get on with the other calls, just wanted to check you are OK. We can have a long post-mortem tonight at my place?"

There was a huge commotion going on in the background, and I could hear Jim in the background yelling instructions. "What the fuck has that got to do with the bleeding court case? Gavin – get your arse over here and tell this idiot that this bloody vase could not possible be *evidence!!*"

"Best get back to it. See you later then. Oh, and Penny – please take care."

"Will do. See you later."

I paused before calling the number for my next team leader. Seeing Simon today had completely rattled me. How was it possible to have feelings for two completely different men at the same time? I could feel my neck tightening even more as I dialed the next number. I just had to push my personal life aside and focus on getting this job done.

My calls to the teams revealed that everything continued to go according to plan, and there had been more evidence culled from two other addresses. When they got to the address for Andrew Barton, he simply went to his office and handed a few paper emails to them. That's not to say that there was no search for materials; lawyers are lawyers and trust in human nature is not something that comes naturally to litigators.

314

Back in Brighton, Phil, still dressed in a jockey suit, sat on a bench on the pier, throwing chips from his newspaper wrapping to hungry seagulls.

After being evicted from the house by AJ and suspended from duties for the day, Simon dropped Phil off at his house, gave him his phone, some cash, and his spare key to the house. Phil had toyed with the idea of wearing something from Simon's wardrobe, but the clothes were simply too big for him. In reality, he no longer cared a jot about his appearance.

In his colourful attire, he sat in the back garden for a few hours, calling Lisa's telephone number over and over like an obsessive compulsive maniac. Realizing the futility, he decided to talk a walk and get something to eat. He had walked the entire length of Queens Road wearing nothing more than a frown earlier that day, so this time, dressed in his jockey suit, he felt positively overdressed.

When he arrived at the long pebbled beach, it was as if he was seeing it for the first time. This beach had always been here, but how many times had he been here to breathe in the salty air, bask in the warmth of the sun, and share the moment with Lisa? Lisa was right not to return his calls and would most probably never give him another second of her time. She was the only true friend he had; a lover, friend, and now mother of his child - he had let her down, absolutely and completely. He had never felt so alone.

Despite multiple calls he had made to his so-called friends, nobody had called him back. He was hurt by that, believing that at least one of his mates would have picked up a phone to check if he was OK. The stag night had been a disaster, and he had no idea whether there would be a wedding. In truth, he would not blame Lisa if she called off the wedding. It was one thing to be the father of her child, but he did not deserve the privilege of being her husband. He wondered whether he was even employed? Presumably AJ would calm down and allow him back into the fold, but there was no guarantee that this would happen. Maybe Penny would replace him? God knows she was capable enough. Although he felt wretched, he also felt free for the first time in a long time, staring at the waves, reliably breaking along the shoreline, as sure as eggs were eggs.

We continued the search, stopping briefly for a packed lunch. I cannot say that the experience was one that I would likely want to repeat. Digging through other people's homes and effectively their lives, is an extremely intrusive process. Most of all, I felt sorry for the wives, who in the main part, were clueless as to why the court had given us permission to go rooting through their underwear drawer.

We were able to stay until 5:30 p.m. according to the terms of the Order, but by around 4 p.m., I was receiving calls from various team leaders informing me that they were heading back to the office. At that time, I was still stuck at the Gatwick address. So I called Andrew and his team, told them to take a cab from the Crawley address back to the office and charge it to the firm.

I felt totally exhausted, physically and mentally. A feeling of anti-climax had come over me, as often would happen when a major event was over. AJ had called an hour previously telling me that the client was completely elated at the success surrounding our execution of the Order, and I had arranged to meet with Gavin, but actually did not want to talk at all.

Driving back to the office in total silence, I felt like a wrung-out rag. It had been a successful but also a horrible day. Sifting through every drawer, inspecting every note, card, or item under the careful watch of the householders had been dreadful. We all knew the Anton Piller Order was a draconian method of enforcing the law, but none of us had any idea of just how draconian it truly was. You had to stand there, see the fear in the faces of the people affected by it. At least a burglary was an anonymous act and the victims didn't have to stand watching the process, utterly powerless to stop it from happening.

I couldn't stand the silence any longer and turned on Radio 3 to listen to some opera. I would have killed for a massage and a huge glass of brandy at that point, yet the day was not yet over. I still had to report to AJ and all the teams back at the office. What on Earth possessed me to pick law as a career? I was already feeling the effects of a stressful career and wondered what would I be like after a further 10 years of practicing law? Maybe it was just the stress of working closely with Phil? How would I feel if I no longer had that burden to bear?

When I arrived at the boardroom, most of the other team leaders had arrived with their teams and the room was pulsing with positive energy. I opened the door, and a hush came over the room. Immediately feeling self-conscious, I began to brush my hair back into place with my hand. Suddenly, my colleagues turned to applaud and congratulate me, making me feel even more uncomfortable.

I looked around the room hoping that AJ had not yet arrived, but saw him in the crowd, also applauding. A blush rising from my neck, I nodded in appreciation until the applause subsided and made my way to the drinks cabinet to pour myself a glass of Perrier water.

After a minute of going through the motions and receiving verbal and physical pats on the back, thankfully AJ got started. We went over the day's operations. "Well, what a day it's been!" Everybody started cheering.

"This is the first time an Anton Piller Order has ever been executed by the firm, so well done everybody! Richard Montgomery has asked me to personally thank each and every one of you for your hard work and dedication. We've managed to cull an impressive volume of evidence to assist with our case. In short, I believe that with this new evidence, we can now apply for Summary

Judgment and put an end to the litigation involving the football club. Again, I congratulate you all!"

There were a few cheers from around the room and somebody (I assumed Andrew Barker) shouted from the back of the room, "Drinks all around then, is it sir?" AJ pretended not to hear, but continued.

"I could not end the day without a very special thank you to Penny Banfield. Her exemplary legal skills, conduct, and dedication to this project have undoubtedly resulted in the successful outcome we've achieved today. You're a credit to the firm Penny, and I for one, find myself extremely fortunate to have you as an associate at Pilkington, Isley & Simeon." More applause ... "If you keep this up, we'll have to make you a partner, Penny."

I felt almost detached from what was going on and began to stare at the faces smiling at me. Raj was applauding and nodding with appreciation, and even the partner with the biggest ego in the room, Tim Fairhurst, seemed to be smiling in recognition. *Make you a partner, Penny ... Hmmm. A partner of the firm ... but that would mean being a partner with Phil, wouldn't it? How many could I look at with admiration and how many would bring out the best in me, and help me thrive as a partner?*

Gavin entered the room to witness the applause seemingly proud at my achievement, but I wondered why my heart had not stopped at the sight of him the way it had with Simon earlier that day? *Maybe it's just been a very long day.*

As Gavin also then started to applaud, I just wanted it all to end. I wanted to go home, have a bath, and a good cry. I often felt that the relief provided after a good cry was far better than any alcoholic drink. I so rarely cried, except when stressed, angry, or frustrated. Anger had always been my preferred emotion when it came to showing my hurt – not exactly the best way to show pain and certainly not if you wanted anybody to provide you with comfort. Maybe I'd inherited this from my mother?

Someone started to call, "Speech! Speech!" from the back of the room.

"Thank you everybody, thank you for your incredible support." I tried to quieten them down. "This was always a team effort, and I am glad to say that each and every one of you fulfilled, and in some cases, *exceeded* expectations. Well done team!"

Somebody shouted, "Hip hip hooray for our team leader," and they started up again. I looked over at AJ to see if he would kindly rescue me from my embarrassment and thankfully he came to my rescue.

"OK everyone, there is food on its way, and I hope you will all join me in a glass of champagne, courtesy of our client." The sound of applause subsided to the sound of corks popping in the background. I smiled in gratitude to AJ and made my way over to Gavin.

"Hello Miss Banfield. Quite a day, wasn't it? Congratulations on a job well done," he kissed me on the cheek.

"Thank you Mr. Preston. God what a day – my head is throbbing. I rolled my head from side to side."

"I'll give you a neck massage when we get home."

"Oh my God, that would be sooo wonderful."

"But first, we need to grab a glass of champagne each." He pulled me toward the crowd mulling around the champagne.

"Absolutely, I think I've earned at least one glass."

"Oh, I'd say at least *two* glasses - don't you think you earned Phil's share, too?"

"Poor Phil. Wonder what he's doing right now?"

"I, for one, don't care a jot about Phil. My focus is entirely on you for the rest of the evening."

"My my, what a lucky girl I am." I raised my glass to him, not caring who might be watching us.

Jim was in his office at the football club, lying low until his wife Lillian had calmed down. She was seething with anger, and he was likely unable to change that for a while. The usual trick of promising a trip to the spa or the use of his credit card for a shopping spree were not going to work this time. She seemed about ready to walk out on him when she had said, *"I never want to set eyes on you again. How could you bring this upon us? This is our home, our HOME for Christ sake, Jim!!"*

He'd packed a small overnight bag and decided to stay at the Club overnight. Maybe after a while she would calm down and let him back in the house. *What a fucking awful day.* He could not believe that Tony Jarvis had gone to court and got a search warrant. By now, they would have all sorts of incriminating evidence against the Club, confirming backhanders had been paid in addition to transfer fees for a lame dog of a player, effectively rendering judgment against the Club a foregone conclusion.

He poured himself a large scotch, slammed it back hard, and picked up the phone. "Hi Julie. It's Jim. Is Stevie there?" There was a short pause before Steven Graham came on the line.

"Jim? I've been trying to get hold of you all day mate, what the hell is going on?"

"It's over Stevie. They have all the evidence. *Everything.* There's no way we can deny anything about the deal now."

"What do you mean they have the evidence? I thought you told me it had all been destroyed, Jimmy?"

"It was as good as destroyed. I thought it was in a safe place and wasn't counting on Tony Jarvis getting a fucking Anton Piller Order and ..."

"What the hell is an Anton Piller Order?"

"They got a search warrant, raided the homes of the Club directors at the same time, searched high and low for evidence, and they bloody well found it at Davie's place."

"Jesus Christ, Jim. What the fuck am I going to do now? My career is over."

"Yes, yes it is, and so my friend, is mine."

"Oh, trust you to think of yourself. Do me a favour and go fuck yourself, OK?" Steve hung up, and Jim let out a huge sigh. *Just as I said, another fucking awful day.*

When Gavin and I got back to my flat, I dropped my bags, kicked off my shoes, and threw my coat on the chair by the front door.

"Do you mind if I run myself a bath?"

"Of course not. You live here remember." Gavin smiled. "Shall I make you an herbal tea?"

"Hmmm. Sounds lovely. But first, I'd really like a glass of brandy."

"If that's what you'd like, just point me in the right direction. I'll get right to it."

"Tea is in that cupboard and brandy is on the sideboard in the dining room. You might just be the perfect man, do you know that?"

"Oh, that sort of praise is always very welcome."

I kissed him on the cheek and then made my way to the bathroom, yawning all the way.

I started to run the bath, added some lavender, ylang ylang bath salts, and took my clothes off. I was so not feeling sexy tonight and really hoped that Gavin was not expecting anything too energetic from me. As I slipped into the bath, I felt the envelope of silky water soothe away the day and wriggled my toes with contentment.

Gavin knocked at the door. "Can I come in?"

"Of course you can," I smiled at his level of consideration.

He came in with a small glass of brandy and handed it to me in the bath. "Just to keep you going while the tea brews."

"Gavin Preston, I think I love you. Oops!! I mean ..." *What the hell was I saying? It came out all wrong. I wasn't sure yet how I truly felt about Gavin. How could I until the Simon thing had been resolved?*

"It's OK, Penny. I'm not going to run to the nearest exit sign. I've been feeling it, too. It's just I thought it a little early to confess. In fact, I almost told you this morning on the phone." He laughed, looking a little embarrassed.

"Really?" I smiled a little uncomfortable smile. *Oh well, it's too late now Penny – you've well and truly let the cat out of the bag, haven't you?*

"Does it make you feel uncomfortable?" He played with the shower curtain as he spoke.

"No, no, it doesn't worry me – not in the slightest. In fact, it makes me very happy."

"Well, happy is good. Happy is very good." He bent down to kiss me in the bath, and I felt instantly calm.

"I think I'd best get out of here and let you have some space, it's been a busy day. How about we just cuddle tonight?"

"My God, you really are perfect, aren't you? When do I get to see the chinks in your armour, Mr. Preston?"

"You will find them soon enough, believe me." He closed the door behind him.

He really did make me feel special, and we had so much in common. But as much as I tried, Simon kept popping up like an annoying piece of hair that just would not lie straight.

Phil had been pleading with Lisa to let him into the building. He knew she was home because he could see that all the windows to the flat were open. After around 20 minutes of trying the buzzer to the entrance door, he resorted to screaming at the top of his lungs up to the top flat. She finally caved under pressure from the neighbours demands for him to *"Give it a bloody rest."*

Inside the flat, he was about to put his advocacy skills to the test. This was going to be the plea of a lifetime. They were due to fly from Gatwick to Las Vegas tomorrow morning for the wedding. He had no idea where his in-laws had gone, but they were nowhere to be seen.

"Where are your Mum and Dad?" Phil looked around the flat for evidence.

"Do you honestly think that I'd allow them to be part of this bloody shit-show?"

"Where are they then?"

"They've spent the day in Arundel, but should be back around nine tonight."

"Lisa, I've never begged anyone in my life before ... please don't let this one day ruin things for us. It was totally out of my control."

"No it wasn't, Phil. It was totally *in your control* – all you had to do was to say, '*NO!*' No to one blasted drink, which would have prevented you from having another and *another*! Perhaps if you had said, '*No*' Phil, we would actually be having dinner with my parents, and perhaps they wouldn't now believe that you are some sort of ridiculous wanker. Perhaps if you had said, '*No, I* would actually be looking forward to marrying the love of my life, rather than wanting to kick him in the balls right now. Perhaps if you had said, '*No,*' I could stop worrying about you acting like a baby and actually take care of the baby I am expecting. Your baby, Phil. *Your Baby!*" She burst into tears.

Phil moved closer to Lisa and stroked her face, wiped her tears away. "I know ... Lis ... I'm sorry. I can't argue with anything you just said. All I can tell you is that I couldn't be more sorry for what I've done, and I love you so much and our baby. I want to be a good father to our child, and I want to be a good husband to you. I realised after sitting on the beach practically all day that the only thing that matters is that you and I are together and we bring up our child *together*. When I really needed somebody to come to my assistance, not one of those useless bastards answered my calls. I can't even believe that I agreed to go for *'just the one drink.'* It just shows how undisciplined I am and how all that has to change and change right now, not just when the baby arrives. I need you Lisa, because without you, my life is meaningless. All I would have is what is left of my career, and that's never going to be enough for me. I want to be a better man for you Lisa, for you, and the baby."

"Really Phil, do you *really* mean it?"

"You know I do. Come on Lis ... let's get married and start our family together."

Lisa smiled through her tears and planted a huge kiss on his lips, demonstrating that Phil Stevens still had the gift of the gab - and always would.

I lay in the bath for about 10 minutes and then pulled myself up, feeling a little heady from the brandy. I slipped into my silk kimono and made my way to the lounge to join Gavin on the sofa for tea. I noticed the phone was flashing, another message waiting. I had no doubt whatsoever that it would be from Simon but it might also be my Dad leaving news of my mother's surgery.

"So Penny Banfield, want to tell me about the day?"

"How about I give you a brief synopsis?"

"Whatever works for you, but why don't you start by telling me about the Phil Stevens show."

"Believe it or not, Phil showed up at his address dressed in a jockey outfit. He'd been drinking with his group of chimps last night, and they got him incredibly drunk, stripped him naked, and left him in a hessian bag in the launderette overnight. As you know, Lisa was worried sick about him. But I guess when she eventually heard from him and he was OK, she flipped her lid and threw all his clothes out the window and onto a tree outside their flat. The only thing that made it to the ground was the jockey suit. So Phil had no option but to wear that."

"But why didn't he just go inside and see if there was anything else to wear?"

"He didn't have his keys, and Lisa wouldn't let him inside the building."

"You're not telling me he went over there naked?"

"No, he went over to Simon's place first and was wearing a bathrobe that he borrowed from him. Apparently, he didn't want to wear a bathrobe to the raid." I giggled.

"I'm not sure which outfit would have been more ridiculous. Not much in it really is there." He laughed. "So he had Simon bail him out then?"

"Yes, I guess Phil must have been totally desperate. He remembered that Simon lived close to the launderette and used his persuasive skills to get him to come to his aid. It was Simon who drove him over to the raid address."

"So Simon came over to your address?" He looked a little perturbed.

"Yep. They arrived around two minutes before AJ showed up unexpectedly."

"Oh my God, poor Phil. So let me get this right, you are there with your gay ex-boyfriend ..."

Laughing, I interrupted. "Excuse me, let's get this right, my *ex-gay*, ex-boyfriend."

"OK, whatever you say. Anyway Simon is there, Phil is dressed up in a jockey suit, and then his boss arrives."

"Yep, a complete nightmare."

"I would have paid money to have seen AJ's face."

"Oh, it was so embarrassing Gavin. Despite everything, even *I* felt embarrassed for Phil."

"Oh, don't feel sorry for him. He brought it all on himself."

"I just feel like today has been a really good day for me, but it's been at Phil's expense. I don't feel good about that."

"Penny, that guy has been taking advantage of your good nature for more than a year now. It was only a matter of time before AJ would realize that Phil is full of hot air."

"I guess so. I wonder where Phil is now? Do you think Lisa has forgiven him yet?"

"What makes you so sure she will *ever* forgive him?"

"Because she always forgives Phil, sooner or later." I started to yawn. *Just like you Penny, you are already spending way too much time thinking about him.*

"Come on Miss Banfield, lawyer extraordinaire ... let's go to bed. It's been a really long day."

"I am not going to argue with that." I let him lead me by the hand to the bedroom, following obediently.

As I lay in bed, being cuddled by Gavin, I thought about the luxury of having a whole weekend of free time before us, no ticking clock, no billable hours. Plenty of time for me to figure out what I was going to do about Simon, Phil, and my future career aspirations. A wise woman would have just shut her mouth and revelled in the luxury of no responsibility for the entire weekend. Wouldn't you know it ... I just had to spoil the moment.

"Gavin?"

"Hmmmm?" He started to nuzzle around my neck.

"Do you think we should start our own firm?"

0.1 Unit - Contemplating new business venture

CHAPTER 13 – SATURDAY MAY 20, 2000

Despite the enormous relief at having successfully completed a project, I slept fitfully. Tired of keeping my thoughts company, I got out of bed, grabbed some jeans, and a T-shirt from my wardrobe and crept into the kitchen, trying not to wake Gavin. I grabbed a juice box from the fridge, called a cab, and then picked up my voicemail:

"Hi darling. Just wanted to let you know that everything went well yesterday – in fact the surgeon is quite confident that we've managed to catch everything in good time, so that's quite a relief. Your mother says Hi. Call if you get a moment this weekend, bye Penny."

Dad sounded very relieved and I too felt relieved, no longer having to feel guilty about not calling. I knew that one day I would need to have a conversation with my mother that was not going to involve my achievements or guilt at having carried *her* secret around for so many years, but it wasn't going to happen today and not for some time, so I pushed it to the back of my mind.

"Penn, it was so good to see you in action today. You were made to be a lawyer, and I'm sure partnership is just one step away. I've no right to be, but I felt so proud

of you taking control of the nightmare you were dealing with, no thanks to Phil. Anyway, hope to hear from you soon. I'll wait as long as it takes."

It felt good to hear his voice and I could feel my resolve slipping now that I was not in full stress mode. I knew I could not walk away from Simon until I had exhausted all possibility of there ever being a future together. I didn't want to become like my mother, trapped in a life she didn't want to live. Gavin didn't deserve to have a girlfriend who was not sure of her feelings

I grabbed a pen and pencil and left a note for Gavin:

Just gone out for some errands - be back by 10 a.m.
Hope you enjoyed your lie-in!
Penny x

I knew that later that day we would be having a very difficult conversation – he may as well get used to waking up without me next to him.

When the cab arrived outside my building, I was relieved that Anil was not the cab driver, as I didn't much feel like explaining myself. I sat in silence until the cab dropped me off outside Phil's place and noticed his car parked outside. I was relieved that he hadn't left for the airport. Maybe there was going to be no trip to the airport, and Lisa had told him to get lost?

I announced myself at the intercom, praying that he was still home. Thankfully, Lisa answered.

"Lisa, it's Penny. I need to speak to Phil, urgently."

"Oh Penny, OK. We don't have long though, we're leaving for the airport in about half an hour."

"I promise, it won't take long." She buzzed me into the building.

Phil came to the door, looking positively normal dressed in a pair of jeans and a red golf shirt. He looked happy. "Hey Penn, to what do I owe this honour?"

"I need to speak with you Phil." I glanced at Lisa awkwardly. "Preferably in private." I noticed that Phil was no longer smiling.

"Wow this sounds serious. Is everything all right?" He took me by the arm into their lounge, leaving Lisa in the hallway with their suitcases. "Sit down. We still have a few minutes before we leave. What is it Penn?"

I sat down but on the edge of the sofa, not wanting to get too comfortable. "Phil – why didn't you tell me about your partnership?" Immediately, I lost eye contact as he stared at his trainers visibly seeking the *right words* to placate me.

Before he had a chance to speak, I jumped in again. "I simply can't understand why you would confide in me about the baby and all that personal stuff, but leave out the one personal thing that affects *me*, and *in a big way?*" The silence filled the room, and I stared him down until he did eventually look up in a sheepish way.

"It's complicated … I mean, I can't really put it into words." He tried his best lost puppy look on me.

"Try me." I continued to stare, well more of a glare really.

"I was told to keep it totally confidential."

"Bullshit Phil. When have you ever *not* told me about confidential stuff that you have heard through the grapevine? You told me about Fairhurst and Raj, didn't you?"

"This is different Penny. It involved me and a huge decision by the partners. Had the wrong word got out, it potentially could have ruined everything for me."

"So what you are fundamentally saying Phil is that you don't trust me?"

"That's ridiculous. You know that's not what I'm saying."

"It makes no sense. The stag party had more chance of changing the partners' decision than I ever could have. I don't buy it. Come on Phil. I need to know. This is important to *me.*" He was visibly uncomfortable now, fidgeting with his hands and staring around the room as if seeking out somebody, anybody to come to his aid.

"Maybe I couldn't believe it."

"Well, I know *I* could hardly believe it. What I find truly impossible to believe is that you would think of treating me this way. We've worked closely for more than a year now and some would say that I should have been the first or at least second person you should have told, after Lisa. I'm so hurt that you didn't think of telling me. In fact, it bothered me so much that it was the one thing nagging at the back of my mind throughout the most stressful day I've ever had in my career so far. I need to know the *real* reason Phil?"

Another long silence followed, until he looked at me with a disgusted look on his face. "I couldn't tell you Penn because, in truth, I was ashamed. I knew I didn't deserve it. I knew I'd relied heavily on you bailing me out whenever I needed you, and that in reality, it should have been *you* and not *me* that got partnership." He stared at me waiting for the full effect of his words to take effect.

"Much better Phil.....I knew we'd get there in the end." I stood up and made my way to the door.

"Is that it?" Phil looked astonished that I did not have more to say.

"I think so." I turned to the door and made my way into the hallway calling out, "Bye Lisa. Hope you have a lovely time." Phil had followed me to the front door.

"What about me? No congratulations to me or even best wishes?"

I felt a surge of anger rise over me, "Not if your life depended on it. Goodbye Phil."

I left the apartment aware that things would never be the same between us. That was a good thing, a very good and essential thing.

0.3 Units Re-establishing self-esteem